PULL
OF THE
VALE

Lorin Petrazilka

FATEBOUND
BOOKS
A WOMEN-OWNED IMPRINT

Pull of the Vale
First Edition
Copyright 2022 Lorin Z Pillai

Published by Fatebound Books
For rights inquires, please contact rights@fateboundbooks.com

FATEBOUND�֍BOOKS

ISBN 978-1-7360622-7-2 (hardcover)
ISBN 978-1-7360622-8-9 (paperback)

Cover design by Alberto Carranza and Lorin Z Pillai

*Dedicated to my Aunt Vicki,
who loved the written word,
and who I'm sure is looking down on us from above,
laughing at all of us jackasses.*

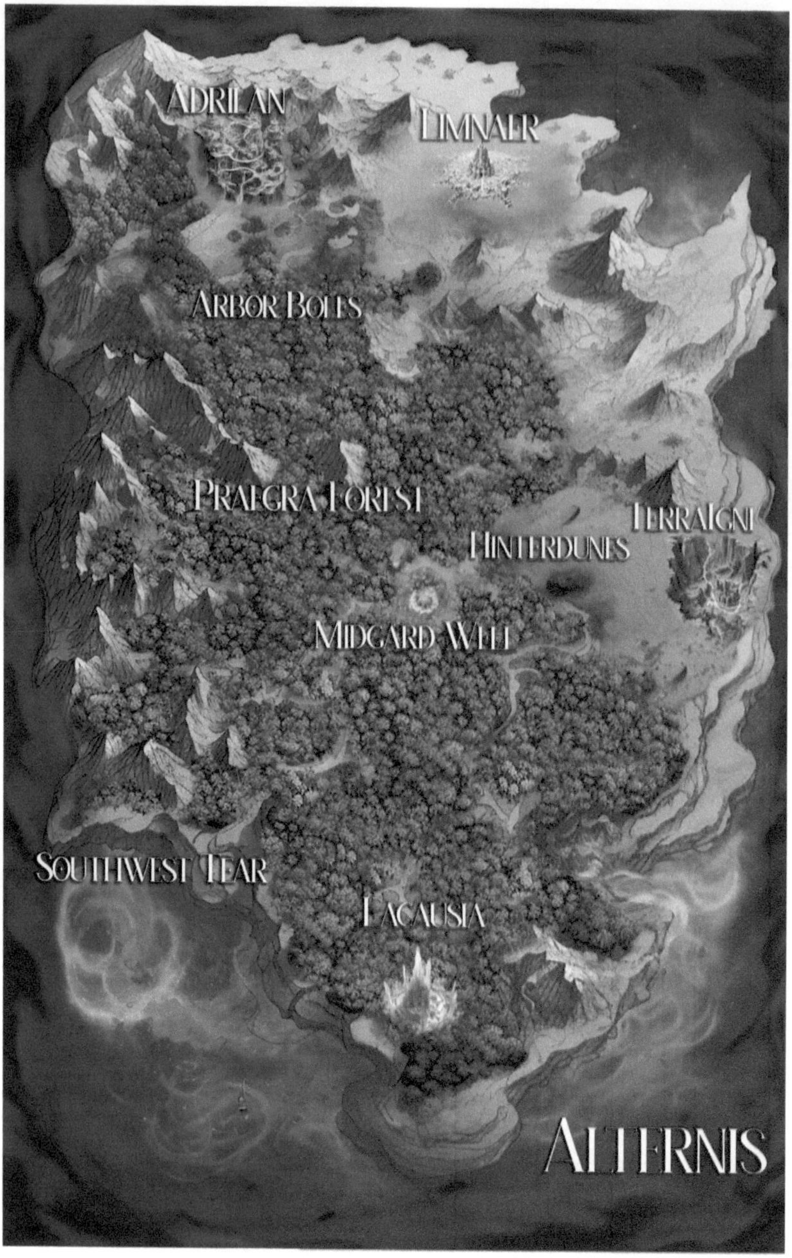

ADRILAN
LIMNAER
ARBOR BOLES
PRAEGRA FOREST
TERRAIGNI
HINTERDUNES
MIDGARD WELL
SOUTHWEST TEAR
LACAUSIA
ALTERNIS

TABLE OF CONTENTS

CHAPTER 1

I nudged the burnt grass with my toe as I held back tears, the withered blades crumbled against the border of the lush growth that surrounded our Southern California land. This was not the homecoming I imagined, not by a long shot. I was supposed to rush through the sliding back door of my family home then hug my mother, who wept at the white tile kitchen counter. Thinking that her grown children were missing, I would ease her worry and show her that we were okay—though clearly we had drastically changed. Instead, I nearly dropped to the ground as I stood in the ash and charred rubble, piles still smoldered wisps of smoke into the crisp, early morning air. Brennanfalk Ranch had burned to the ground.

Felix was slack beside me, he hadn't said a word. My lip wobbled as I looked at him, his pointed ears sagged and his angular face glistened with tears. We had not changed back to our human form. I think we both assumed—both believed—that once we stepped back through the passage into the glen of Black Oak Grove, we would shift back. I looked down at my lengthened limbs and shuddered. There was no hiding this.

Panic started to rise as I clenched my fists and my breath quickened. *No, think this through. Take a breath.*

"Wildfire?" Felix finally asked.

I looked around, the destruction was contained to our land only. "No, I don't see any sign of other sections of land having been burned. Besides, it's spring. It's a good six months until firestorm season."

Fire again. Always fire, fire, fire. And this time it wasn't that I was there and unable to do anything to stop it, it was that I wasn't there and *could* have done something. One cruel irony after another. My anger rose, but it didn't boil to my skin like I thought it would.

I glanced in all directions, using the investigation to stave off the debilitating terror poised to shred my mind. "I'd say maybe an accident, but even the barn is burned down." *Even the barn,* where were the horses? Not a sound came from the rubble, they had either perished with it, or been let out. Apollo, oh no, Apollo. I hoped my horse had been saved. But if he hadn't, that would mean … our mom. Where was our mom? My body shook with grief and worry. There was no way she wouldn't try if she were awake to see what was happening. I muttered a silent prayer that she was not inside the house when it happened.

I looked at my hands, and decided to pulse the embers buried in the last pieces of smoking framing, to see if I could wink them out. Nothing happened, not a tremor of power simmered under my skin. The well inside me was shuttered.

"I can't use my abilities. Can you?"

Felix twirled his hands, in an attempt to whip up one of his cyclones. "I feel like I'm motioning with nothing behind it. It's like it's … hidden."

Shit. *I guess I couldn't have helped.* I gulped down the guilt that I had not been here to protect my home, or my mom.

My eyes darted around, searching for any clue. An illuminated window at the neighboring ranch was the only thing I honed in on.

"Come on, Felix, maybe the Phillips know something."

"We can't let them see us like this!"

It dawned on me why people never came back, when they went missing in the forest like the old stories said. If they were Vale Born and had gone through the passage to Alternis, coming back to this world meant their changes came with them. It was permanent. And re-integrating with humans would prove to be a risk. Beyond what people would say, what if the government found out? Would they take us away, and perform experiments? The blood drained from my face as I realized, it was not that this just wasn't my home anymore, it *couldn't* be my home anymore.

I rubbed my cheek. "We have to try. It's worth the risk I think. They've known us our whole lives. They might freak out, but they won't *sell* us out. Right now we need to find out if Mom is okay. Then, I guess we'll figure it out from there."

We took off running, closing the quarter-mile distance to their home in no time. Walking up to their familiar dutch door, I realized how my altered eyes made things enhanced, more detailed. Every flake of green paint stood out on the wood siding, the rustling of their maidenhair ferns that lined both sides of the faded brick walkway caused my gaze to dart back and forth. It all put me on heightened alert. The doorbell echoed in their house as I pressed it, my heart was in my throat as steps thudded across their worn parquet floor inside. I could picture the interlocking pieces of wood shifting as they were walked across, each movement caused a minute scrape against each other; something my human hearing would never have picked up.

My anxiety spiked as the door creaked open, revealing our lifelong neighbor Barb Phillips' shocked face.

"Hello can I—Lily! Felix? What the … what have you two *done* to yourselves? Where have you been? The entire town has been searching for you! The helicopters have been searching the hills! And your poor mother-"

"Barb, I know this is a lot to take in. Where is my mom? We just saw the ranch. Is she okay?"

Her eyes were round as she stared at us and shrank back a pace. "Yes, she's okay. Very shaken up, but okay. She's here, in our guest room. We helped get the horses out and brought them all here in the middle of the night." Her eyes zeroed in on my pointed ears, and the distinctive, sharp jawline that was so clearly inhuman. Not to mention our otherworldly clothing that didn't belong in Black Oak, or anywhere in this world.

She motioned for us to come in, but paled as we stooped to enter her front door. Going into Barb Phillips' house struck a chord, we were strangers here now—and didn't belong. This house that I had spent my childhood stealing pomegranates from their orchard and then asking to use their washroom to remove the obvious evidence, I no longer fit here.

Barb pointed down the hallway to a closed door. I gulped as I walked towards it, every laborious step sent tremors through my body. Felix and I settled to a stop outside it, I glanced at him and sucked in a breath, before I knocked.

I might as well have been hitting the door with a baseball bat, the thud on the wood hallway door made me wince as my ears twitched. Slowly, the door opened and revealed Rachael Brennan-falk's face, puffy from crying.

"... Kids? Where have you—what have you! What has happened?" She rubbed her eyes and looked again, as if she could fix the distorted image of us. The one that showed us as much too tall and chiseled.

I ducked in and placed a hand on her shoulder. "Mom, I'm so glad you're safe. Please tell us what happened to the ranch. I'm sorry we went missing, I'll do my best to explain."

We took a few steps further into the room, she walked backward until her legs bumped into the bed, then sank onto it as she gaped.

"Mom," Felix said as he shut the door, "please."

I sat down with her and waited, letting her pore over my face with equal parts concern and disbelief.

She closed her eyes as tears slipped over each cheek. "It was an arsonist. I heard the horses, they woke me up. The house was full of smoke, I could barely see. I came outside and found everything burning. The house was engulfed, there was nothing I could do about that so I ran down to the barn, that's when I saw her. Just as she was running away. I only caught a glimpse, but she *smiled* at me. Smiled! She was strangely tall," she gulped as her glance flashed over us again, "long brown hair—straight. And," she reached up to touch my ear, "she had these, too."

A chill ran through my body as her words settled in my mind. I snapped my eyes to Felix. "Oh *fuck.* She isn't dead."

"Holy shit. No. How is Dashelle alive?" Felix exclaimed.

"When I didn't get her power, I just figured you did. How did she find the ranch? How could she … Opius. That son of a bitch! He must have told her, before he died. It's my fault! I told him! He kept asking specific questions and I thought nothing of it!" I pressed my hands to my face and cried.

No, no, no, this can't be happening.

"Kids, stop swearing dammit. And what the hell are you talking about?"

I dropped my hands and looked at my mom's careworn face. She had lost so much. And now this. It wasn't fair, none of it. "We have … a lot to tell you. And it's going to be very, *very* hard to believe." I sighed and scrunched the quilt-covered guest bed with my hands, then proceeded to tell my mom everything that happened in that crazy, beautiful world. Well, almost everything. And why Felix and I had to go back to it.

"Lily Mae Brennanfalk, get your head out of your ass."

"Excuse me … what?"

"You can't be serious. First off, that all sounds ridiculous. And second, we have things to handle here! The ranch is gone! What about the horses? This is your home! You belong here."

"No, I don't. I know this sounds unbelievable. What, are Felix and I supposed to just hide out here in Black Oak and pray that none of the residents let our secret slip? It will only be a matter of time before someone finds out—the wrong kind of someone."

"You're going back? You're just going to leave me here? What about Apollo?"

"Look at me, Mom! How can I stay? And that arsonist is *much* more than just that. She's a murderer, and wants to kill Felix and I for what we can do." I squeezed my eyes shut, chastising myself for blurting out that piece of information. I didn't intend on telling her that part and making her even more worried. I looked at my limbs as it settled in my consciousness how big I actually was now. The horror written all over her face as I glanced back made my stomach clench. "And Apollo," I gestured to my legs, my torso, "I can't even ride him anymore, he'd be sway-backed in less than a year. I love him, I love you, and Black Oak. But … " words evaded me as tears gushed from my eyes.

This was my fault. Foolish Lily, telling Opius anything he wanted to know. Letting him pour glass after glass of Fae wine and spilling all details about my home, for him to turn around and regurgitate it to Dashelle. Selling me out bit by bit so that he got his end of the deal with her. Deliver three Vale Born, and get rulership over Lacausia in return. All the while I was thinking he was interested in me. And now Dashelle was … *somewhere,* either in the human world or heading back into Alternis. I had no way of knowing where her home might be. All she had said was "hick town", that could mean anything. Who knew? It didn't matter, I wasn't about to go hunting her down. Tricked, I had been thoroughly tricked, and now my mom was paying the price.

I looked at Felix, his face was stearn and unreadable.

"I'm so very sorry, Mom. I can't believe the ranch is gone. Our family home-" I shuddered, I couldn't even finish that sentence. "This is not what you deserve, but now that we know this person is still alive, I have to get back to Alternis and warn them. She … killed Josie. Josie was like Felix and I. And she killed her so that she could absorb that power and become stronger. If she finds me here, I have little chance of defending myself. She's a trained fighter, and vicious. I'm safer—we're all safer—if I go back. I can't let the Fae we met get hurt, I care for them. I … fell in love. I can't let anything happen to him. There, in that realm, I'm powerful. I make a *difference.* In ways that I always struggled to here. I wish you could come and see it for yourself."

She shook her head and covered her mouth. "No, this has to be made up. This can't be real. I'm finally having a meltdown. You two going missing, my house burning down. I've lost my mind, that's what this is. I must be making up some ridiculous story to convince myself you're still alive." My mom squeezed her eyes shut and sobbed; horrible, choking sobs. Each one went right through my ears and cut to my heart. "You can't leave me! You two are all I have now." She shuddered as the words spilled out.

I reached forward and clutched her arm, forcing her to look up at me. Her face was so much smaller than I remembered, her wrist felt diminutive in my grip. She looked at my hand, probably noticing the reverse, how much coverage my enlarged hand had on her arm. I smiled at her, which she gasped at. I realized with a wince that it was the first time she had noticed my canines.

"Mom," Felix said softly, fortunately tearing her attention away from my teeth. "I will help you figure things out, before I go back as well. Lily is right, we can't stay here. It's not safe. But I will make sure everything is okay. Have you talked to Aunt Maureen yet?"

"Yes," she sniffled. "She wants me to come stay with her. She even said she would have our horses trailered there. But it's so far, and Ithaca isn't my home anymore. Black Oak Grove is. I told her no, I couldn't leave, not when I didn't know where you two were."

"It's a good option while everything gets sorted here." I said. "Insurance, rebuilding, it will all take a long time. Plus … you'd be with her."

"You mean so I'm not alone, because you two won't be here." She tugged at her chestnut brown hair as she hung her head.

"I understand you are … well I can't even imagine how you feel."

"No, you can't."

My heart shattered for her. I had been so selfish when we lost my dad and Maris. It was all about me. How it affected *me*. Maybe it was a lack of emotional maturity to begin with. But whatever the reason, I failed to realize how my mom had been affected until much later.

"Why is this happening? Our house, you kids. None of this makes any sense," she said as I rubbed her shoulder. She was right. It didn't make any sense.

"We'll find a way to make this all right. I don't know how, but I promise you, I will do it."

"If you'd just stay, you wouldn't need to make that promise. We could figure this out together," she pleaded.

I opened my mouth to respond and glanced out the slatted wood blinds, as dawn was breaking over the chaparral hills. There was no explaining that this wasn't really a choice for us. I had an immediate longing to glimpse the cluster of rocks far out in the east, that one that marked the glen with the passage to where I needed to go. A thread tugged in my core, pulling me toward the place I couldn't see. My home.

Guilt wracked me from my traitorous heart. So quickly I was ready to bolt back there, and leave my mother here to deal with this new reality, abandon the place I grew up and the woman that gave so much of herself to raise me.

Felix was staring in the same spot as well, as a thrum went

taut in the direction of the Vale. A beckon, a demand, "Come back now," it said. He and I snapped our eyes to each other.

"The Pull," I whispered. He nodded. Rannoch had warned us about the Pull, but he didn't know how long it would take before it began drawing us back. It was why the Fae couldn't leave, the Pull was too strong for them. The Faeries could ignore it the longest, but even they weren't immune to it.

I gulped as I looked at our mom. I had to say goodbye, at least for now. "It's calling us back, Mom. It won't let us leave the realm for long. I have to go. I'll come back when I can, I'll find some way to visit you in Ithaca."

Tears slipped over her cheeks again as she crushed her eyes shut. "I can't believe this is happening."

"We will find a way to help you, Mom. Somehow, this will all be okay and will all make sense eventually." I brushed a kiss on her forehead, then stood to leave with Felix.

"How can you promise that? You're telling me that you're leaving to go live in some fantasy world—which can't possibly be real. How can you make this all right?"

"I don't know, but I will find a way." I couldn't manage any more words, couldn't look at her pained face any longer. There was so much I needed to do, people whose lives depended on me getting back to Alternis. I would return someday. But now, I had to go. The Pull was probably one of the most intense reactions I had ever felt, an unyielding force that demanded I return. I wrapped my arms around her and gave her a long, tight hug. Felix joined the embrace, I kissed her cheek as we released. There had to be a way for us all to be together.

I motioned to Felix with my chin. "I'll be back soon, Mom. I won't be able to stay long, though," he said to her. She swallowed a whimper as we left the room. I looked at her one last time, before Felix and I silently left the Phillips' house.

We ran the full two miles out to the gateway.

11

CHAPTER 2

We arrived at the glen, nestled below a towering rock face of moss-covered granite. The oaks beneath the angled sedimentary layers hummed with the sounds of peaceful insects warming in the newly risen sun.

"Lily, have you thought about this completely? You are one of the best people at looking at things logically," Felix asked after we hopped the creek.

I pinched my nose and exhaled loudly. "Felix, what are you trying to say?"

"Are you sure you don't have Stockholm Syndrome? You did admit that you were captured by them."

I blurted a laugh. "Come on, seriously? Yes, I was captured by them, and I made the deal while under duress. But then, it was not long before Rannoch rescinded the whole 'captive' situation. He apologized, and gave me the choice to leave. *Nothing* had happened between us at that point. So, I hear you. But no. Everything I did from then on was *my* choice. Even though we look completely inhuman and don't seem to have a choice about staying here because of it, I had already chosen that I was going to return to Alternis."

He folded his arms and leaned against a tree—the last tree before the perfect circle of oaks that marked the entrance to the passage through the Vale.

"Look, this is all fucked-up," I said. "Dashelle has done her damage here. What if she comes back to take your powers while you're here tending to things? We may not be able to use our abilities here, but that doesn't mean she can't kill you for them, then go back into Alternis and have access to your power. And in that scenario—which I refuse to let happen—Mom and I will have lost yet another family member. Do what you have to do, but come back soon. Once Mom is settled in Ithaca with Aunt Maureen and the horses are sorted, there is no good reason for you to stay."

"I have my own reasons for wanting to come back, and I will," Felix said as he tightened the fold of his arms. "Plus, the Pull is intense. Every fiber in my body is wanting to go into the Vale. But I think that Mom needs an adjustment period. I know I can't stay. Besides, only one of us is enough to go back and warn the Ignisfae. And I'd bet Rannoch is ready to pummel anyone in his path until you get there."

"Oh I'm sure Kerenza has had it up to here with him since I left. How long will you stay here? I don't know how you can ignore the call, it's so strong my body is shaking."

"It is for me, too. But I'm going to try to hold out. At least for the day, longer if I can."

"Maybe I can send Faeries, and give you an update," I suggested.

"Do you know how to do it?"

"Nope. I'll figure it out."

"Listen." Felix shifted uncomfortably. "I have something to

tell you."

"Okay."

He waited a beat. "Nevermind. It's … not the right time."

"Seriously? Now I need to know!"

"No, I'll tell you soon. Too much has happened today. I need to think about it more." He tightened his arms around his waist. I had never seen him so guarded.

"All right, Felix, next time then. Be safe." I wrapped my arms around him and squeezed him with all my might. My brother. My wonderful, caring brother who was strong enough to ignore the Pull and go back to our mom for a little while longer. He was the best of us. I released him to look at him again, then turned to follow the insistent call to enter the Vale.

CHAPTER 3

The air flurried inside of the trees before I stepped in. Everything fluttered rapidly in a nervous, erratic jitter. Standing just on the outside, the leaves barely shifted above me. I pushed in, knowing exactly what I'd feel. The air thickened and resisted, the invisible border flattened out the planes of my body, just before swallowing and spitting me into the center of the circle. Was that the test? Only Vale Born could pass the film? Or was what followed the real metric, being able to call the opening to enter the passage to Alternis. I looked back to Felix, frozen in time on the other side. I imagined he'd see barely a flicker of me, before I disappeared due to the frequency shift.

I sucked in a breath as I waited for the next stage to begin, colors bloomed inside the membrane. Each plant glowed with its own aura, as the dappled light danced on my skin. There was a thrum that I could not only hear, but also feel against my body as the spot of light appeared; an opening, the rift that called to me. I raised my hand to the flicker that widened toward me. A beckoning that tugged at my fingers, and a longing I couldn't deny drew me toward it.

The air rushed as I stepped in further, uncomfortably bright colors burned themselves into my sight in haphazard patterns. The world funneled down to a narrow passage, and sucked me in. I slid into a chaotic tunnel.

Flashes assaulted my senses as wind whipped past my ears. My hair flapped over my shoulder, straight out in front as I blew through the vortex I had entered. My chest tightened and breath quickened as I slipped further in, swept along like a twig in a raging river. The loud cracks and strobing visuals were overwhelming as I fell deeper through the gate.

I lost all sense of time while I was in the passage, was it ten minutes—an hour? It took all my will not to have a full-blown panic attack. Holding my arm up to my face did little to block the clamor. I could see the stimuli through the minute gaps of my hands when I tried to cover my eyes. The intense pain I had felt during my initial journey was thankfully absent. That should have been a clue when Felix and I came back to the human world. It hadn't hurt, therefore we hadn't changed.

Eventually the turbulence started to quiet and the flares subsided. My heart fluttered with relief as I blinked my eyes open to the view off the precipice. The tops of the Praegra Forest bobbed high in the atmosphere. Inhaling a huge breath, I flexed my fingers and stretched all my limbs as my power surged. The dam on my well had been released, and the simmering strength that waited to be used heated my blood. Powerful, I felt truly powerful. I debated whether I could jump straight off the lip, and guide myself down the length of the vertical vines in the blink of an eye. The blink of a Fae hybrid eye. I could do it, I knew I could.

I took a half breath as I retracted a pace. *Absolute power.* I gulped as Felix's words echoed in my memory. I realized how intoxicating the power was, the sickening understanding struck deep. I hadn't noticed it on my first arrival. Maybe it was the pain of the transformation, and the raw, ragged state of my emotions as I slid through the tunnel uncontrolled. Based on how I felt now, Dashelle's lust might have almost made sense. And with her absorbing more and more of it, there was no telling what that would feel like. Fortunately when Felix and I had bonded with the Maeder tree, she had sipped off a portion, tamed some of the fire that boiled inside me when my sister, Maris, had rejoined her. Maris had been fire. I would have thought her water, with her graceful movements and easygoing personality. But she wasn't. There was a piece of her we didn't get to meet, maybe it would have shown itself as she grew older. Seeing her coalesce with the tree—a healing so profound and complete—was the greatest gift I had ever been given.

When Felix and I had finally climbed out of the Well to head home, I had felt it. The strength—the depth that churned within me begging for an escape, it had ebbed. Tempered by our creator and returned to its source, perhaps. The energy beneath my skin was still considerable, the gradual lead up to testing its limits had trained me how to sense it, manage its reserve before I would collapse completely.

I flexed again as I stared unfocused in the distance. If this was me now, what did Dashelle feel? I shook my head, *She's a completely different person, it was her choices with the power, not how much she had.* I thought about all she had taken from me; Josie, our house—the last link to those that I had lost, burned pictures of the proof of my human upbringing with my family. All gone. All for her greed and power lust. I couldn't be like her, I wouldn't. And I wouldn't let her take what good I had found. I would fight fiercely. I steeled my resolve and walked to the edge of the dropoff, then jumped.

CHAPTER 4

I swung down in fluid arcs, just as I had pictured. It was as easy as I imagined—easier—as I cascaded down the weaving vines. My skin prickled with the rush of cool, sweet air against it. I scanned the ground as I continued my descent. Multitasking had never been so natural; navigating a treacherous downwards traverse while looking for foes, and also thinking about which direction to start off in. I landed silently on the mossy ground as I finished estimating the best path. My gaze fell on the cluster of rocks, the same ones where Opius stood when I met him. Prick. His dashing smile flashed in my mind. I shook my head as I went in the opposite direction, away from Lacausia territory, leaving the memory of him where it belonged.

TerraIgni would take many rotations to get to, Rannoch had to head back there as soon as I had left before. Hopefully I would happen upon Faeries that might aid me in getting the message to him that I was back already. *I was in the human world for ... six hours? That's about seven rotations, I guess.* Having never been to his homeland, I didn't know if they would have already reached it. They were most likely still traveling, based on what he had told me about its location.

I hit the trail at a sprint, constantly scanning my surroundings as my thoughts churned. Where to go, what to seek out, what should be my first goal? Faeries would be a score if I could find some, but so far not a single being had caused my ears to prick up. North I would go, until there was reason to go elsewhere.

The forest thickened as I pressed on. The chirping of unseen birds—or mammals—told me there were at least no predators nearby. The air was heavy with moisture, as the moss grew more slick underfoot. Water, there was definitely water nearby. The lights of the Praegra Forest glimmered high in the trees. Were those Faeries? They didn't sing, and took no interest in me. I sent out a thought, like a spear in the early morning air to whoever was nearby. Maybe it would strike someone, hopefully not the wrong kind of someone. I was pretty sure I was heading well away from the Umorfae borders, that was my primary concern. Happening upon any of them was the last thing I wanted. I should probably stop the mind-javelins, who knew who I was throwing them out to. Especially if Dashelle was in Alternis, and hunting for me. If I felt the Pull, she did, too.

After hours of running, I still was not out of breath, and hadn't seen a hint of another creature. Alone in this world. Who was I here? Physically this was where I belonged, emotionally too, but how could I fit what I was before into it? It all had to mash together, what I had learned from my upbringing needed to find a place in this new reality. The Vale clearly would not allow me to live outside of it, even just a few hours away and it began pulling me back—demanding that I return. As I ran across the lush ground, I resolved that I would honor my human mother by retaining who I am while I was here. Alternis was alluring, consuming. But I couldn't let it overtake who I was at my core. My past and where I grew up had to have a purpose, I couldn't let that just fade away and be forgotten.

I slowed to a walk as I approached a stream. My ears twitched as I determined a stronger volume farther off, my magic sensed it; a wide river that traveled northwards, from the southeast. Ancient and wise, the waters conveyed knowledge, an understanding of something more. I called a runnel of water to drink from, when I sensed someone approaching, the faintest ripple alerted me to their presence.

I retreated three paces and obscured myself behind a tree, as the head of a creature emerged from the water in the distance, and let only its eyes above the surface. It moved as fast as lightning, in half a heartbeat it was across from me.

I stifled a gasp as my eyes fell on familiar dark hair and large, black eyes.

CHAPTER 5

Naiya. How could it be her? I blinked rapidly to clear the image. She couldn't be here. She crept out of the water on whisper-quiet legs, her long dorsal fin dragged on the ground as she emerged completely. I could hear the minuscule rocks being picked up by her scales and scraping along the larger riverbed rocks. I tracked her for several steps, silently climbing over the massive roots of the tree to peer at her from the other side as she passed by. Could it be some shape-shifter that took on the appearance of someone you knew, using the familiarity to lull the viewer into a false sense of security? *Questions, questions, it is always questions with you.* I shook my head, *Dammit, Opius, get out of my brain.*

In my digression my hand frayed a piece of bark off of the tree, which made enough of a sound to get her attention. She whirled towards me, as our gazes locked to each other.

"Naiya … how?"

"Not Naiya, I am her sister, Neila."

My heart stuttered. She had lost her sister, too.

"I came to warn you. Silvanis, he knows you are back. He lied to the empress, after he slunk back from the battle. He made her believe you had murdered Opius without reason, and convinced her to let him go after you when you returned. He is already on your trail. I am faster in the water than he is on foot, so I used the small window I had to reach you first."

"I don't know who that is, I'm guessing one of Opius's henchmen."

"Yes, he is the one you healed. Silvanis told the empress how you and your brother wounded him, then intentionally healed him so he could return to inform her that you intend to take over the realm. To deliver the message that it was time for another Vale Born to rule."

"What the-! That was what Dashelle was doing! Not me!" My thoughts spun. I had been framed for Dashelle's hateful deeds, and now a pissed-off Umorfae was hot on my trail.

Well, fuck, Rannoch was right. "Why did you come to warn me?"

"We Syrenni are desperate. Naiya lost her life trying to free us. Now it is up to me to protect her embryo before it hatches, and to hide it from the Umorfae when it does emerge. They control when we breed, taking our eggs before they can be fertilized. This one, it is different somehow, very different. Larger than any Syrenni embryo I have ever seen. And I have sensed power from it. Keeping it safe was the last thing Naiya made me promise. This was my only chance to do something, before it would be too dangerous. Naiya helped me break the Taming, but there are many others that have not been able to."

My stomach dropped as I remembered Opius devouring his breakfast, his Syrenni egg breakfast. "What is the Taming?"

"Vitus Augustus—the Vale Born that ruled—he instructed

the Umorfae on how to shield our mental powers, so that they could control us. Before then, we were formidable. Only those that have broken the Taming can remember our prior strength, so most are in placid servitude. Even though I can remember it, I cannot access it."

"What else can you tell me about him?" I asked my former friend's twin. "Dashelle wants to be like him, to take over this realm. We thought we defeated her but she tricked us."

"I tend to the Palace library, and read in secret whenever I can, in the hopes of finding a clue to unraveling the Taming. I found a book on his history. He was ruthless. He discovered he could absorb other Vale Born's powers and grow in strength, leaving none to challenge him."

I fidgeted and looked around, how long did we have before Silvanis found me? I didn't have time for information I already knew.

"By adding to his well, he could avoid the threat of death from delving too deep in the power and burning out."

My eyes snapped back to her. "Death? From burnout?"

"Yes. Fae simply run out of power until their well refills, but Vale Born can borrow against it, draw more and more to the point that they lose consciousness. And if too much is drawn or burnout has happened too many times, they can die."

Shit. I had reached burnout … twice? Rannoch must not have known, he'd never let me go that far if he knew I could die from it. He would have cited that as a reason to not heal enemies after the battle.

"You must go, there is no time left. I came to implore you to find a way to help us. I believe you may be the only one who can break my people's bonds."

I gulped and nodded, remembering the last time I had seen Naiya, and hearing the heartbreaking wail she had let out. It carried her ultimate failure to save her kind, and apparently, the knowledge of a child she would never get to meet. "I will." More questions, I had so many more questions.

Her eye membranes flashed as she backed towards the water. "Stay safe, Lily. Do not stop until you are with someone you trust. And stay hidden from any Umorfae."

Obviously. "You were never here. I don't want them doing to you what they did to Naiya."

She dipped her head, then disappeared into the water. I waited to see if she resurfaced, but she never did. I turned back towards my prior path, when I heard ground plants rustle off in the distance.

CHAPTER 6

My eyes went round as I realized who it might be. I wasn't going to wait around to find out. Based on my location, chances were pretty high it wasn't a friend. It couldn't be Felix, he was heading back to our mom for at least the rest of the day, if he could hold out. That would be seven to ten rotations. I took off at a flat-out run. I lowered the angle of my head, each of my mighty strides cleared ten feet at a time. I chopped my bent arms in rhythm with my near-silent footfalls.

As I bolted through the forest, my mind rambled over what Neila had told me. Absorbing that much power prevented burnout, that would mean Dashelle could just wait me out in a head to head stand-off, until I lost consciousness. The extra abilities would be a boon of course, but the true advantage was the ability to have her well never run dry. My thoughts reeled, how could we fight against her if her well was already the depth of four Vale Born combined? *With allies, that's how.*

Neila's plea echoed in my mind, it seemed I was fated to help those who suffered the injustices of the Umorfae. But in truth, I wanted to help. If Naiya hadn't been brave enough to seek out

Rannoch and damage the Imperiductus, none of the events that followed would have happened. I would have been delivered to Dashelle without a hitch, a lamb ready for slaughter. Just as Josie had been handed over, probably still in Opius's thrall. And I wouldn't have met Rannoch, or Kerenza, and discovered my true strengths. *I will find a way.*

I hoped I was going in the right direction, the forest was so dense that it gave no indication as to where I was actually headed. Maintaining a straight path was difficult, the massive trunks caused significant detours. Though hopefully they also concealed me from the one who tracked me. The bright daylight and pleasant atmosphere belied what was after me, as if the forest had yet to catch on to the evil charging behind me. Perhaps I had gotten far enough ahead that I had given myself a solid buffer. I thanked whatever Gods watched over this realm that Neila had warned me in the nick of time. I adjusted my course to avoid another tree, when my ears twanged, picking up the sound of a bowstring snapping; followed by the thud of an arrow burying itself in the bark of the tree, near where I had just passed.

My chest tightened as I realized how close he was, how close I had come to getting hit. It was a low shot, probably meant to take out a leg. *So he could finish the bargain that Opius had struck, no doubt.*

I pressed on faster, and used a burst of fury at the thought of Opius's deal to release a swath of flame behind me. I cringed, I hated starting a fire, but it was the only thing I could think of to slow him down. I laid down four more burning hurdles after that, to waylay my pursuer.

The telltale hiss of water dousing a flame confirmed that he was an Umorfae, even though there was no question in my mind. Neila's warning combined with the direction the foe had come from, I knew it had to be him. Hopefully the smoke and steam would help disguise my path. I released two more ahead of me, then I veered off and headed east. The diversion might buy me a little time. I prayed the crackle of twigs igniting would be enough sound to cover any movements I made. Faster, I needed to go faster.

Three had been put out, that left four more burning blockades—as long as he took the bait of the last two. The sounds got further away as I raced, I heard another slosh of water. Then another.

I pushed on, my lungs were near-bursting from how much air I inhaled. I gritted my teeth, *I will go faster!* I drew from my well and willed strength to my legs, they heated and quickened to a speed I had never tapped. The forest became a blur as the distant sound of the last two fires were put out in sequence. He fell for it. I didn't let the relief slow me down, as I ran headlong deeper into the forest.

I screeched to a halt, as I peered up into the tree in front of me. A pair of beady eyes stared back.

CHAPTER 7

I could have screamed with elation. I had found the Amabilis. I projected a thought, "Please, help me. I'm being hunted by an Umorfae. You know me, please, escort me away from here." I was burning precious seconds. If he did not agree to help me, it could be a fatal error. I swiveled my head, searching the trees for signs of his approach.

I looked back to the Amabilis, still silently watching me. "Please! You know my mind. I endeavor to help innocents of this land. I need to find Rannoch … Prince Rannoch Ashwani Albericus." My breath hitched at his whole name.

A twig snapped, which echoed through my ears. I flinched, then realized the sound was not from Silvanis, it was the Amabilis bursting forward while inflating, not waiting to clear the branch before he grew. The bough cracked as he leaped from it and flung his arms out.

He sailed down, in one fluid motion he encircled me and wrapped his membrane wings around me. As he finished encasing me, I glimpsed the Umorfae, at the same moment that he released an arrow. I spun and shrunk with the Amabilis a millisecond before the arrow arrived. Silvanis's angry howl was the last thing I heard, before I entered the chaotic sublayer with my guide.

I clenched my eyes shut at the sudden barrage of bright lights, it took every ounce of my willpower to force myself to breathe slowly. My fists balled as I tried to maintain my composure. I wanted to cry with relief at my narrow escape. It had been too close. Emotions surged as we hurtled along the strange path. The pulsing energy of the nebulae threads strobed as we raced. I wanted to both stare at the wondrous beauty, and turn away from the overwhelming vastness of it. I closed my eyes and pictured Rannoch, I couldn't wait to collapse into his arms.

"Do not worry, we will escort you safely," the Amabilis's voice finally echoed in my head. "We are searching for him now."

I reminded myself that they could hear my thoughts, and to keep my imagination from straying into lustful territory. I bit my lip as my skin flushed, I couldn't help it. The memory of him alone was enough to heat my blood. Plus, I just needed him close, to know he was all right and to feel his warmth surrounding me. *He better be okay.*

"Take heart, young one."

I nodded wordless thanks as we sped through the flashing sublayer. My mind spun as we tunneled further into the realm. I wished I could close my mind to them, and not worry that my mental wanderings were being monitored by a race that could read and disseminate all of my thoughts. Shutting down further postulations about Rannoch's whereabouts was my only recourse. I was left to wonder where we were headed, and how long the journey would be.

My daydream ended as we expanded into a forested area, the

trees surrounding us shrank as we inflated. The visual disparity caused my mind to wobble, the trees of course hadn't changed size, I had. But the change gave me pause as my rational mind worked to order what had actually happened with what my senses had told me. Human brains were not equipped to deal with a proportionally altered reality.

The Amabilis held a paw to my shoulder as I faltered. "Get your balance. We have brought you to where we believe you need to go."

I gulped as I tried to keep myself from bending over at the waist and retching. I had run for so long before being whisked away by this savior, and then our travel through the electrified passage, it was enough to make anyone overwhelmed. Let alone someone that constantly had the threat of debilitating panic attacks waiting to take hold.

The area resolved into clarity, tall trees with an unmistakable birch-like pattern came into view surrounding me. The outermost edges of the Arbor Elves forest spread out before us.

The relief at the familiar sight made me release a breath I didn't realize I was holding. I looked around, anxiously waiting for another Amabilis to appear, with my love in tow.

"He has not been located yet." The din sounded between my ears. "We are still searching, but we suspect he is in the Hinterdunes. That is the only region we do not go, it lies beyond the Praegra Forest and must be crossed to reach TerraIgni."

My heart sank. Hopes for a reunion were blown away as thoughts of endless, harsh sand dunes came to mind. I blinked tears away, how would I find him? I needed to warn him. I unclenched my hand and counseled myself to calm down. "Thank you for bringing me here. I surely would have been captured by the Umorfae without your help. I was very lucky to find you." I placed an arm across my chest and bowed.

"It was not luck, we heard you before, when you sent a thoughtwave out. We admire you for what you did to save the Ignisfae children, and are glad to help in this way. If we are successful in finding Rannoch, we will bring him here."

As the Amabilis shrank back into the sublayer, the familiar electric portals exclusive to the Arbor Elves appeared. Two fenestrams opened in front of me.

CHAPTER 8

The bright white opening edged in multi-hued colors crackled in front of me, forcing wide the endpoint and revealing two friendly faces on the other side. Dendris and Illaran spun then stepped through, coming to a rest right in front of me with weapons raised.

The fact that they arrived with swords at the ready was no surprise, it seemed to be their default approach to whomever crossed their borders. I knew they were old friends there to greet me in my time of need. Though truthfully, if Dashelle really was alive, it was all our time of need.

"It's great to see you both! I bring important news. How is Aurelian?"

Dendris held up a hand to halt further questions. "She has vastly improved, Lily. It is good to see you again as well." Her face had barely a flicker of a smile, but her brilliant green eyes sparkled in genuine happiness. "She has not returned to official duty yet, but she is up and about, though moves slowly."

I nodded, mulling over what I had to tell their Venitor. I didn't want to cause her stress as she was trying to recover. "Perhaps I should give the news to Tenaraen, and she can relay it to Aurelian as she sees fit. May I enter with you? I am unarmed."

They replied wordlessly with a single dip of the head, Dendris guided me through the portal, into the majestic tree lined hall. The expansive room was remarkably cozy, with appealing warm light and gentle chatter from all who sat at the long banquet tables. Returning to their common room imparted an instant sense of calm. It was most welcome, considering how concerned I was about the Amabilis not being able to find Rannoch.

"Please sit and rest, I will alert Tenaeran that you are here," Dendris said as she deposited me at a sparsely populated, long wood table. My gaze wandered around the room, until it fell on an individual across the way. Piked ears, and a larger build than the Arbor Elves, definitely some sort of Fae. The stranger twirled a drink in the air with his fingers as he stared at me. It rotated slowly, the clear glass levitated above his fingertips as the pink liquid inside wobbled slightly. He didn't tear his eyes away as he released the magic and snatched it out of the air to take a sip. A mischievous smile spread across his pale face as he lifted his beverage in my direction. A drink being set to my left startled me out of the moment. Illaran set a plate of fruit down next to it as she glanced at where I had been looking. I raised my eyebrows with a silent question.

"Don'Li, a Caelifae that has come to visit. He has been here three rotations. Each one feels longer than the last," she muttered the last part under her breath. She winced, then said, "He is kind enough, he is just a bit … loud sometimes."

"What is he doing here?"

"I came to find out about the rumored battle!" his voice thundered, now only two paces away from me. The wind from his flash movement breezed past a moment later. I hadn't even seen him get up.

"Don'Li, this is Lily, the Vale Born who fought against Dashelle."

He swung his leg over the bench and seated himself without an invitation. Vapor wafted in tendrils around him as he leaned closer, inspecting me. I tilted my head and cocked an eyebrow as he studied my face, the mist swirled closer and glided over my hand which rested on the table. I resisted the urge to pull back as it grazed my skin, causing the tiny hairs to stand up at full attention. The mist measured me, testing me somehow.

"Interesting, your well is deep. You are powerful, strong. When we Caelifae heard of the battle between two Vale Born, I was sent to find out more information. We do not need another Fae war on our hands. The death of Vitus Augustus and the subsequent coup of the Umorfae nearly shattered our realm, that is something we want to avoid at all costs." He narrowed his cloud-blue eyes, the irises rimmed in brilliant prismatic rainbows.

My breath hitched. "I wasn't the one that started this conflict. Dashelle was the one who-"

"Yes, yes, but now that she has been defeated, what are *your* intentions?"

"I have no goal of ruling, if that's what you mean. She wanted to rule, and was destroying other Vale Born to do it. She tried to kill me, I fought along with Ignisfae and Petrafae, against her and the faction of Umorfae who had joined her."

"So then what *is* your goal?"

Someone rushing up to my side distracted me from the question. Ten's vivid eyes were wide as she glided toward me. "Lily!" I stood to greet her, she lifted her hand to press against mine in a warm hello.

"The Amabilis brought me here, I was trying to find Rannoch, I needed to warn him—warn everyone."

Her eyes darkened, I flashed a questioning glance in Don'Li's direction. She nodded for me to proceed. "I'm not sure how much you know about the battle, I assume since Don'Li knows Dashelle is Vale Born, you know as well. We didn't know that fact, until after Rannoch and I had been captured." I sucked in a breath, thinking of all that had happened since I had seen the Arbor Elves last. "Contingents of Ignisfae and Petrafae came to help us, led by Kerenza. We thought we defeated Dashelle but she tricked us. She survived, and escaped. She went back to the human realm and burned down my family home. I assume she found it because Opius had been her Umorfae ally."

I winced, not wanting to think of my home's destruction, my history with him and all of the precious information I had unknowingly spilled.

"Alive!" Don'Li roared.

I cringed as it reverberated in my eardrums. "I believe she is coming back here, to garner more resources and reattempt a takeover. I wanted to tell you, so that you could decide what to tell Aurelian. I didn't want to jeopardize her recovery by adding concern over this matter."

"Fortunately," a voice came from behind a tree trunk support beam, "I am well enough to still be stealthy." Aurelian stepped around the obstruction, her cane clicked on the solid wood flooring as she approached. "I appreciate your concern, but I need to know all issues that might involve my people."

"Of course, Aurelian. I think Dashelle may be ... a vengeful person. What other reason would she have for burning down the place where I grew up?" I gulped, thinking about my mom and our memories now being piles of ash. "You and your people had helped us, and fought against her allies. If she manages to rise to power, she may take out her revenge on you as well."

Her face didn't so much as flicker, she stood a little taller, easing herself off the cane. "Our choice to help you was the right one, even if there were or will be consequences. We will be prepared for whatever happens."

My eyes stung with tears, though I had done everything I could to aid in her recovery, the guilt that gnawed at me from the result of the Arbor Elve's assistance threatened to undermine me. Their losses of Aolis, Fenlaen, Auroris—and Aurelian's current physical state—haunted me.

"We will fight again, if it comes to that," she said as she stepped to Tenaeran. "Eat, rest, we will talk further later."

She placed her hand in the crook of Ten's bent arm, then headed to the other side of the great room together.

I turned back to Don'Li, who sat staring at me. "Well, I can see they trust you. I shall give you a pass, for now."

Oh wow, thanks! I had to stop myself from visibly rolling my eyes. "So what's your story? What's this great war you mentioned?"

He paused as several Arbor Elves delivered food and drinks, waiting until they had dispersed to say anything.

He picked up the fresh glass of wine, then inspected it as he said, "Before Vitus Augustus's rule, the Fae peacefully coexisted. He changed everything, introduced greed, hatred, and most of all distrust. He ruled here for over fifteen hundred cycles. It was the Umorfae that took to greed readily. After his death, they struck.

The Petrafae were the worst hit, losing their castle to them and they were nearly obliterated in numbers. They started a new city, the refuge of Adrilan off to the north, but they never quite recovered. My people, the Caelifae, fared better but not by much. The Umorfae killed many. The Ignisfae were the least affected, largely due to the location of TerraIgni. Crossing the Hinterdunes is dangerous, and makes the perfect buffer against a water-reliant race. However, the Ignisfae still rely on trade so they were not spared the wrath of Empress Caldine, Celestine's mother." He knocked back a gulp of the wine, draining the entire cup. He held up the glass and motioned to a nearby Elf for a refill.

I looked at my own glass and I mulled over his words. I took a sip before asking, "So if this Vale Born was so bad, why does anyone here trust me at all?"

He lowered his brows. "Some do not. Probably most who lived during the time of the war."

"Did you live during the war?"

"I was a young filio, but yes."

Noted. "How do you get to the Hinterdunes? I need to find Prince Rannoch."

He flashed a devilish smile and arched a brow. "Oh do you?"

My cheeks flushed and I cleared my throat, trying to side-step his suggestive tone. "I also was hoping … I want to learn how to talk to Faeries. I need to send a message. Do you know how?"

He blew out a breath, which caused my hair to rustle and the vapor flow faster off of his flossy white hair, which resembled cirrus clouds.

"Yes, I know how."

"Will you teach me?"

He tipped back on the bench. "Share a few drinks and a meal with me, then I will teach you on the next rotation."

"Deal."

An Elf delivered more drinks and food, we drank as I peppered Don'Li with more questions.

"You are a curious one. I should get some sleep before your lesson. I may not be ready for the Fading, but I am not as young as I used to be."

"The Fading?"

"When we pass to the next realm, we Fade into it. Visible age only happens just before the Fading, when our hearts accept we are nearly ready to move on."

I thought back on all the Fae I had encountered, only one had appeared older; Illyana, the Ignisfae female that had made the nourishing tortams. I frowned, realizing that one day Kerenza and Rannoch would Fade as well. *As all beings do, I guess.*

"Do not make that sad face, I will be around much longer!"

His comment startled me out of my thoughts. He bellowed a laugh as he took another slug of wine. Don'Li flexed his arm muscles. "And we live in perpetual youth until that time!"

I chuckled as I finished my glass. "Well, I should get some rest, too."

"Alone?" He cocked an eyebrow at me.

"Yes, alone. That is until I find Rannoch. We are together."

"Just as I thought. Smart of him."

"Why's that?"

He shrugged. "Well, a Vale Born as an ally is a considerable boon. As he is prince of TerraIgni, it shows he is wise. Though King Ashwan may prefer an Ignisfae female at his side."

I dropped my brows and scowled. "I don't think Rannoch cares for me *because* I'm Vale Born. And he had plenty of opportunities to select an Ignisfae mate as I understand it. It wasn't what he wanted. Besides, he does have an Ignisfae female he can rely on. Kerenza."

He smirked. "Perhaps. Well, I suppose I should get some sleep. Shame it will be unaccompanied."

I rolled my eyes after he turned around. *Whatever.* I saw through his ploy, trying to weed out insecurities and introduce doubt. *Not cool.*

I got up to find an escort to wherever I'd be sleeping. I found Dendris sitting cross-legged on a bench, gazing at the mural on the far wall of the hall. I startled her as I came to a stop by her side.

"I didn't mean to disturb you."

"Not at all. I often come to the vision wall to think. I see something different every time I sit. It brings me solace."

I gazed at it for a few minutes with her. Indeed, different colors than the last time I had looked at it came to the forefront. "Last time I saw so many violet colors, purple and also blue. Now I see so much yellow."

"That is because you are in a different place in your life, what you need is what is presented."

I stood a moment and absorbed the feeling of a painted sunrise, with a deep red smear on the horizon. Like a slash of blood on a blissfully unaware victim. One of my dad's sayings jumped into my mind as I tore my eyes from the brilliant image. *Red skies at morning, sailor's warning.*

"Come, I will guide you to your room. Will you be staying long this visit?"

"Unfortunately no. Once I send a Faerie to message Rannoch I will set off to find him."

She nodded. "We are glad to see you again, even for such a brief time."

A tear pricked my eye. Being around the Arbor Elves soothed me. Anxiety was a memory when I spent time with them. And their wondrous home in the trees, such a refuge in a realm where dangers lurked was a rare blessing.

"I'm so thankful to be here again. I was nearly captured by an Umorfae before arriving. I am terrified to think where I could be at the moment, if I hadn't been brought here by the Amabilis." I shuddered as I imagined myself in the throne room, thrust before Empress Celestine being tried for crimes against the Umorfae.

Dendris stood, then pulled open a fenestram, wiping away my momentary descent into the what-ifs of being caught by Silvanis. She guided me into a room; a lush retreat where I could gather my thoughts and calm my concerns. But until I knew Rannoch and Kerenza were safe, peace would evade me. With no way of knowing where Dashelle was at the moment, hypervigilance would be my friend.

Dendris handed me a communicator band before reopening a portal to depart. I clutched it as I watched the sparking oval close to a speck, as she disappeared from view.

CHAPTER 9

Sweat beaded on my skin as I startled awake, I gasped for air as choking sobs heaved out of my shaking body. Images of my haunting dreams flitted through my mind; large black eyes staring vacantly into the distance, before being swallowed in a plume of flame, an identical female cradling a growing egg in the wake of her sister's loss. Droves of amphibious beings trudged with heads bent toward a pit of certain death, with Umorfae towering on both sides, forcing them to their doom. Dashelle's maniacal laugh echoed as I went over the edge of the abyss with the Syrenni, into the darkness. Far below, bodies piled up in endless heaps. The last image was the most disturbing of all, the one that cut to my heart so completely; Josie's bloodless face and broken limbs lay mangled atop the others.

I sobbed and clutched the blankets I was safely tucked into, the Arbor Elf comforts were a small relief from the dark night-mare. I brushed the hair from my forehead, plastered in place from perspiring all night, the knot that had formed between my brows ached as I rubbed it. I peeled off the sheets that clung to my body, desperate to wipe the residue from the fitful sleep. Fortunately, the bathing chamber was a few steps away and ready to wash away the salty layer that coated me.

Showered and dressed in the Elven camouflage pants and fitted tank, I twisted the blocks of the summoning cube to alert an Elf. Illaran appeared, then guided me to the dining hall.

Don'Li turned as I arrived, and flashed a cocky smile in my direction from across the room. He was in front of me in an instant, the wind from his movement billowed past me a moment later.

I blinked in surprise as he bellowed, "Well, up at last are you? Arbor Elf clothing suits you, you look quite appealing."

I winced at his deafening tone and shielded my ears. "Can we start my lesson on calling Faeries, please?" I asked, ignoring his comment.

"All right then." His tone was now a barely audible whisper.

I lowered my hands from my head. "Do you not have a regular talking tone? Is it just full volume or almost none? I have to admit that when you're loud, it's too much for my ears."

"I apologize, that is a common complaint amongst even my brethren. It is probably one of the reasons they are always sending me out on errands, rather than keeping me around." He sagged and cast his eyes down momentarily.

"If you could keep it on the quieter side, I'd appreciate it. Now, what do we do?"

"Outside is best, Faeries are more likely to come if they do not have to pass between walls. A dedicated Faerie would come regardless, but it is best to make it easy for them to find you."

"What do you mean "dedicated"?"

"Some have a Faerie that has connected with them. When that happens, that Faerie will always respond when called, even within walls."

I nodded. "I see. I plan on leaving right away. Since we're heading out, I'll let the Elves know."

I marched over to Dendris and Illaran, who were laying out trays of food. "I will be leaving now. Would you mind escorting Don'Li and I outside?"

"Aurelian and Tenaeran requested to be notified when you were departing. Eat something while I retrieve them," Dendris said as she finished sliding the platter in place.

Oh, right, food. I inhaled a breath, it took considerable effort to quell my nerves and force myself to sit. I bounced a knee as I ate some fruit. I could barely swallow as I thought about Rannoch, worrying that somehow I was already too late and Dashelle had found him. *Stop it, she'd have a hard time finding him.* I couldn't help myself though, as he didn't know she survived, he also didn't know about the threat of her likely return.

I closed my eyes for a beat, when I opened them again Don'Li had just finished seating himself at my table.

"You should smile more, you are such a pretty filia, a frown does nothing for your features."

I slammed a fist on the table, rattling the dishes and shaking the glasses of the Elves that sat on the far end. I planted my hands flat on the wood and leaned toward him. "Look, I appreciate that you are going to teach me to call Faeries. But that does not invite you to comment on my features or my body. I have made it clear that I am with Rannoch." My skin prickled with heat and my eyes flashed, the fire churned from the inside out.

He flinched and shrank back. "I am sorry, I … I am alone in this world," he whispered with his shoulders slumped. "I lied before. I am near Fading, but I have held it off. I never found a mate, I made mistakes in that area, grave mistakes. I pined for one that was already mated, and ruined her life in the process. Our relationship caused nothing but grief for … several important Fae. I thought perhaps I still had a chance to redeem myself." He avoided looking at me as his face creased in anguish, and guilt.

I blew out a breath and lifted my hands off the surface, a blackened imprint was left burned into the wood. *Great.*

"You can Fire Bring," he breathed.

"Yes, I can. And I'm sorry to hear that you never found a match. I'm sure you'd make someone—the right someone—a good mate. But as I said, it's not me."

"I did not mean to offend you with my comments. I admit I have become desperate as the Fading nears. Though I still have youthful good looks and appeal, I know they will be gone soon."

"Can I give you a little advice?"

He sighed and motioned for me to proceed.

"You're very handsome, but looks alone are not what a female is drawn to. When I met you, you tried to get me to doubt Rannoch's intentions. I suggest just being yourself, being real."

He nodded and exhaled, wisps of mist feathered off of him as he did. "You are right. It was a tactic that I should not have tried. I had too much to drink, and was not making sound decisions. I am glad though that nothing happened between us, it would not have been the first time I damaged the royal familia of TerraIgni, even if it was an eon ago. And my earlier comments, they were only meant to be compliments."

I regretted lashing out at him, even though his approach with me was less than honorable. He was clearly distraught over his lack of companionship. I couldn't imagine wandering a realm for hundreds of years alone. His own kind didn't even want him around. I did wonder what he meant by "damaged" but I also wanted to let it go and leave it in the past.

I reached forward and patted his hand. "Friends?"

He perked up and boomed, "Friends!"

"Dammit, Don'Li! That was loud!" My ears rang for a moment after, the searing noise caused my eyes to water.

He cringed and whispered, "Sorry."

I chuckled after the shock had passed. "I think I might be risking my hearing by being friends with you."

He grinned sheepishly. "I will try harder to be quiet."

Aurelian and Ten appeared, followed by Dendris, who carried a loaded pack.

"Dendris alerted us that you will be departing," Aurelian said when she came to a stop. Her cane shook in her hand, which I did my best to ignore. "We wish you well in your quest, Lily. Should you ever need anything, call on us. We will come. Grow with purpose."

"Grow with purpose, Aurelian and Ten. Your hospitality and aid is once again my saving grace."

Dendris handed me the pack she carried. "Food and essentials for your expedition. We washed your garment as well, and included extra clothing. I will guide you to the border of the Arbor Boles closest to the Hinterdunes."

I smiled at her, though she rarely returned the gesture, her eyes squinted at me as she cracked a smile of her own. Thoughts of when she had braved the cave with me resurfaced, the trials we had endured together to knit us as unlikely friends. "I will miss you, Dendris."

Her face hardened. "Be safe. Stay vigilant."

I nodded as Illaran stepped over with Don'Li. "Right, ready then," I said.

They opened fenestrams, then we stepped through to the border of their realm. Dendris gave me one last long look, before wordlessly stepping through back to the hall. I glimpsed Aurelian and Ten on the other side of the portal. Ten raised her hand in farewell as the doorway closed.

I turned to Don'Li as I adjusted the pack on my back. "Okay, let's get to it."

CHAPTER 10

"So, what do I do?" I asked.

"Well, you start by ... what is it that you do? You blow out in a whistle, well not quite a whistle. And you flutter your tongue, no, your throat."

"You have done this, right?"

"Yes! I have to do it myself to be able to explain it. I have never instructed someone before. And I am bonded to a Faerie, so my call is a bit more specific. Have you ever met a Faerie that took an interest in you?"

"Actually, yes. There was one that peered into my eyes, and I realized that I could see them more. Then later they slept on my hand."

"They? Was there more than one that took a liking to you?"

"Well, no. I said "they" because the Faerie shifted from female to male while I was watching."

"This is magna news! You bonded with that Faerie. Picture them, remember the facial features, close your eyes and weave your sight through the forest, imagining that you can see exactly where they are in Alternis."

I watched as he closed his eyes, a slight wobble emanated through the air around him, and rippled in a wave that distorted our surroundings. Finally, I heard it. The faintest hum came from deep inside him, high pitched and rhythmic. After an overspent outward breath, he blinked his eyes open.

"Now we wait. You try. The call comes from the back of your throat like a beacon, waking up the pulse the first time can be difficult."

I closed my eyes and tried to copy him, thinking of the Faerie's beautiful face, picturing them floating peacefully through the glen. But the glen was empty, they were not there.

I cast my vision farther, searching through the trees of the great forest. A ping called my attention closer, not far from the Arbor Elf territory. I scanned until I honed in on them, swishing through the air in a cadenced murmuration. I opened my mouth to call, to whistle out to them, but the sound was absent. I tried again, no tremor emitted from me. I opened my eyes as my panic rose. "I can't do it!" My breath quickened and my chest tightened as terror gripped me, afraid that I would be unable to tell Rannoch what I desperately needed to. "I can see them but I can't start the call." I rubbed the creases in my forehead as I racked my mind for a solution.

Don'Li placed a hand on my shoulder and murmured, "It will be okay. The first time is not easy. It is awkward to initiate. But you *can* do it."

Moments later, a bluish light zipped through the air and circled around him. He laughed as the Faerie ran across his cheeks in greeting. "It is good to see you old friend!" Tinkling bells answered back. "Will you take a message to the Caelifae? We have word that the Vale Born, Dashelle, lives, and will most likely return to Alternis."

I winced at hearing the news again, my failure at ensuring she had been handled, and my faulty assumption that she had destroyed herself. The Faerie flashed away, leaving Don'Li gazing at the vanishing path of light.

"One of my few friends here, she has never shied away from me when others did. Come, try again. When I call, I give myself a moment to focus inwards, to hone in on the source of the signal."

I sucked in a breath, and closed my eyes as I slowly exhaled. I sent my sight out and searched the forest for the Faerie again. Finding them was easy this time, I knew right where they were. Then, I followed the line back to myself, watching as my vision tunneled into myself. My sight went through my body, and shrank down to view it on a microscopic level. I zeroed in on a cluster of nerves that surrounded a node. I reached for the bundle, which sent a shockwave outward. I pulsed it, as a hum built in a cascading crescendo. I followed the path back out as it radiated in a cresting wave. I took another breath before opening my eyes as I felt the surge reach the Faerie. I smiled at Don'Li, who beamed at me.

"You see! You can do it!" He bellowed, then recoiled. "Sorry," he muttered, "I became excited."

I laughed. "It's okay, I wanted to shout too. Hopefully it won't be too-"

The Faerie arrived before I could finish my sentence. As they circled me, my heart burst with elation and relief. It was not only that I would be able to send my message at last, it was also that I was rejoining with a reassuring presence. I giggled as they kissed each of my cheeks with their dainty feet.

"Will you take a message to Rannoch? I think he is crossing the Hinterdunes to reach TerraIgni. Tell him Dashelle lives and will most likely return here, her threat is imminent. And I am on my way to him, I will be crossing the dunes to find him."

They wavered back for a moment, seeming to hesitate before bowing, then skittered away at a blazing speed.

"Crossing the dunes, eh? Dangerous. Asking your Faerie to enter the Hinterdunes was a large request. They must care for you, it could be deadly for them as well."

I blanched as I dropped my jaw. "Oh no! I didn't realize that. I should call back and find another way."

"No, do not do that. The Faerie would have said no if they did not want to take the risk. Though bonded to you, they have their own mind and will."

My forehead creased with worry as I sent a silent prayer that they would be okay, deliver the message and then return to safety as soon as possible.

"Don'Li, I have a request. I was hoping you'd escort me to the Hinterdunes. I don't know my way there."

He blew out a breath which rustled my hair. "I would be glad to, though I cannot cross the boundary. My race perishes quickly in the dunes. I would be of little use to you. Are you sure you can cross it? The peril is considerable."

"It's what I must do. I need to tell you, an Umorfae, Silvanis, may still be looking for me. I escaped him because of the Amabilis, but I would bet he is still hunting me. My hope is that the Arbor Elf territory is so far from where he was last that he has little chance of finding me." I bit my lip, I sure hoped he *was* still far off. "Why are the dunes so dangerous?"

"I have never entered them myself, I know the heat is beyond what my race can survive. We Caelifae turn into mist and disappear. The Petrafae sink and cannot control the sand. Umorfae wither to dust. I believe the border senses if you have fire, it will allow you to pass, but I do not know for certain. I will take you to the dunes, regardless of the threat of the Umorfae. Perhaps this may be a way for me to redeem past transgressions." He placed his palm on his chest and bowed.

I could have collapsed with relief. Being hunted prior to my arrival at the Arbor Boles left me apprehensive about being all alone as I continued my trek. My eyes welled as I looked at him and returned the gesture.

"We should depart immediately," he said. "The less time we spend traipsing the Praegra Forest, the better. You fought the Umorfae with the Arbor Elves before. It is conceivable Silvanis would come straight here as soon as you evaded him."

The blood drained from my face. He was right. As Opius's trusted Praetor, he would have known the Elves had aided me. It would be a natural assumption this is the first place I would go as soon as I escaped his capture. I tried to reassure myself that at least there was no way into their sanctuary without the assistance of the Arbor Elves. With their dwellings nestled high in the trees and tucked out of view, someone could walk underneath and be unaware of the majestic city hidden in the leaves and branches above. Here on the ground, at the edge of their guarded domain, we were wholly exposed and unprotected.

I captured a breath and steeled my resolve. "Let's go."

CHAPTER 11

We took off running straight east, weaving through trees on an unmarked path. "Stay on this heading," Don'Li shouted, "I will give us a boost from behind." He dropped back, then a current of air pushed against me and propelled me faster. The wind curled around me in a blooming corona, obscuring objects that rushed by my outermost peripheral vision in a haze. My feet were a blur beneath me as I worked to keep up with the assist. Trees streaked by as we hurtled around the trunks.

After what must have been several hours, the horizontal current sputtered out. I slowed and looked behind, Don'Li's face sagged as his steps faltered. I spun around then caught him just before his knees hit the ground.

He opened his mouth to speak, but his voice cracked and only a rasp escaped.

I eased him to the ground, then sat by his side. "Don't worry, I may be able to help. I'm amazed how long you kept that up for. We must have made our way through half the forest already!"

He gulped down breaths. "Not half. But we are almost to the Midgard Well. I hoped I would be able to get us all the way there on the first burst." He squeezed his eyes shut.

I rubbed his shoulder. "You did great. We'll get there." I pulled him over to a ring of rocks, which provided some protection from the exposed forest. I pulsed a thread of healing light, in an attempt to weed out what needed regenerating. I frowned as I burrowed deeper. Every cell in his body felt depleted, like an evenly wilting flower. There was so much that required attention, I didn't know where to focus the beam. I stitched haphazard threads into his joints, but the surrounding tissue was equally taxed. I cast out as much soothing energy as I could, before I backed out and my vision returned to normal.

"I'm sorry, I thought I could do more to help."

"It is okay. The Well will help, but I will need some time before I can attempt to move again."

I nodded. "Next time, maybe not using as much of your element would be wise. You've exhausted yourself."

"It is not just that, my body is starting to fail me. I may not have the visible signs of Fading, but I have the internal clues. It aches horribly some days." He cringed and cast his eyes down.

"Don't worry, rest and regenerate. I'll try and help you more in a moment." I rummaged through the pack Dendris gave me. I found clothes, food, a waterskin, and something hard wrapped in bark. I handed Don'Li the water, then unwrapped the food bundle. I rifled through the many parcels inside, portioned off for each leg of the excursion. I opened one and split it. "Here, eat something," I said as I passed him his half of a bread baked with shredded vegetables. I unfolded the husk from the weighty item, and found a brilliant silver dagger inside.

"An Arbor Elf blade! Quite a gift," he said as he handed back the waterskin. I traded him the blade, letting him inspect the finely crafted detail.

I swigged, noting the reduced weight of the container. "We'll be able to refill this at the Well, right?"

He shook his head as he handed the knife back to me. "No, we will have to find a stream. Taking liquid from the Well is forbidden. Besides, it is not water exactly. It is the lifeblood of the Maeder Tree."

"Oh. That makes sense." My face fell. We would need to find water at some point. We'd be okay for another rotation, but I'd definitely need to replenish before entering the Hinterdunes.

He grimaced and adjusted against the rock, trying to find a more comfortable position.

'What hurts the most right now? I can hone in on that."

"My back, and my knees. Those seem to ache the worst."

"Okay, you just relax. Close your eyes and imagine handing some of your burden to me. Picture it like it's a weight you're letting go of."

My sight narrowed into him as I cast out the golden filaments, binding them in unison around the most inflamed areas of his back. I could see the inflammation lessen as I worked down along his spinal column. Several bulging discs righted themselves and slipped properly into place. I backed out, then focused on his knees. The cartilage was severely depleted, leaving bone to scrape against bone in multiple places. Minute fragments had chipped off, and were cutting into the fleshy tissue like tiny pieces of glass. I moved them back into place and welded them to the head of the femur. Several ligaments were frayed, I lashed around them and tightened the cord to rejoin the fibers back together. I recoiled the threads back up my arms, which snapped into place inside me as my surroundings speckled back into view.

"That was … how did you *do* that? That is some skill!"

I smiled at him. "I'm just glad I could help you feel a bit better."

His face fell again. "Never let the Umorfae get ahold of you, no matter what. They could use that for evil. Knowing them, they will find a way. Fortunately they probably do not know about it, right?"

I cringed. "Well, yea they do. The first time I discovered I had the ability I healed an Umorfae guard. Several witnessed it, though I don't know if any of those guards still live. Then after the battle with Dashelle, I chose to heal the injured, even the enemies. Silvanis was one of them. I was told that he informed Empress Celestine what I had done." I clenched my hands, my damn bleeding heart may have risked more than I thought by being sympathetic.

He gave me a reassuring pat on the shoulder. "Do not beat yourself up. You have found an ally in me, I will do whatever I can to prevent anything from happening to you. I feel better than I have in a long time, thanks to you. We should press on." He stood and stretched. "Good as new!"

I chuckled as I slung the pack across my shoulders. "Just running this time, no magic. I need to let mine regenerate as well. How long do you think until we reach the Midgard Well?"

"Nearly one half rotation. Without the wind assistance it will be considerably slower."

"It's better this way, rather than to fall apart trying to get there faster."

Without another word Don'Li took off at a jog. Not nearly

the blistering pace we had first set out at, but some movement was better than none. We ran until my chest heaved, my skin prickled as we came over the rise to a secluded valley below. I could feel the magic nearby and glimpsed the glittering gem of the Well for a split second, when my eyes fell on an unwelcome and familiar sight.

CHAPTER 12

*S**hit, shit, shit!*

My terror strangled me as I retreated a step. Don'Li followed my wide-eyed gaze down to the north shore of the Well, to a creature floating eerily back and forth, waiting for prey.

"Ah, not good. It has been some time since I crossed paths with the Pythonnisamul," he whispered.

"Not good is right! She's going to kill us if she gets close enough!"

"Not if I can help it."

"What does that mean? What can you do?"

"Just follow my instructions, and we will be okay. I need to dive into the Well, but I only need a moment in there to repair. And with you preparing to cross the Hinterdunes, you should jump in also. We should split up, you head down along the south path, keep your eyes averted. Then I will flank her. Once I do, jump in and swim to the east edge. I will meet you there."

"This sounds like a dangerous idea, even Opius couldn't defeat her with three armed guards. If I'm not mistaken, you're not carrying any weapons. And I only have that dagger. You should take it if you're going to do something crazy."

"I do not need to defeat her, but I can distract her. Now go."

He disappeared in a flurried gale and left me gaping after him. I snuck along the side of the ridge to approach the Well from the farthest side, away from her terrifying vortex and haunting call. Fortunately, she hadn't spotted us, and the light remained where it belonged in the sky. Her deadly siphon had not been initiated, which told me she was not alerted to our presence.

I wove through the trees, using the trunks to hide me from her line of sight for as long as possible, until finally there was nothing left to obscure me. I stepped out onto the shore directly across from her. She snapped her head in my direction, and started the tunnel to attempt to draw me in. I kept my eyes glued to the east, to the spot where I would rejoin with Don'Li. My hands shook with fear as she approached me. *To the east, to Rannoch. Stay strong, be brave.* I jumped in the Well, just as Don'Li overtook the fearsome creature. *Oh no, I jumped in too early!* He said to jump in once he had overtaken her. I glanced back, and nearly stopped paddling at what I saw.

He blew a forceful gust and knocked her off balance, which caused her whirlwind to abate. Don'Li looped an arm around her waist, then spun the Pythonissamul towards him.

And he kissed her.

I dropped my jaw as she now appeared in her maiden form, gone was the ghostly and hideous demon. She was now the beautiful trickster, the one I had seen on the first occasion when I crossed paths with her, the one that had tried to call me so that I could be consumed. Only this time, there was no beckoning song, and Don'Li was the one in control. Her electrified hair was now smooth and silken, as she kissed him back.

I realized as I floated in place—staring at these two beings kissing at the edge of the mystical Midgard Well—how strange my life had become. I shook my head and reminded myself of my task. Don'Li had done his part, he had distracted her and given me the time I needed to escape. I swam to the east shore, then climbed out and glanced over to them.

Don'Li released her, then dove in without looking back. She cried out after him, but instead of restarting her vortex in an attempt to catch him, she dropped her arms and stared as he vanished below the Well's luminous surface.

I turned around then ran into the trees, away from the creature and toward the next stage of my journey; the trek through the remaining Praegra Forest, to my love that—hopefully—knew I was headed to the dunes. Don'Li appeared a moment later.

"What the hell was that?" I blurted.

I expected a sly grin, or a snarky response about being dashing. Something. Instead his face hardened.

"I understand loneliness."

The comment speared my heart. Here I was, heading toward the male I had fallen in love with, who loved me in return, and I was accompanied by someone who never found that. In eons he hadn't found someone who returned those feelings. Guilt washed over me as I considered what that might be like.

"It was a dirty trick I pulled, to kiss her like that. It is not the first time I have done it, either. Though I wish for a mate, I had no intention of it being anything more than a diversion to get us both to safety. The Pythonissamul can, sadly, never be trusted."

"Are you sure about that? She could have tried to catch you

with her vortex after you stopped. She didn't."

He shrugged as we jogged further into the forest. "I would not trust her."

"What is she?"

"No one really knows. She has wandered Alternis for much longer than I have lived. It was said that she was once an ally of Vitus Augustus."

I almost halted in my tracks. "Wait, she allied with a Vale Born?" My mind reeled. I remembered what she had said to me, that she had not had a Vale Born in ages. Did she mean something other than consuming one?

"Well he betrayed her, so I would doubt she has much faith in anyone."

Maybe there is a chance, some way to change her. Or to help her. We ran for some time while I mused over who she might have been, if she had a name—other than what she was called—or what she was like long ago. Was she always a fearsome demon-witch? The smell of water tore me out of my curiosity about the Pythonis-samul. A stream came into view through the trees. I slowed as I scanned the area for threats.

"Water ahead, Don'Li. We should drink as much as we can and refill the waterskin."

I handed him the soft jug and called a runnel directly from the stream to drink from.

He raised his eyebrows as he lifted the vessel to his lips. "Water ability also? You *are* formidable."

I smirked as I released the water back to the source after drinking. "I must admit it's my weakest skill. Fire seems to be the one that is always barking to get out, and the one that takes the least from my reserve. In fact sometimes I have to spout a little bit, just to tame it. Water is … awkward, but it's there. It definitely saved my butt when rescuing the Ignisfae children."

"I would be interested to hear more, but for now, we should press on."

We took off running, and stopped only when we required a short break or to sleep. Fortunately Don'Li knew a few places to collect water along the way. When I had made the trek to the Southwest Tear with Rannoch, Kerenza, Felix, and the others, I had been glad for the great expanse of the forest. Without our group pushing at such a fast pace, it took us much longer to cross. It had given Rannoch and I time, a chance to court each other as we traveled. And with us being chaperoned, we were forced to temper our lust.

CHAPTER 13

After ten exhausting rotations, great rocky outcroppings grew on the horizon to the northeast. My heart froze as I realized with dread that I had been near this area before. The multicolored ore grew in large boulders surrounding the wide azure lake, the same lake that had been stained by Umorfae blood during the battle outside the cave. The familiar mountain towered from the center, with the entrance to the cave submerged in the water below.

"This is where the Umorfae held the Ignisfae children," I whispered to Don'Li without looking away. "Deep inside that mountain in the lake. It was horrible, what they did."

He nodded. "I heard. The Ignisfae owe you a great debt, Fae children are uncommon. We celebrated for the Ignisfae, when we heard how many they had been blessed with, all within just a few cycles of each other. We believed it was a sign we were finally healing from the great war. What the Umorfae risked by taking them, if they had been lost … that would have been a crime against the Maeder Tree. There is no greater sin."

"Empress Celestine was apparently unaware, so it wasn't all Umorfae. But now she has that snake Silvanis in her ear, spreading lies about me." Saying her name reminded me of my time lazing around the castle, mindlessly being waited on by their slaves. Slaves. I had taken part in their atrocities by enjoying myself there. Reveling in it. Letting the Syrenni wait on me, serve me food. Their eggs. I nearly bent over and threw up at the memory.

"There are more injustices that need to be righted before this is over," I said with firm resolve as I turned to him. "You asked me what my goal was when I met you. What my intentions were here. I'm going to change things. I'm going to change *everything*."

"And I, for one, cannot wait to watch you accomplish it." He pointed to the east, south of the tainted reservoir, to barren hills beyond. "We are almost to the point where we must part ways, the Hinterdunes lie ahead."

I twitched a smile. "One last sprint then."

He flourished a bow, inviting me to start the run.

We ran along the border of the rocks to the south, the heat increased drastically as we neared the boundary. Don'Li slowed significantly as the temperature rose, before he finally stopped.

"I cannot go further, Lily, I must turn back now. Call your Faerie and send word to me when you have an update, or if you need assistance when you come back this way. I will be there to help you."

I placed my fist on my heart, I could only imagine the missteps I might have made getting to this point alone. His guidance to the border of the wasteland had been invaluable. "Stay safe, Don'Li. I'll send word when I can."

I turned toward the empty landscape and started my trek. I looked back one last time before I was too far away to wave at Don'Li, in hopes of one more glimpse of a friendly face before I began my treacherous journey. Right at the same time, his voice bellowed across the expanse.

"Lily! Run!"

I panicked as I saw opal hair glinting in the light, just ahead of him. I fumbled for the dagger and shouted back to him. "Take the knife!" I threw it with all my might in his direction. He cast out a cyclone of air, pulled it toward himself and then used the funnel to fling the blade further along its trajectory. Silvanis feinted to the side to avoid it, but was a moment too late. It buried itself just above his collarbone and sunk in deep, all the way to the hilt. Silvanis hollered as he staggered from the grave injury.

Don'Li was a blur around Silvanis, and spun the Umorfae in a chaotic tornado which lifted him off the ground, before tossing the enemy further away. Don'Li halted for only a beat to yell again. "Run!" He disappeared on a gust of wind, off to the northwest, back to the Praegra Forest.

I didn't wait to see if Silvanis moved again. I sped off as fast as my legs could carry me, into the Hinterdunes.

CHAPTER 14

Sand bit my face as a hot blast of air blew against my skin. I squinted my eyes as I pushed further into the harsh environment. Each laborious step resulted in decreased movement forward, as I climbed the first lengthy dune. My legs burned as I struggled to reach the top. I looked back, to the lake far behind and to the boulders of that ill-fated mountain. The mountaintop had diminished on the horizon behind me, and would offer little guidance as a landmark for much longer. I spun, looking all around for anything else I could use to retain my bearings. Nothing lay to either side—or ahead—that could help me in making sure I was heading in the correct direction.

I groaned, I could easily end up walking in circles. With no path of the sun to follow, and no distinguishing features, each dune traverse was no better than a wild guess, a shot in the dark that I had chosen to go the right way. I closed my eyes for a moment, and straightened my arms with my fists at my sides. *I will find you, Rannoch.*

I slowly opened my eyes to the hills ahead of me. To the way I knew in my heart I needed to go. All indicators of direction for crossing this land that I would search out as a human were not available. But I had more. And I was not human anymore. A thread tugged to the one I loved, an inclination that told me what I needed to do, how I needed to connect at a root level in order to survive—in order to reach my goal. I needed to focus inward, follow the lead rope that was there, even if it was immaterial and spirit only. It existed, a link that we had not yet solidified, but one that was there nonetheless. I could feel him—cloudy and indistinct—on the other end. I needed to follow that line, hand over hand and pull myself along, until I reached him.

I would find him. I would warn him, no matter what. I would reach the male I loved and protect him from the hateful evil that threatened us all. I charged ahead, down the bank toward the next rise, and the next. I pumped my arms as I ran. Perhaps an infinite number lay ahead of me, but I could feel the way—sense it with a cord that was new and unknown. Similar to the Pull, the one that demanded I return to the Vale. This one was gentle, and welcome. Wanted. On the other side of this treacherous expanse my destination—my destiny—awaited. I grimaced as I blocked off another burst of gritty wind. I couldn't let the harshness of the Hinterdunes waylay me from my endpoint.

I raced down another hill, and charged ahead with the speed of a nimble Arabian horse in its natural environment, how their graceful hooves can navigate the sand with ease. I pictured myself practically in flight, barely needing traction in the shifting land below my feet to keep moving.

Though I held no power over earth and sand, I was a force of mighty strength. I coursed through on a gale of my own will, propelled by the thread that bound me to Rannoch, and spurred forward by my own churning determination. I would not be distracted, would not be reduced by the constant sapping of energy that the wastes attempted to draw from me in relentless, ebbing waves.

Dune after dune, I pressed on toward TerraIgni. Rows of sandy, windblown ochre ridges were all there was to see of the land, and an uncomfortably bright sky, still somehow shielded by mist in spite of the heat. Sweat beaded on my brow, which just as quickly evaporated as I raced through the endless hills. I stopped infrequently to take a sip of water or eat a nibble of food. Supplies were running short anyway, I couldn't afford lost time, and I didn't know how much further I had to go.

The heat blared as I faltered on the descent of yet another countless dune. It had been perhaps three—maybe four—rotations without rest since I entered the expanse. Who could say for sure. The constant blazing light and radiating heat belied how long I had trekked through the remote territory. I closed one eye as I continued onward. Exhaustion and confusion nudged aside my will to continue. Maybe I could lay down, just for a bit.

I slapped myself on the cheek. *No.* If I lay down, would I get back up?

The light had waned, though night was approaching the heat had yet to lessen. I smacked my parched lips together, checking my empty waterskin yet again for the slightest drop. Nothing. I was going somewhere, toward a lake perhaps? Water for sure, that was what I needed. It was just a little further. I rubbed my brow and continued, *it must be over the next rise.*

Darkness only deepened as I pushed on. I struggled to reach the crest of the ridge, then tripped at the top, which caused me to tumble down to the valley of the dune after it. Disoriented from the fall, I rooted around in the sand for a moment, did I lose something? I was holding onto a thing. A rope maybe? I searched the sand to no avail, frantically pushing aside swaths of grain. I gave up, and sat there confused and exhausted. I could have sworn I lost something. I finally pulled my feet underneath my body and struggled to stand. *It's over the next hilltop.*

I staggered up the rise, every step half-slipped backward. *Just a little further, water soon.*

Each step became less effective than the one before. I slumped further with every trudging footfall. *It's over there, just get to the top.*

I looked over the curving windblown lip of the dune to spy the lake below. It shimmered with a brilliance I had never seen. Glistening water spread out before me, waiting, offering cooling relief in the hot night air. *I knew it!*

I brought my legs below me—which were no better than wobbly noodles now—to push me the last few feet to my salvation, to the life-saving liquid that waited at the bottom. I collapsed over the top, then fell the rest of the way down the slope, only to be greeted by dusty and depleted sand, devoid of life and moisture.

I cried waterless tears as I clutched at nothing; sand which held no mass, water that wasn't there. Bright blue lights circled my peripheral vision as I retreated from the harsh reality, and imagined the form of someone familiar approaching from the dune beyond.

CHAPTER 15

Wind howled in rhythmic droves, as the sound of millions of fine particles rushed and pelted. I cringed as I woke up, expecting the barrage of sand to impact any exposed surface of my skin. Instead, I realized it was striking a buffer between me and it, a soft surface that buckled yet held steadfast against the driving force. A light flickered in the darkness, the tiniest filament from within glass illuminated the area. I sat up as broad shoulders blocked the light for a moment, before small torches lit up, one by one from a quick funnel of flame.

I gasped as Rannoch turned to me, though his jaw was set and his lips were pressed together, his eyebrows softened as he looked at me. I threw my arms around him and squeezed him with all my might.

"How did you find me?" I cried against his neck. He hugged me and nestled in tighter, before he pulled back to look at me.

"You could have died, Lily. You almost did. I almost lost you. I could feel you slipping away. Even though I was still far off, I could feel it. That Faerie of yours, you are lucky to have one so committed to you."

"I'm sorry, I had to find you. Plus, I was being hunted by an Umorfae. The Hinterdunes was the only place I could go to escape him anyway. I needed to make sure you were okay. None of us are safe. Dashelle is alive."

He nodded. "I know, the Faerie delivered the message. I had just returned to TerraIgni and immediately left as soon as I heard you were out here. I followed the Faerie to you, though I think I might have been able to find you anyway."

"I felt it, too," I whispered, then grabbed onto Rannoch again and wrapped my arms around him. I needed to be close. To hold him and know for sure that he was there. That this was not some fever dream just before I wasted away in the punishing drifts.

I glanced around at the softly lit, generous space, the leathery walls sighed and snapped as the wind pummeled them.

"Did you carry this tent all the way with you? This thing is huge!" It looked like it could comfortably house ten to twelve Ignisfae with ease.

"No, we have caches along our route through the Hinterdunes. Stores with food, water, shelter. Anything you would need to wait out a sandstorm—which, by the way, we managed to narrowly avoid by the time I found you. I was able to get us to the closest cache and have the tent built by the time it arrived. The Faerie had to leave immediately to escape it. The heat out here is one thing, but the storms are the deadliest part."

I released him and pulled away so I could look him in the eyes.

"I went crazy as soon as I heard you were in the dunes, Lily. I was in the middle of speaking to my faeder, giving him the update on all that had happened when I found out. I left without another word, and barely gave Kerenza enough notice that she had to go in and complete my task. I imagine he is furious. But I do not care. I had to find you."

Tears pricked my eyes, I cupped his face with both hands. I almost couldn't speak; the relief at finding each other, that he was safe, how we had trudged through this wasteland to reunite. Together at last.

"I had to get to you, I didn't mean to worry you. When I realized Dashelle was alive … I was already missing you *before* I found out about her survival. I had to know—first hand—that you were okay. There was nothing more important."

I couldn't wait another second. I sat up on my knees and leaned forward to kiss him. He slipped his hands behind my back and caressed my spine, as I pressed my lips to his. A sound from inside his throat made my heart stutter. A drop fell on my cheek from his eye, then slipped down to my chin. I released his mouth to wipe his tears. He shook his head as more spilled over. His hands clenched my sides as he shuddered.

"I was terrified I would lose you. You were delirious. I poured water in your mouth, and you didn't drink it. You slipped further away and I screamed at you. I pounded the sand for you to wake up and take a sip. I hollered so close to you, and your face did not so much as flinch. I cried and begged the Gods. I have never done that, not even when my maeder was lost. I never asked them for anything before. Then, you made a sound. You twitched and I poured more water in, I have never felt such relief when I saw you drink at last." More tears cascaded out.

"I'm so sorry, Rannoch." My brows contracted, as adequate words evaded me to express my regret at scaring him so completely. I leaned forward and brushed my thumbs against each damp cheek, then kissed him gently. He took one more shaky breath, before he kissed me back.

He pulled away, then closed his eyes and took one long, slow inhale through his nose to steady himself. When he reopened them, the embers in his pupils blazed bright. Alive.

"I offer myself to you, Lily. If you would have me … as your mate. I will forever work to be enough for you, to be a coniunx that values your goals and supports your dreams. To be someone deserving of your faith, if you accept."

My breath hitched. "Enough? Rannoch, you are *more* than enough. More than I could ever hope. I don't know your ways. I'm not sure what I'm supposed to do or say. I do have some questions first."

His eyes widened ever so slightly as his body went utterly still. I saw the unmistakable look of fear flicker for a moment, as I realized he thought I might be saying no.

"How old are you?"

He looked at me quizzically. "One hundred and sixty five cycles."

I reeled as I tried to wrap my mind around the age, and attempted to reconcile the fact that he looked no older than a man in his mid-to-late twenties. But then, he wasn't a man.

"Actually, with me being twenty one human years, maybe I'm older!" I mused. "With twenty eight rotations to one human day, if you calculate-"

"Really, Lily? Math? Now? Also, no. I am older, one cycle here equals one human cycle. There are over ten thousand rotations to one cycle."

"I'm just trying to sort this out in my head. In the human

world you'd be long dead. Expect more questions from me and nerdy postulating, always."

"... Nerdy?"

"Nevermind. Why did you never take a mate before? Kerenza told me many tried."

He puffed his lips and blew out a breath through them. "I had several females that I was involved with at different times. They always wanted more, and I felt that they were with me for the wrong reasons. None of them ever saw the real me, or if they did they did not even like who I was. They liked how I looked, they wanted my status. But they did not actually want *me*. There was pressure, from my faeder, from them. They were in league with him, constantly calculating. It was one reason I was always volunteering for the hunts. So I could get out of TerraIgni and away from them."

My heart faltered at that. To hear that someone had tried to use him to their advantage, to commoditize him. My face darkened at the thought of scheming females angling to control him. "Does that mean I'd have to deal with your crazy ex-girlfriends?"

He huffed a laugh. "Not sure exactly what that term means, but you have nothing to worry about with them."

"What about your faeder, King Ashwan? Is he going to have a problem with me? I'm inherently different from any of those females he would have chosen for you."

"I love that you are different. I fell in love with you, in part, because of it. Not because you look different, but because you never treated me the way they did. They were selfish, you are *selfless*. If he has any sort of issue, it will be his to deal with. He cannot break a mating link, no matter how he may feel about it."

I chewed on my lip as I looked at him. The fire in his eyes

dimmed as he waited, completely still. But I had chosen long before I had even seen him again, before he found me. The pull that I felt to him was undeniable. Even if we might have obstacles to overcome in TerraIgni, he was worth it. If we had to fight tooth and nail against endless foes, and had to battle forces until the end of time, *we* were worth it.

I leaned in closer. "I would be honored, thrilled, and excited to be your mate. To call you my coniunx and shout it to the world."

He audibly exhaled as his eyes flashed to life again. Whatever thread held him at bay snapped, as he practically lunged forward and swooped his arms around me. His kiss was frantic, feverish. I opened my mouth to his and arched my back. The subtle movement made him tighten his grip as he groaned, unable to hold himself back any longer.

He whipped off my shirt in one fluid motion. I nudged my swelling breasts against his bare chest as I reached into his pants. I needed to feel him, to hold him in my hand. I gripped his silky smooth hardness as he clenched my hips. His growl into my mouth turned my core instantly hot. I pushed his pants down, then bent forward and wrapped my mouth around him. His throat clicked as I slid all the way down, taking him all in. I ran my tongue against the back of his generous length, grazing the tip once before I glided down again. I savored the taste of him as I continued, making each pass slow and deliberate. He moaned as his grip on my shoulders tightened, the sound in my ears caused my skin to ignite. I tried to keep going, but he gently pushed me back and guided me onto the bed.

The loose fitting sleep pants he must have dressed me in were off in the blink of an eye—so fast I didn't even see where they went. He arched an eyebrow as he wordlessly moved aside my bent knees and lowered his face between my thighs. And licked. Long, sweeping, gentle strokes. Like he had all the time in the world. He placed one hand just above where he worked his tongue, and tugged in rhythm. Rannoch slid his other hand up and cupped my breast, gliding his fingers over the tip of my exposed skin.

I hung on for as long as I could, but the moment he growled against me, I exploded. Light and stars and fire and ice, everything momentarily filled my vision as I clenched my eyes and shrieked in pleasure. He didn't stop.

He kept going until the world tilted around me again. I gasped his name and shot up to sitting, clawing to get Rannoch closer to me, on top of me, in me. I needed him right then.

He kissed his way up my stomach, between my breasts, then kissed and hovered over my lower neck.

"May I bite you?"

"Bite?!" I exclaimed between shaky breaths. The question surprised me, though I had felt the drive for him to bite me before, something buried within me, a strange compelling need for it.

"Yes, bite. It is how we initiate mating. The female has to agree to it."

"You don't just take the female?"

"Long ago, yes. But not anymore. May I bite you?" he asked again, his voice husky and insistent. His focus on my response was so honed he could not be bothered with more words. He only wanted one word from me.

Would I be agreeing to some age-old Fae covenant, with intricacies I had yet to discover? His body was like a coiled spring while he awaited my answer, his eyes shifting from mine to my lower neck. Whatever the bite meant, I knew I wanted to make that promise.

"Yes, bite me, Rannoch."

He quickly sunk his teeth into me just above my collarbone, his canines latched under the tendons as he let out a low growl against my skin. I gasped in pain, and at the same time, pleasure. So intense that it almost made me climax. It shook awake something feral deep within me, an animalistic instinct to bite him back.

I gripped his shoulders with my fiery hands, and scraped my teeth on his muscled neck. A guttural moan reverberated from him as he pressed himself harder against me. The sheer size of him made me ache.

I nudged my hips toward him and opened them wider, insisting he give me exactly what I wanted. A faint whine told me that the wait for my return pierce was torturing him. That without my bite he would drown, be lacking in confirmation from the female that he had professed his love and unending commitment too. I bit down at last, giving him just what he desired, the primal, deep-rooted sign that I had accepted him. That he was mine and I was his. There was no one else in any world that I wanted, that I would spend the rest of near-immortality with.

He let out a roar that was muffled by my neck as he slid in. It felt like it took an eternity until he was all the way seated inside me. I panted against his skin, with my teeth still in him. He released his bite at last, allowing me to mimic him. I laughed at the elation as the invisible yet tangible link thickened between us, the link I had felt when I had searched for him. I sensed cord after cord looping, knotting, casting us closer and closer. He bent down and kissed me as I adjusted to being so completely filled by him, a deep but gentle kiss that was careful and considerate. I tasted my blood on his lips, mixing with his blood from mine, coupling together and merging as one. And then he started thrusting, and I thought I might die from loving him so much. The warrior that had come for me, found me in the Hinterdunes. But more than that, he had helped me find myself, face myself; look at my mistakes head on, and move forward. It had been years—sad years—that I had floundered. Years that I wasted and wandered. Wandered in one world and then the next. Until I found him.

His potent strokes matched the beat of the blasting sand against the walls, the wind whistled as we both heaved loud, gasping breaths. I flipped him over in one movement, and was on top of him, riding to the same pace as before. He gazed at me, stunned for a moment, when I bent down and kissed him with all the fury and love and hope and mirth I had because of him, because of us.

Fire churned down my arms, he sat up and clutched me, giving one more hard thrust into me. He howled as he reached his ultimate release and unloaded his surge into me. I gasped his name in return as I found my completion at the same moment. Everything illuminated as light shot through to the very core of the world, to the pulsing and nebulous sublayer that connected everything. A bright flash radiated out in a brilliant shockwave. The tent walls bowed out momentarily, stretching from the mighty blast we had sent out.

We both shook, panting as we held each other. I couldn't

help it, I sobbed as I clutched him. We had gone through so much, nearly lost our lives, fought and fought and survived. Now finally, we were together and mated, and the release was so intense on every level. He stroked my back in soothing comfort.

I pulled away and pressed my forehead to his. "I love you, Rannoch," I whispered.

He let out a restrained whimper and finally said, "For a moment I thought you were going to say no when I asked you, and I was sure I was going to die from it. I thought I would Fade in my heart and instantly disappear."

I leaned back, then brushed the tendrils of hair from his dewy face, and just gazed at him.

"I love you, Lily. And I will never stop appreciating that you accepted me."

I nearly started crying again, but he hugged me and twisted us to the side, then lowered me carefully down. He cradled my head and threaded his broad fingers through my hair, then made slow, passionate love to me until we were both spent again.

We glistened as we laid exhausted next to each other, our legs tangled and the sheets in a knot around us. The storm raged outside, while we lay in bliss, protected within the tent walls.

"I meant to take my time with the bite, if you said yes, I was going to savor it. I thought about it over and over, on exactly what I would do if you accepted me. It's a singular moment in a Fae life. But as soon as you said yes that all just disappeared. It was like I could not do it fast enough."

I laughed. "Afraid I'd change my mind?"

"I think so. Instinct just took over."

"I knew I'd say yes, even if I had questions first and made you wait. There was no doubt in my mind. I felt our bond forming long ago, I think ever since we told each other how we felt. I didn't quite realize it at the time, but looking back I know it was there."

He squeezed me closer and sighed. I closed my eyes and listened to his breathing, his heartbeat. I lay next to him, with my head atop his chest, until I drifted off.

CHAPTER 16

The smell of hot coffee roused me at last. The wind still slammed itself against the leather walls as I pulled the sheets around my bare skin.

Rannoch smiled at me from across the tent, where he stood warming a pot and preparing something to eat in a simple kitchen. He motioned to the opposite side of the tent. "There are things set aside for you there, to wash if you want."

I gave him a sleepy smile and dragged the sheets with me over to the heavy draped partition, then stepped in. I dropped my jaw as I looked around, he had set up neatly folded towels, warmed water, soaps and oils, a hairbrush, and fresh clothes. "Um, Rannoch? Is there a bathroom in here?" *I need to pee before I burst!*

"Next small chamber over, push aside the far wall," he called out from the other room.

I stifled the audible relief as I found the sectioned off area, detached and with no flooring over the sand, unlike the rest of the homey yurt. I cleaned up, dressed, and brushed my hair before I returned to the main tent.

He had just finished setting out food, carefully arranged on a tray on the floor, with poufs to sit on across from each other. I smiled at how hard he was trying, to make it special, to use whatever he had to celebrate our time. I seated myself as he started serving.

"Capuli first, of course." He flashed his dazzling smile, the one that would definitely have me dropping my panties in no time. I accepted the steaming mug and sipped, hiding my sideways smirk with my cup as my eyes gleamed at him.

His ears twitched as he sat down across from me. By the slight, quick arch of his eyebrow, I knew he sensed my body warming at the thought of him. We smiled at each other as the air charged. I bit my lip, it took considerable effort to continue eating when all I wanted to do was toss the tray aside and leap on top of him. But, I needed sustenance, and he probably did too.

I decided to sidestep the tension with conversation, so that we could try and get food in us before I attacked him. "When I went to the human world, I didn't change back. Did you know that would happen? I had thought I would turn back to a more human appearance, but I didn't."

He shook his head. "I do not know much about the human world, other than it is there. No Fae can cross the boundary of the Vale, so all we know of it is what we have learned from Faeries, or Vale Born. What did you look like before? Much different?"

"A bit. Not nearly as tall, and my face was a little softer, rounder. And short ears. Enough of a change that I was clearly not human, I couldn't have stayed because of it. I was there only a short time when I felt a demand from the Vale that I return. It wasn't going to let me stay there. It started pulling me back. I don't know how my brother is resisting it." I realized with sudden dread that he may not be resisting it at this point, and might have come back through the tear. *I need to request a message from the Faerie once this storm passes, and tell Felix about Silvanis.* Felix would be just as much in his crosshairs as I was.

"I think you may have been lucky it let you out at all," he said around a mouthful of jerky.

I ate some food while I mulled it over; my nearly immediate departure after returning to Black Oak Grove to run back to Rannoch. "What you said earlier, about me being selfless. I'm really not. I left Felix to deal with everything there so that I could get back to you. Dashelle burned down my family home. My mother—maeder—is now displaced and I just left them there. I'd call that pretty selfish."

"No, Lily. You *are* selfless in a lot of ways. The fact that you obeyed the Pull does not make you selfish. And that you wanted to protect me, and Kerenza, I think that is more proof. I am sorry to hear about your maeder's home. Will she be all right?"

I nodded, though I knew in my heart, it was also self-protection. I couldn't bear to lose him. I'd had too much loss already. I had to know, and was ultimately compelled to know he was safe. "She is going to live with her sister. It won't be easy, but she'll be okay. She's moving to a place called Ithaca, where she was born."

"That name sounds familiar."

I didn't want to talk about the human world anymore. I cleared my throat. "About the past females ..."

He stopped chewing and went still, then struggled to swallow his bite. "I do not want to think about any female other than you."

"It's okay, Rannoch. I'm not weird about prior relationships. I don't expect or want you to pretend like you were never with someone else. I just wanted to know what you meant, by saying that I'd have nothing to worry about with them."

"Oh. They have all since found their match. It is a little awkward around their mates, because they all know that their female tried to choose me first. More like force me. But, they are all much better off. With me, they were not their best selves. I did not bring out their good side. All of them mated with someone who allows their best version to shine. I think it is proof I was not right for any of them."

"I see. Did Kerenza … was she on your side about all of that?"

"She hated the whole situation. She—like me—believed one should mate for love, rather than power. One of the females had even been her close friend, prior to that. Kerenza felt betrayed by it. She started coming on the hunts, too, after that. Then she fell in love with Kenneder, they mated. He was not who my faeder would have preferred she chose. So she has already broken that barrier for us."

"Thank you, for telling me all this. I know it's uncomfortable. I have a lot to learn about what it's going to mean being your mate. I just want to be prepared for when we go to TerraIgni."

"You have some time, the sandstorm probably will not pass for at least five to seven more rotations."

I picked up a piece of dried fruit off the tray. "You mean I get to enjoy bedding you in this tent until then? Fantastic." I raised it to my open mouth, but it wasn't in my hand anymore. My empty fingers hit my lips as I realized we were now in bed, and Rannoch was already undressed.

"Hey! I was eating that!" I laughed as he tugged at my pants, his eyebrow cocked as he waited for my approval. "Absolutely. Rip them off."

They were gone before I finished my sentence. So quickly I was ready for him, needed him. Burned for him. He was on top of me in an instant. I gasped as he buried himself in me. I reached up and ran my hand along his jaw, down his chest as he moved in an ardent, slow rhythm. *My mate.*

He stopped, wide-eyed. "I heard that," he breathed. "Say it again."

This time I said it out loud. "My mate. I love you, my mate."

Rannoch dropped his eyelids shut, then opened them again to reveal a fire within burning brighter than I had ever seen before. He lowered his face and kissed me as he ran his hands over my body. He was gentle, slow, planting kisses on each eye. But the moment I ran my nails through his hair at the back of his head and dragged my teeth on his neck—right where I had marked him—his tether snapped. He growled and sat up, hauling me on top of him. My ears tingled at the sound and sent a shiver down my spine. I couldn't get close enough to him, as he pulled my hips down harder with each indulgent stroke.

I fell back, gasping after we finished as I trembled. Rannoch adjusted himself next to me, laying on his side and watched me while I caught my breath. I rolled over to face him, and admired him as he smiled back at me. I breathed a sigh as I finally cooled, the fire that had moments before been simmering on my skin had quieted.

CHAPTER 17

"I kept imagining this," he said. "I would dream about what it would be like, with you. I have to admit my imagination is severely lacking. The reality is far better than anything I pictured. Though, the musings helped with the long trek back to TerraIgni … or made it worse because it made me miss you more. Still undecided." He laughed as he ran his fingers through my hair. "Your hair, it is unlike anything I have ever seen. No one in this world has hair that color. It feels like … like the finest thread. I cannot believe how much sand was in it when I found you. It took forever to brush out."

"You brushed my hair? Rannoch! That is so sweet!"

"I did more than just that, you were pretty dirty from crossing the dunes. I have to admit, I enjoyed brushing it. Once the sand came out, I kept going. It ended up being what calmed me down at last. Finding you like that, you nearly slipping away, then struggling to get to the cache and build the tent fast enough before the storm hit. Once everything was settled and taken care of, I could relax at last. But you had not woken up yet, and I could not unwind. Brushing it soothed me. Is that strange?"

"Not at all. I'm glad it made you feel better. That all sounds … stressful."

He twisted his mouth. "It was. But, we are safe now. It was all worth it."

I pressed a kiss to his lips. "I'd love it if you brushed it for me, when I was awake."

He flashed a smile and was out of bed in a heartbeat. He returned with the brush and a damp towel. I sat on my knees as he settled himself behind me. My skin warmed as he carefully picked up my mass of hair and looped it around his hand, then ran the washcloth along my upper back. I closed my eyes as he made soothing passes over my skin, all the way down. He blew against it, to dry it faster. It caused the surface hairs to rise in delight. Rannoch kissed the nape of my neck, then released my hair with a swish. He glided the brush through, the bristles reaching in to graze my scalp. I shivered as he made countless strokes. To just spend time together, unhurried, in relative safety, it was a blessing I would forever be grateful for. I savored each moment of it.

I turned to him at last. "I want to do something for you now. I don't know if this is something Fae do, but it's done in the human world. Called a massage. After everything you did to get us to safety, I'm sure you could use one."

He squinted an eye. "Haven't heard of it."

"I always love it when you use contractions. It's so cute. Okay, lay down on your stomach and relax."

He lay down and adjusted himself around the pillows. "Now what?"

"Just breathe. Close your eyes, and release your worries. We are safe, we are together, and I am here to take care of you."

Rannoch blinked his eyes open wide. "No one has ever said they were going to take care of me before. Well, not since ..."

He went to turn to me, but I stopped him with a caress to his face. "Close your eyes, I'll be right back," I said softly. I rose, then went to the partitioned room and grabbed the oil. I returned and knelt beside him, and rubbed the smooth liquid between my palms to warm it. I worked it into his muscles, rubbing it into the tense cords along his spine and around his shoulders. He groaned as I let a little burst of fire to my hands and sent a healing thread out. I glided the heels of my hands over him, pushing them deeper into the tissue. I admired him as I kneaded. He worked so hard, he always seemed to be doing something for someone else: his fight to get Emblyn back for his sister and rescuing the other children, going on hunts to provide for his people, trying to do what his father wanted of him—even though it was not what he wanted for himself. And then what he did for me, coming to find me in the desert after just returning home. He must have been exhausted, and yet he came directly out to look for me, built our shelter and protected us from the storm. *He* was the selfless one, not me. As I continued, I resolved that I would forever endeavor to be more like him, to be a mate that was as considerate and committed as he was, and to use every skill the Vale had gifted me with, to be a force of change. To take what my mother had taught me, to use what I was given for the good of all. I had given up on that, before coming to Alternis.

I realized his breathing pattern had changed, lightened and slowed. His eyebrows arched softly as he slept. I smiled at the expression of peace on his normally stoic face. I shifted off my bent knees before they went completely numb, then eased up next to him and drifted off to the sound of his content exhales and the relentless storm.

89

CHAPTER 18

I rooted through the makeshift kitchen to prepare some food. Rannoch still hadn't woken, and the storm had yet to lessen. I scurried to do the same for him as he had done for me: prepared the bathroom items, organized and cleaned up the main tent, and arranged some food for us. Just as I finished I looked over to find him sitting, watching.

"Bonum mane." I grinned.

He stretched and stood. "I cannot remember when I slept better."

"I'm glad you enjoyed the massage. I'll have to make a habit of it. You deserve good sleep."

He sauntered over to me, then wrapped his arms around my low back and nuzzled my neck, pulling me close. "Something *else* you do gives me good sleep as well."

I giggled and pulled away, motioning with my chin to the bathroom. "If you want to freshen up, I'll make us some capuli."

He sighed. "You win, my love."

I fluttered my eyes then pecked him on the cheek. "Food first, flirt later."

He chuckled as he disappeared behind the partition. I finished arranging everything I could find on the tray. Our supply was starting to diminish, and the same rations of dried fruits and jerky were becoming tiresome. But, it was something, and at least we had plenty of capuli. I didn't bother with setting the typical heating station that he had used before. I filled the pot from the waterskin and held it in my hand, using my own fire to heat the pan.

"Well that's convenient," he said as he exited the bathroom.

His skin undeniably glowed, I couldn't help my physical reaction to him as I glanced at his chest. *Calm the fuck down, Lily.* I laughed to myself at my own internal discourse.

"What's so funny?"

"Nothing," I said sweetly as I poured in the ground capuli, then pressed it through the sieve to strain out the granules. I transferred it into two mugs, then placed everything on the tray and brought it to the seating area.

He swung a leg over the pouf and seated himself, quirked a brow and cocked a positively male smile at me as he ate. The look was enough to burn my underwear.

"Stop it," I said over the lip of my capuli mug, "or you won't get any food in you."

"You started it." His grin widened. "Besides, I would rather fill you with something besides food right now."

He barely finished his sentence. I tossed my capuli cup and pounced on him in one motion. We didn't even make it to the bed.

I released him, panting as we both fell back, then laughed

when I saw the coffee cup on its side. "Well I finally did it, spilled my precious capuli for you. I hope you know that signifies ultimate love and attraction for you."

He belted a laugh that captivated my ears.

I held my hands to the sides of my head, feeling the sensation diminish. "I love when you laugh. I think it's the best thing I've ever heard."

He put his arm around me and pulled me close. I closed my eyes and hugged him. I never wanted this to end, I wanted to stay in this tent and have this be our entire world.

No hiding, Lily.

My eyes shot open, even my own internal voice wouldn't let me fall back into my old ways.

I sat up and inhaled sharply.

"What is it? Are you okay?"

"Yes, I'm fine. I just … had a weird thought. Come on, let's actually eat something this time." I stood up and dressed quickly, then picked up the scattered food from the tray.

He finished tying his pants as he strode over to me in two paces. "Tell me."

"I just had a thought that I wanted to never leave this tent, and have us be safe in here forever. In here, it's just you and I, and endless love and everything wonderful. My mind instantly told me I couldn't hide. That's what I did before, bad things happened and then I hid from life. There's inevitable danger waiting for us out there. Just for a moment, I wanted to pretend like it wasn't there." My lip wobbled, I covered it to try and hide it from Rannoch.

He hugged me as I fought back tears. If we faced Dashelle, I could lose him. Or I could die. There was the considerable possibility of death. I closed my eyes and counseled myself back to calmness. *We fought her once, we can do it again.*

I leaned back and looked at him. "Rannoch … will you tell me about your maeder? You've never said what happened. Was she the one you almost mentioned before, that had said would take care of you?"

His eyes darkened and he pressed his lips together. He released a sigh and sat down on the floor cushion. I sat across from him as he said, "Yes, of course. It's not easy to talk about. But you deserve to know. My faeder had been successful in establishing good relations with the Petrafae and Caelifae. He thought that enough time had passed since the war, that perhaps the Umorfae would be willing to consider a trade alliance. He wouldn't listen to anyone that it was not a good idea, to anyone that said the Umorfae couldn't be trusted. He sent my maeder as an emissary with a contingent of guards to present the offer to Empress Caldine, along with a trove of blades made in our forge as a gift. The Umorfae slaughtered them all with the very weapons we had given them, and left their bodies in an indiscernible, mangled pile at the border of the Hinterdunes, the weapons stuck in a circle with my maeder's crown on top. I was nineteen cycles at the time, it has been so long I barely remember her face. I was so angry with him when he had sent her. I did not think we needed more trade, we were doing well and there was no reason to expand. I accused him of having greed that matched the Umorfae, he nearly threw me out of TerraIgni for that."

I gulped, and fought back the urge to heave. I pictured Celestine's mother, ordering the execution in the same throne room I had stood in. Had it happened in that same spot? My vision speckled with the threat of passing out from the horrible image.

"That is beyond terrible, I'm so sorry you endured that." I reached over to hold his hand. He squeezed it in return. Making such a decision that would ultimately mean the loss of my mate's mother, it was beyond incomprehensible, and made me start to wonder if I wanted to know his father at all.

"I hated him for a long time, in some ways I still do. But … he is my faeder, and I do still try to do right by him. Or at least do right by my people. It wasn't just his choice, she could have said no. I think that is what she was doing, trying to do what was best for the Ignisfae. Better trade meant more resources. Water *is* scarce, we rely on underground aquifers. The Umorfae's haughty belief that they hold sway over all life because they control water was probably the reason they reacted so harshly. Why do they need us when they have their fields of grain that they don't struggle to water, fish hatcheries, and an endless supply of Syrenni? It was a message. "We are better than you, we don't need you." The lack of respect for our lives was stunning, to say the least. They had killed the queen of TerraIgni without a thought beyond "show them their worth to us." It made her loss even worse."

A tear slipped over my cheek for him, for them. For his mother. Robbed of her time with her children, she was taken too early by a race with no regard for the sanctity of life. "I see your worth, I see your beautiful lives and know that you have so much to bring to this world, for a positive change." I cupped his face, remembering how he had done the same for me when we were with the Arbor Elves. He told me that dealing with loss had been the hardest task of his life. I had no idea then how much he had gone through.

"I avoided telling you, because I go to such a dark place when I think about it. And then when I thought there was a chance we would mate, I worried that you would not want to be bound to a family with a faeder that had facilitated something so terrible. I shouldn't have done that, I should have been more forthcoming before you decided."

"It would not have changed my answer. I would still choose you, choose us. Life is messy, in any world. Things go wrong, mistakes are made, lives are lost, and we incur wounds that need to heal. But then, life is beautiful, too. Sometimes, the sadness we've endured helps us to appreciate the happiness before us."

He closed his eyes and leaned into my palm. When he opened them again it looked like a lead weight had been removed from his shoulders. I realized he had promised no more secrets, and may have been worried that I would group this with holding back information.

"I understand you waiting to tell me, I understand how painful it must be to talk about," I said.

He heaved a sigh and gave me an appreciative look.

"Come on, let's do something lighthearted. What do Ignisfae do in these tents for fun, to pass the time during the sandstorms?"

A mischievous grin spread across his face. "Fun? Oh, I have just the thing."

CHAPTER 19

He went to the other side of the tent, then pulled out a fat waterskin and a leather-wrapped bundle. "We play this, it's called luden palas." He unrolled it between us, which revealed scores of finely etched stiff leather cards, all with three notches evenly spaced along the bottom. He organized them into five different piles in a fan shape, then placed a six sided die with strange markings in the center. "You start with five random cards. Then you roll, and pick up a card indicated. If you want to exchange your card you can trade two cards for one of your choice. Then we build in turn, if you roll well, you get either corner notch to build. Roll poorly, and you must use the center notch to stack the next card. It's a game of chance, skill, and strategy. Build a structure that will not fall … on your turn. But before you can build, you take a drink." He lifted the waterskin to indicate it, apparently full of vinirubrum.

"Holy snacks, a complicated Fae drinking card game? It's on." I stretched my fingers.

"Think you can win? Keep in mind I've been playing this game for over one hundred and fifty cycles."

"Oh yea? Well keep in mind, you have no idea how competitive I can be with games like this. I'm a jenga champion."

He chuckled. "What does that even mean?"

I rolled my head side to side. "You'll find out. What does the winner get?"

"Planning your spoils already?"

"Heck yes I am."

"Winner's choice, of course. Now here is another layer of the game, if you roll either the ludens or the palas side of the die, which are both corner builds, the other players get to say only that word—ludens or palas—to distract you. In whatever creative way they can think of."

"Now *that* gives me some ideas. Tell me, who usually wins at this game?"

He narrowed his eyes. "… Kerenza."

"I knew it!" I slapped my knee and laughed. "Oh you are so going down." I studied the cards, and the markings which were unrecognizable to me. "Okay first, which card is which? I've never seen these characters before."

"Ludens, palas, clava, adamantem, and regina," he said, pointing at each one in turn. "They all have equal value, but you will see the difference when you start to build. Adamantem is strong, thicker. Good for a base. But also heavier. Enough that it can bring down a structure if improperly placed at the top. Regina is light, flexible. But not suitable for a strong foundation."

I gazed at the female carved into the thinner card, her supple lines and grace were apparent even in the few strokes it took to make her form on the game piece. "Sounds sexist to me. I'm gonna prove that wrong."

His eyebrows shot up.

"She's the only female of the bunch that I can see. And she's the weakest? I call bullshit."

"I … did not make the rules. My views and beliefs do not translate to this game. And I did not say weakest, I said flexible."

"Interesting how you stop using contractions when I call you out on something." I stared him down for a beat, then laughed. "Relax, Rannoch, I wasn't trying to say it was *you.* But, as a forward thinking female, I do think it's not a fair reflection on my gender. I took it as maybe a challenge. But, I guess we'll see. It is just a game after all." *Or is it?*

He smiled. "Well then, let's start."

I rolled first, the die righted itself on the marks corresponding with regina. I smirked as I picked up the card.

"You can exchange for a more … substantial card to start out with, if you wish."

"No, this will do great, thanks." I took a swig from the skin as I flashed heat from my palm onto the card without tearing my eyes from him, then curved the leather rectangle around my fingers as it cooled. Once the bent form held, I settled it in the center of the game board.

The corners of my mouth tugged up as he dropped his jaw. "Your turn." I smiled as I leaned back in my seat.

"I think I'm in trouble." He laughed and shook his head.

"I could have told you that as soon as you opened this game. And you know, winner's choice with the outcome of this, I wasn't about to let that go."

"I might just forgo that and let you have your way with me."

"Nice try, as much as I'd love to tackle you again, I prefer to see where this goes first. I'm going to play this with you, dammit!"

We played round after round, the structure of cards rose up before us, all centered on the foundation card I had placed with my initial regina. Everytime he placed one on his turn, I saw his eyes flash to it. I had to admit to myself, I liked it a little too much that it had held the branching system we had piled on top of it. He rolled a ludens, then went to place his card. I edged dangerously close to him and dragged my tongue up his earlobe.

"Ludens," I whispered in his ear, drawing out the 'S' as I traced my fingers too high up his inner thigh. He struggled to put it in place, but I didn't stop my upward momentum with my hand.

He hissed as he tried to drop the card safely in its spot, but he couldn't. The whole thing toppled from a breaking point further down, at an adamantem card he had set earlier.

I cackled as it all came crashing down. With wine still on my lips from my last turn, I jumped on top of him. "Winner's choice, right? I intend to make the defeat an enjoyable one."

"Who's to say I didn't do it on purpose?"

I waggled my finger at him. "Now, now. Accept your loss."

"I actually am shocked you won, but I guess I shouldn't be."

"Beginner's luck maybe. Now, take me to bed."

He scooped me up, then laid me down again in an instant. "Now, what would you like, my mate?"

"I want it all."

CHAPTER 20

I awoke to the sound of the storm, or rather, the sound of the storm abating. I looked up at Rannoch, who was watching me, his face stern. I knew without him saying anything what it meant. He tightened his embrace as I settled back in with him. I didn't want it to be over. I didn't want to return to the dunes. They had been so punishing, so harsh, endless. But, maybe with Rannoch by my side, they wouldn't be so bad.

Just as I resolved within myself that I could brave the shifting hills again, the desert responded with its answer. The wind stopped, and the sand halted its blast against the walls. I clenched my eyes, soaking up the last of our magical time; the beautiful moments we had been gifted while sheltering from the elements. I took a breath, and counseled myself to have the strength to walk beside him. TerraIgni waited for us, whether his people knew I was coming or not, and whether they would accept me, only time would tell. It dawned on me that as I was Rannoch's mate, TerraIgni was my new home. I hadn't processed that fact, hadn't even considered what our lives might be like once we left the safety of our tent. My breath hitched. *My home is wherever he is.*

"Rannoch, I just realized that TerraIgni will be my home now, with you. But what about my brother? Will he have a place there?"

"Of course he will. He will have his own room and place of honor. He won't have a title, like you. But he will be welcome."

Title. I tried not to blanche as I internalized that statement. Instead I angled my face up to him and smiled. "Thank you for welcoming him also. I suppose it's time. I'm ready."

"I'm not sure I am. I've never had peace like this. In all the cycles of my life, nothing has come close. I can understand why you had that thought, about wanting to hide in here."

"Whatever comes, I am by your side." I pulled myself up, then gave him a long, deep kiss. *Together. We will face it together.*

I pulled away at last and gave him an inquiring look.

"Together," he whispered as he pressed his forehead to mine.

I realized he had heard me again, our connection grew with each joining, every intimate moment made our link stronger. I grasped his hands, and finally pushed myself up to standing. We had to start moving, to make that initial effort to prepare to leave. I could easily fall back down into his arms, and ignore the call to go. But, our food supply had dwindled, water was becoming scarce, and we needed enough to reach the next hidden store of supplies.

"How long will it take to reach the next cache? And how long will it be until we reach TerraIgni, for that matter?"

"Three rotations to the next one, we have two more caches ahead of us before we reach the city. It's about ten rotations total from here. You made it nearly halfway through the Hinterdunes on your own, which is quite impressive really. And you were not dressed well for it, half exposed in your Arbor Elf clothing. What you did is noteworthy, though dangerous."

"I was motivated," I said in all seriousness. I recalled how frantic I had felt at needing to find him, to know for sure that he was unhurt.

He stood and faced me. "Promise me that you will never cross the Hinterdunes alone again."

My face hardened. I couldn't truly be sorry for doing what I believed needed to be done. The Hinterdunes offered me protection from Silvanis—at a price. But, I was sorry how close to death I had come and that I had terrified him so thoroughly. "I promise, Rannoch. I won't do it again."

He squeezed my hands and forced a smile. "Let's get to work then. Time to break down the tent and pack the cache. But first, we need to dress for the dunes, and ready the supplies we will take."

I nodded, and released his hands to go clean up behind the partition. After I was refreshed, he helped me dress in a protective wrap garment that covered everything except my eyes. He tied his own, then unlaced the tent flap to reveal the bright wasteland surrounding us. I squinted against the light as we stepped out.

CHAPTER 21

We made quick work of disassembling the tent and rolled it all together. A pole four times my height with three red tattered flags marked the location of the underground storage chamber. The sand had built up considerably around the hatch. Rannoch unstrapped two shovels from the base of the marker, then handed one to me. I smiled to myself as we started clearing the opening. It was such a small thing, to give me a tool to work alongside him. There had been no question in his mind, I was capable and strong. I couldn't help remembering a certain someone who treated me differently, as if I were a frail female who had little to offer in a situation which required some muscle.

I swept the thought from my mind as we finished shoveling the blockage from the entrance. Rannoch pulled open the door then climbed down inside. I dragged over the weighty bundle and helped lower it into the alcove. He hoisted himself out, then latched it shut again.

He stopped abruptly and turned to me. "Lily, do you know about the Kakodaimons?"

"No."

"Another reason you should never cross the dunes alone. They are evil spirits that wander the desert. You can hear them coming, they have a distinctive wind sound. If you hear them, drop to the ground and shield your eyes. Just don't look at them and you'll be okay."

"What. The. Fuck. More evil spirits? Dammit, this world I tell you! Okay, wait. I need to know something right now. Are there also giant spiders anywhere in Alternis?"

"What?"

"Giant spiders! In fairy tales and fantasy books back in the human world, there are always giant spiders! And I just cannot deal with that. So tell me now."

"What is a spider?"

"An insect, with eight creepy legs, big gross butts and beady compound eyes. Usually venomous. They spin thread and make webs to catch their prey." I shivered and instinctively brushed my arms off at the thought of them. "Ew, I can't even think about them."

He laughed. "No, not that I know of. Are they giant in the human realm?"

"Well no, I mean I guess it depends on where you live. Where I lived they are about this big," I said, using my fingers to show approximate size.

"So tiny! That doesn't sound fearsome."

"Says the guy that has never crossed paths with a black widow. Trust me, I think the fact that they are somewhat small makes them worse. One bite can kill you, and you might not see it until it's too late. And then there's the orb weaver spiders, the wolf spiders. Okay, no more talk of spiders." I gagged and shuddered, remembering how my dad actually used to name the ones on the ranch that got disgustingly huge.

The ranch that's no longer there. I sagged, hoping my mom and Felix were doing okay.

"Before we go, I need to send a message to my brother." Rannoch motioned for me to proceed. I settled myself and closed my eyes, picturing where the Faerie was in the realm. I was surprised to find them quickly, waiting in the Praegra Forest at the closest point to the Hinterdunes, perhaps waiting for me. I tunneled into myself, toward the node in my throat that could emanate the call. It started so smoothly this time, the sound rolled out in effortless waves then rippled in a strong current toward the Faerie. I waited for some time, it was quite a distance to reach them. Before long, the familiar blue light was circling me in a happy tinkling cadence. I laughed as they seemed annoyed that they couldn't reach my cheeks to run over them. Instead, a flutter against my eyelashes was my greeting. Little flecks of glitter were left embedded in their wake, sparkling in the bright early light.

"Hello, my friend! Thank you for braving the Hinterdunes for me again. I need to request a message. My brother Felix will be coming back into the realm soon, he may already be here. He doesn't know about the danger of the Umorfae, Silvanis. I hoped you would find Don'Li of the Caelifae, and ask if he would go toward the Southwest Tear to find him, then warn him. I want Felix to head toward here, hopefully Don'Li will agree to guide him as he guided me. We will find him at the border and help him cross the Hinterdunes into TerraIgni."

The Faerie bowed, then flashed away. Their blue trail lingered for a moment before vanishing on the horizon. I turned to

Rannoch, who stood like a stone as he stared at me. "What? Is something wrong?"

"Don'Li Calbaeric? He guided you?"

"Oh, geez, yes. I forgot to tell you that. When I arrived back through the Vale, Silvanis was quickly on my trail, I found the Amabilis while evading him. They took me to the Arbor Elves. The Amabilis had tried to find you, but said you must have been in the Hinterdunes because they couldn't locate you. I met Don'Li there, who told me a little about the history of the war, and also taught me how to call a Faerie so that I could send you the message. Then he guided me from the Arbor Boles to the border of the Hinterdunes, and protected me from Silvanis there, who had managed to find me again."

"That is a long journey. Did anything … Don'Li is notorious. With females."

"Jealous?" I searched Rannoch's worried face. "Nothing happened with him. He did try, sort of. More like just made passive comments, and it was only when we just met. I was very, *very* clear with him from the get go. I said you and I were together, and don't try any bullshit with me. He stopped the comments altogether, and was nothing but helpful to me. You owe him your gratitude, not your distrust."

He visibly relaxed. "I am sorry. Males can be possessive, particularly after joining. I will … work on it."

I walked over to him, then rubbed his arm. "I understand, sort of. Though I'm a little mad at the implication. Because *I* wouldn't have done anything. My heart belonged to you long before we became official. I wouldn't have even entertained the thought of someone else."

He lowered his head and cast his eyes down. I could barely see anything of him under that wrap, but I could feel his shame at allowing the insecurity to creep in.

I lifted his chin with my hand. "It's okay, Rannoch. I'll get over it. This is still new, for both of us. Maybe this was a good thing. I didn't feel the need to prove my devotion to you. But maybe you did—in a way. You were involved with females that were careless with your heart. That would inevitably leave an old wound."

He nodded his head, but said nothing.

"I say we let it go and chalk it up to what it is, a learning experience," I said, though I could still feel his unease, and truthfully I was still a bit upset that he would think I could be lured away. "Now, back to these evil spirits, does their wind sound different from the Hinterdunes wind? It's always kind of windy here. How will I know the difference?"

"You will know, it sounds like … a sucking sound. Like a funnel drawing inward."

I recalled how the Pythonissamul had the strange vortex and rushing wind. I mused about the possible similarity as we settled our packs in place. Rannoch lifted his hand to shield his eyes, and scanned in the distance.

"How can you tell which way to go?" I asked, my voice muffled from the covering.

"I'm searching for the next marker now. They are spaced at the limits of Fae vision. It can take-" his eyes flared with pride. "Found it!" He pointed in the direction he had spotted it.

I squinted to see it, far off I caught two flickers of red against the ochre dunes. "Okay, let's do it. Three rotations? Let's make it two."

He let out a single laugh. "Slow and steady, my love. We cannot rush it. I know you're anxious to get me into that next tent."

"I can feel you smirking under that wrap, smartass. Okay then, slow and steady it is."

We set off in the blistering heat, loaded with just enough supplies to get us to the next checkpoint.

CHAPTER 22

Time dragged on as we crossed the dunes. I frowned as Rannoch seemed to be torturing himself over his momentary doubt. I could sense his revulsion as we trudged, it seethed through our link. We finally stopped for a break to have some water and food. I loosened the wrap from my face, then lifted the waterskin to my lips, but halted before taking a drink. "Are you going to kick your own ass the entire way to the next cache?" I swigged as I looked him in the eyes.

"I feel like a stultus."

I swallowed, nearly choking. "What the heck is that?"

"A faexhead, foolish. I feel terrible about how I reacted to hearing that you traveled with Don'Li. I am a stultus for even worrying."

"Well, I've forgiven you. It'd be great if you'd forgive yourself too. Listening to you beat yourself up through our link is distracting me from appreciating all this beauty surrounding us." I opened my arms to the wasteland.

He cocked his head, clearly not catching my attempt to lighten the mood.

"Come on, that was funny! Not even a little laugh, just for me?" I walked to him and poked his nose. "Boop."

He grabbed my finger and wrapped his other arm around my waist. "How dare you," he said, drawing me in closer.

"Oh, I dare." I leaned forward to kiss him.

His face softened as he went to brush his lips against mine, when he froze. Rannoch's eyes flew open wide as he went rigid.

"What is it?" I sensed his sudden panic through my heart. That was when I heard something hurtling toward us, with a tumultuous, inhaling sound.

He pulled me to the ground and shielded our faces. It was upon us in an instant. The sensation of large, rigid fingers scraping my body made my skin crawl. Not fingers, I realized with dread.

Claws.

I screamed as I jerked my limbs away from them, the racket drowned out any noise I made. I tried to keep my eyes shut, but from a gap under my arm I saw them for a moment. Black vapor whipped around us, as bipedal beasts that were all talons, teeth, and horns charged in a frenzy. Creatures the size of large dogs with a single eye in the center of their unsightly heads tried to break us apart. I clenched my eyes as the claws raked at my legs, trying to haul me away from Rannoch. He held tight, he wouldn't let me slip even an inch, at least at first.

Their drag became stronger, more insistent. A talon hooked itself in a fold of my pants, gaining enough purchase to drag me a short distance. Rannoch grunted as he struggled to pull me back.

I twisted to the side and thrashed my legs. I was tempted to sneak a glance, so that I could aim a kick at the hideous thing that was attempting to tug me away. I fought back the urge to look, and wound up another flailing kick. My foot swished through the air, not connecting with anything of substance. Terror suffocated my lungs as Rannoch lost his grip on me.

Focus. Three. Two. One.

I took a breath, and centered myself. *I don't need to see. I can feel.* I sent a probing thought to the awful monsters, on the off-chance I could connect with them like I had with the arthropods in the cave. But these beings didn't have minds like the beetle-scorpions. The mind-spear didn't connect with anything, and just shot off into the ether. Like nothing was there. The beasts flickered around us, flashing between locations with a funnel vortex surrounding the pack. Their forms were murky and ill-defined. I sensed the one that was gaining traction against me, with the frequent tug to my legs. It would be there one moment, and then the next it would dissipate, fading into nothingness before reappearing again. I noticed a pattern to the pull, and that it would start from a specific direction each time. Three yanks, then circle.

I took a slow breath in, waiting for it to jerk me the now-expected three times. I counted, then kicked in an arc with all my might in the direction it would have been coming from, if it kept up the previous order. I used my base—my hips—to add strength to the kick like Kerenza had taught me, and put all my force into it. My foot connected with a mass which quickly gave way, and made whatever tugged at me falter. I scrambled back toward Rannoch, his solid forearms were ready to retract as soon as I came in contact with him.

Just breathe, and wait. I realized the words were not mine, I had heard them through Rannoch. I struggled to relax, but finally convinced myself to settle into the sand. *Playing dead is safer than fighting back.* With our interlocked hold on each other, there was little chance the Kakodaimons could get Rannoch and I apart again.

I am one with the sand. I am one with the sand. I said to myself, then expelled all my breath as I let all my movement stop. I sunk further into the ground, allowing it to envelop me. A hooked talon snagged my wrap and ripped into it. *I am … sick of this.*

I unleashed a helicopter kick with both legs. My heel impacted with a fleshy head as I rotated through, catching it squarely in a nook behind a bony protrusion. I clenched my eyes as I slammed it to the ground, being careful not to allow myself to peek even for a moment again. A loud crack echoed in my ears as it shuddered up my shin bones.

A strange yelp, followed by a shuffling sound of something twitching in the sand tempted me to look. I fought the urge and buried my face back down again, as I tightened my grip on Rannoch.

The wind quieted just as quickly as it had started. Gone were the clawing talons, the chaotic noise, and the sense of a malevolent and angry evil. After a moment, I hazarded a glance at our surroundings, then stood and dusted myself off. I took a shaky breath to try and steady myself. My hands trembled from the lessening surge of adrenaline that had pumped through my system. My knees nearly buckled underneath me as I spun, looking for any sign of the horrible beasts.

"Let's hope that's the last time we see them, they're terrifying."

"Yes, let's hope," Rannoch said in a stern tone. We picked up our scattered supplies then located the cache marker again, ready to restart our trek after the unnerving encounter.

CHAPTER 23

We reached the cache without further incident, though Rannoch didn't seem as relieved as I thought he'd be. Inside the tent, we'd be safe from the desert spirits, and spared the constant sapping of our energy from the dunes. I had expected the apprehension that gnawed at him from within to abate, but it still stewed below the surface.

Though I was exhausted, we worked together to assemble the tent and load it with the supplies we would need for a rotation or two of rest. I threw down blankets and arranged a bed for us, while he hauled waterskins and food bundles into the makeshift kitchen. I couldn't wait to get my dusty clothes off and flop down in the covers. I was depleted from the experience of the Kakodaimons, the thought that some spirit could suddenly materialize and whisk you away was beyond terrifying. It had left me hypervigilant for the rest of the journey to the cache, I half-expected them to return and steal me into whatever dark realm they inhabited.

Rannoch laced the tent shut, then turned to me, loosening his clothes to allow the top part to fall around his waist. "We need to talk about your impatience, Lily."

"What?" I asked as I tugged at my protective wrap. "I thought we discussed this. I think I am being patient, personally I thought I was pretty cool about the whole Don'Li issue." The garment came off awkwardly and left long tails hanging from my hands.

"That's not what I'm referring to. I'm talking about how you rush everywhere. Wanting to race to the next cache, deciding to fight against the Kakodaimons instead of waiting them out. All you had to do was wait. Fighting them was a risk."

"Maybe you're not rushing enough!" I exclaimed, the fabric pieces swished in the air from my sudden motion. "We have threats on our heels, and my brother is out there somewhere. I lost Josie due to inaction. My dad and sister, too. I won't make that mistake again."

He helped pull the wrap off, it finally fell in a puddle on the floor. "You had said you probably would have died as well, if you had gone after them. Didn't you say it was your equus-creature … horse that wouldn't go in? And what if you had come through the Vale when your friend did? You may have lost your life then, along with her. Everything would have been different. Maybe Opius would have made quick work of his deal, gotten ahold of Felix next, and Dashelle's rise to power would be imminent. Perhaps your inaction was the key."

I closed my eyes as tears welled. "I can't ever be okay with the fact that I didn't search her out right away. I only looked there, in the human realm. I didn't know this world was here, but I did feel *something*. And now her power is bound inside that bitch Dashelle, while she continues to wreak havoc."

His face softened and opened his mouth to speak. Instead, he wrapped his arms around me as I shuddered. A wave of tears flooded as I thought about my friend, my stand-in sister that had been there for me when I was at my darkest moment. The person that had made living in the aftermath of loss at least a little more bearable, for a time. It had been her and I against the world. Then, she was gone.

"I am sorry," he said as he stroked my back. "I only meant … Fae live for so long. So very long. The cycles can be unbearable if you are always hurrying somewhere. It just becomes so tiring. The biggest reason some Fade earlier than others is that they burn themselves out. And I see you, always in a rush, it worries me. I began to be concerned that you would Fade before your time."

"To be honest, it's hard for me to think so long term, especially when we have danger lurking and near-immediate threats."

He stiffened. "Do you not think we have a future?"

The pain of his words plucked in my chest, from his heart straight into mine. The sudden fear of his that I hadn't thought we would live, that mating would only be temporary anyway, such that making the promise was not a difficult decision.

I pulled back to look at him. "I do think we have a future, I believe in us. I hope you don't ever feel that again. I don't know exactly what that thought was, but I could feel it. I want an eternity with you. I only meant I hadn't thought so far ahead, to think what our lives could be like. I was human for twenty one years. Life is *fast* as a human, a fraction of what a Fae life is. It's somewhat ingrained in me, even if I didn't always act that way. I think you might need to have patience with me, in that regard."

I wove my fingers through his, then tugged him toward the blankets we had tossed down. "Come, let's clean up and go to bed, I need you close. I need to feel my mate as close as we can be."

We stayed in that tent for a full two rotations, and barely slept for most of it.

CHAPTER 24

The last part of the journey across the Hinterdunes was a blur of long days in the hot desert, with another short respite in a temporary homestead wedged in between. I spent most of it lost in thought, mulling over Rannoch's words, all stirred together with my various bubbling emotions. My dark past, combined with my nebulous future left me unsettled. I couldn't determine who was right, or if it should be a compromise of the two. Did I rush everywhere as Rannoch said? Perhaps one reason we were mates was that we were meant to gain understanding from each other. That was the one thing I could keep landing on, that we were together for more than one purpose; I could learn from him, as much as he could learn from me.

He slowed, pointing ahead. "We're here."

Relief flooded at the thought of being able to rest. My legs felt like they couldn't carry me much further as it was. I squinted to where he motioned, I couldn't see anything beyond more sand. "I don't see it. Are you sure?" I took another step closer and realized there was a split in the land, from our vantage it seemed to be no more than a hairline fracture across the desert.

I followed his lead as he proceeded, we crested the rise of one last dune. The terrain beyond terraced down to a yawning canyon. As we dropped down each expansive steppe, the city unfolded before us. Built entirely into the vermillion chasm wall, countless windows and doorways spread across the half-moon stronghold. Balconies with cascading succulents dotted the facade, which wrapped and wound along the entire citadel.

We came to the edge of the last terrace before the drop off, marked by two flaming columns. I looked over the wide ravine, to peek at the canyon floor far below. A carved rock staircase wound its way down to the base, thousands of stairs down, then approached a massive entrance to the city. Burning torches lined the whole way, ending with giant sculptures of carved Ignisfae, each with one hand held high and cupping active balls of flame.

Rannoch took my hand as he turned to me, he had already undone his covering to below his collarbone. "Ready?" he asked.

My stomach clenched as I nodded. The moment was finally upon me, where the people I would live among would see me with Rannoch, as his mate and partner.

He gently removed the wrap from my face, then pulled my bright blonde braid free and adjusted the wrap around my shoulders. "Do not worry, my love."

I tried not to let the concern show, but I couldn't help my apprehension.

"Many of them already owe you their gratitude and allegiance," he continued, "because of you those with young ones that were taken have now been reunited. You have already proven yourself to the Ignisfae. You deserve your place here, not because you are my mate. Because of what you have already done for them."

I took a breath and held back tears. Guilt gnawed at me, so quickly I had a new home, my family house and human life were gone, and I was so swift to move beyond it. As I gave him one slow nod, I resolved that I would somehow make it right with my mother. There had to be some way, a reconciliation that I could provide that she had not raised me just to have her daughter vanish into another world.

Rannoch smiled at me, a knowing and understanding smile that told me he sensed my conflict, and knew of the hardship I carried on my shoulders. He raised his hands and stoked the flames of the spires to our sides, sending the plumes high in the air. A drum beat responded from a battlement at the top of the city, alerting all within of our arrival.

He offered his arm and motioned to the descending path ahead. "Ready to make a big entrance?"

I gave him a quizzical look and proceeded down the walkway with him. As we approached each set of torches, he charged them both up into the atmosphere, creating spouts of fire to line our aisle. I flinched momentarily, the heat of it brushed my cheek as we continued. And yet, here I was not in danger of succumbing to the sheer power that fire could inflict. Instead, I was its master. I smiled at him. *Together?*

He chuckled, as we reached the next one, we each lifted a hand and sent the plume curving up from one side to the other over the path, creating an arched walkway. It became our rhythmic march that moved with us as we approached the city, every four steps was another torch to continue our hallway of fire. It hid my view of the surrounding area, and lit Rannoch up in a luminous glow. I focused on his warmth, his solid and reassuring presence that told me no matter what happened, we'd be okay.

As we reached the platform to enter the city, we let the flames die down. I looked away from Ranncoh to glimpse the entryway into my new home. My heart leapt when I saw Kerenza, standing alone at the entrance, with her unmistakable sideways smile. She beamed at us as the fading flame glinted on her bound dark hair, with its contrasting brilliant ruby highlights. She rushed forward, her exquisite clothing flowed in soft waves and billowed around her as she came to a stop in front of us. The finely woven luster of rich yellow satin complemented her tan skin perfectly.

"Oh my Gods," she belted out a laugh as she looked at us. "Did you two save any energy for the trek here? You look beyond exhausted." Her smile lit up as she glanced at our marks, at the proof of our mating. "Let me be the first to congratulate you both. This makes me immensely happy, you deserve each other."

I tried to laugh and thank her, but I was so tired I could have collapsed. I straightened my back. Falling over on the doorstep of my new home was not how I wanted the Ignisfae to first glimpse me, mated to their prince and utterly useless at the moment. I would show them I was strong, and resilient enough to brave the Hinterdunes; that I would be a force to be reckoned with, for them. I drew from my reserve to lift my head higher, as I stood with Rannoch.

Hundreds of Ignisfae started appearing along the battlements, in the plazas, and on recessed balconies. To welcome their prince home, and spy the newcomer which probably none of them ex-pected.

Kerenza glanced over her shoulder. "Your people await, my sister."

My sister. I nearly buckled and let tears fall at those words, but I bolstered myself and remained steadfast. I sucked in a breath as she got down on one knee and took my hand in hers, making a visible display for the people of her acceptance as she bowed low. Rannoch took my other hand in his, and raised it high for them all to see. A cheer erupted, colorful banners whipped in the wind as I stared at them all. So quickly they celebrated our union. There was no doubt they could see—even from this distance—that I was not an Ignisfae like them. I gulped, part of me was terrified that they would take one look at me and question my loyalty, or my heritage. Kerenza stood and released my hand as Rannoch lowered my arm. I placed my fist across my chest and bowed in deep appreciation for their acknowledgement.

But on one balcony, the biggest and most grand platform, a lone figure stood immobile. He watched, and waited, before turning to disappear inside the great keep.

Rannoch and Kerenza both noticed as well. She narrowed her eyes. "What a culus. Come on. Time to get you settled and introduce you to your city."

My stomach fell as I realized it was their father, perhaps the first sign of what I would face with him. My exhaustion was getting the best of me, it pecked away at the self confidence I had, the part that would list off all the reasons I was a solid match for Rannoch—and why King Ashwan should be happy for his son.

She put her arm around my shoulders. "Do not worry about him. I am sure you would like to clean up and get some rest."

I tamped down the disappointment, the distant first glimpse of their father had already filled me with foreboding. Perhaps our biggest hurdles as a couple were not between the two of us, but rather between family as we figured out how to bridge the gap. Inherently I *was* different. There would be a learning curve for all involved. As much as I wanted it to be just Rannoch and I, it wasn't—and could never be just us. I had joined with a prince, I knew even the first time I found out about his lineage that this would mean complications.

I leaned into Kerenza, at least she believed in us, and was sympathetic toward our union. I quirked a tired smile at her, I knew in my heart I would never stop appreciating how she had lent her support from the very beginning. It was she—the first time we met—who had softened first. She had turned a kind eye to me and facilitated the start of an adventure I could never have imagined. Granted she had her need, the driving reason she strove to do most everything she did, after the birth of her child. Emblyn became the reason for most of her endeavors. But I could never forget or discount what she had done for me. She had looked past what I was dressed as, what I appeared to be on the outside, and gave me the chance to show myself.

"All right, you big sap, I will take you to your room before you start crying on me."

"They'd be happy tears." I sniffed, my raw emotions begged to be released. We walked toward the towering entrance, dwarfed by the sculptures of the warriors bearing flames. Though they were at least thirty feet tall, the height of their flame did not reach the top of the fortress. My glance swept to each side, taking in the hundreds of windows carved into the rock face, with soft, woven awnings to shelter them. It was incredible that I couldn't see anything of the tall city from the Hinterdunes until I finally arrived, hidden by the last steppe. The top of the fortress was equal to the level of the land, perfectly masked by the dunes around it.

Kerenza guided us to our quarters, though Rannoch knew the way. He gave her clear lead to walk us through the city, amid the throngs of people who reached out to greet their sovereign's son, and his new mate. Their smiling faces and open hands made my heart weep, though I held myself up as I smiled back at them. I wanted to stop, learn their names, and say hello. But Kerenza moved us quickly past, and in truth, we needed to. I had only enough energy to make my way through the winding paths of the red stone city. Light from high above punctuated the tile walkways, soft coverings draped over various entryways, all woven from vibrant cloth.

At last we reach a guarded entrance, clearly the gateway to the palatial center. Rannoch waved to the people that trailed us, I mimicked him and waved as well. I frowned at the separation, that there was some distinction between them and us. I had been raised on a ranch in simple, equal terms. Neighbors were just that—no better, no less. The palace marker that separated us and the crossed spears in TerraIgni made a clear delineation. *This will take me some time, Rannoch.*

His face hardened as he looked at me, clearly he had heard my comment. Whether he understood it, I didn't know. But he would need to understand that I was not brought up to think this way, even though it existed in the human world. The difference was, back there I was just average. Not exalted, not revered. Just me. I would take that authenticity and meld it with this life.

CHAPTER 25

Kerenza swept aside a heavy cloth doorway embroidered with glinting gold and silver, and intricate red patterns swirled throughout. She motioned for us to enter. "For the happy couple. Emblyn is waiting for me, and I imagine you would like to have time to yourself right now." She left without another word.

"Wow, Rannoch, your room is beautiful. I wouldn't have thought it would be quite so ornate." Silks hung from the ceiling, and draped in cathedrals in the expansive space, all framing a huge bed. A pierced wood partition separated off part of the room. Gold light filtered in from windows covered in gauze. I toed the smooth, clean tile, the cooling feeling soothed my aching feet.

"This isn't my room, this is for newly mated high born."

"Oh." I blushed. *Honeymoon suite.*

He walked behind the carved barrier. Water rushed, followed by steam that billowed over the sectioned off area, as the sound of a tub filling echoed in the room. I peeked over the wood to spy him adding bath oils to the hot water. I entered the bathroom and started pulling off my clothes, when he stood, then crossed the short distance to me.

He stopped me from removing my wrap. "We have a tradition." He lowered my hand, then started slowly undressing me. He motioned with his chin for me to do the same. "In TerraIgni, fabric is a part of life. We weave together, as we weave our lives. Removing each other's clothing is a sign of acceptance of who the other is. That when all is removed, regardless of what we see before us, we embrace the whole of that life." He unwound the top, then guided the bodice down past my waist.

I loosened the pieces wrapped over his shoulders and pushed the panels down off his arms. I undid the ties at his sides, which caused the garment to fall to the ground. He released the knots at my hips, and placed the broad planes of his hands on my skin, then pushed the fabric the rest of the way off.

He looked at me, at my whole body, with a soft smile as he shifted his gaze to my eyes. "I see you, my mate, and accept you for all that you are."

I nearly cried. I hadn't expected there to be a ceremony, hadn't even considered it. But as we stood in each other's bare presence, I was so glad for it. There was something deep, and spiritual about the moment. I felt as if he could truly see beneath my skin, to the person that I was; right down to my virtues, flaws, shortcomings, and strengths. He embraced all that I was without question or doubt.

I took a breath as I looked at him. "I see you, my mate, and accept you wholeheartedly for all that you are."

He scooped me up and carried me over to the tub that was big enough for both of us, then lowered me gently in. The warm water against my skin was like heaven. After countless days in the desert with only washcloth baths, it was a luxury that made my eyes involuntarily close. We washed each other, taking our time with each pass of the cloth. The exhaustion I had felt before melted away completely, as if the wafting steam had evaporated it into the air. He turned me around, then guided my chin up as he poured water over my hair, careful not to get any of the soaped water in my eyes.

After he rinsed it, I slipped around him and slid my legs to wrap around him from behind. I ran my fingers through his wavy hair and returned the favor, washing his tousled hair that reached to his mid-back, the ruby streaks embedded in the black shimmered in the water. I passed my hands over his broad shoulders, then kneaded into his significant back muscles. He groaned as I worked into the knots around his lower neck.

Rannoch reached up and gripped my hand, then spun to face me. "I don't want to get too tired." He stood, then held his open palm out to me.

"I think I just need sleep. Is … that okay? I know this is like the mating room or whatever. But it's been a long journey and I'm emotionally exhausted."

"We don't have to do anything. Can I hold you?"

I smiled at him as we got out. "Yes please."

CHAPTER 26

I woke up to soft light coming through the window curtain, which rustled from a gentle breeze. Rannoch still slept beside me, the silken sheets were a mess around us. I rose, then went to a cabinet to find something to wear. It had been stocked with a variety of garments. Though I would have defaulted to a comfortable pair of pants and light fitting shirt, a flowy dress hanging from the center rack caught my attention. The finely woven material had clearly been made with care and attention. In the heat of the city, walking around in this cloud-like, lilac satin dress sounded like just what I needed. I slipped it on, and admired the gold embroidered equus running along the wide three inch border which brushed the top of my feet. As I finished tying it in place I turned to see Rannoch watching me.

"Time for us to find some capuli," I said as I adjusted the wide straps around my shoulders.

"I couldn't agree more. You look beautiful. TerraIgni fashion suits you."

"I like it too! I was never one for dresses, but there's something about it, it's comfortable, functional, *and* pretty. Just kind of ticks all the boxes for me."

He laughed. "I'm guessing that's another human expression." Rannoch stood, then strode to the cabinet to get dressed. I bit my lip as he walked over. His ears twitched and he raised an eyebrow at me.

"Sorry," I said, " I couldn't help but admire you."

He slipped his hand around my waist and brushed his lips against my cheek. "Are you sure you want capuli right now?" he whispered in my ear.

I pulled back and batted my eyelashes. "You're merciless. But yes, we should eat something. I'm starving."

He dressed quickly then guided us to a moderately busy dining hall. It reminded me of how the Arbor Elves served their meals, family style with plenty of long tables. The design naturally encouraged people to sit together. I glanced around the vast room; warm red walls and floor, accented by translucent drapes around the windows that allowed the light to peek through in shafts. Everyone halted their conversations as we walked in, all eyes shot to us. Banners that hung from the ceilings were the only movement, gently swaying while everyone stared. I averted my eyes and looked at the banners that displayed an insignia of a flaming scroll, all woven with gold filament on a burnt red background. My gaze landed on an expansive buffet table laden with food. We walked over and began picking out our meal. From across the hall, I spotted two familiar faces.

"Is that … Dhirdre and Dhiren?" I asked as I filled a plate with intricately carved fruit.

Rannoch looked over his shoulder as he poured capuli from a carafe. "It is! Would you like to sit with them?"

I nodded as I tossed several braided baked rolls onto the already full plate. He motioned for me to lay it on a tray that was loaded with several other plates he had made, and the capuli. I hesitated, it looked to be too much for one person to carry. He wordlessly insisted again, I shrugged and set it on the tray, carefully finding a spot amid the clutter.

Rannoch lifted the tray and balanced it high overhead. "Direct me to our table, my mate."

I pointed to the open seating next to our friends. I schooled my face into neutrality, though it took considerable effort to keep my cringe at bay. I didn't want my concern to show as all Ignisfae in the hall stopped to watch him navigate with the unwieldy tray. He swooped the platter down with a theatrical flourish, it spun and settled to a stop in the center of the table.

Dhiren smirked. "Magna, Rannoch."

Rananoch grinned. "Have to show my mate I can provide."

"With style, of course," Dhiren chuckled. He and Dhirdre stood in unison, then bowed low to us. "Congratulations on your joining!"

I smiled. "Thank you, but please, sit! You're our friends, you don't have to bow." Rannoch and I sat down on the benches across from each other, as they settled next to us.

Dhirdre scrunched her forehead. "I suppose you will not want us using a title for you as well, like Rannoch and Kerenza."

I grabbed my capuli and blew off the steam. "Sounds about right." Considering social standing and hierarchies before having even a drop of coffee was unthinkable.

"Lily is not used to formalities like that," Rannoch said.

"How have you two been since I saw you last?" I changed the

subject after taking a sip. I sniffed the aroma of the fresh brew, *this is exactly what I needed.* I drank more as my senses started to wake up.

"Well," answered Dhirdre. "Just waiting on orders from King Ashwan. We have not had much to do while you were … busy."

I snorted a laugh, my capuli nearly came out my nose. She grinned at me as Dhiren shook his head.

"Joking about our prince mating, not appropriate, Dhirdre," Dhiren scolded his sister.

"That's what makes it funny, Dhiren," I said as I went to take another sip. I smiled at Rannoch, *inappropriate jokes are always funny.* He huffed a single laugh and twitched up one side of his mouth. "Besides, that's like a one on a scale to ten of indecent jokes. Maybe even a one-half. Barely registers."

"How is Felix? Will he be joining us soon, I hope?" Dhirdre asked. Dhiren narrowed his eyes at her. She ran her fingers through her silken black hair, flipping it at him as she ignored his suspicious glare.

I halted my reach for a roll, my nerves flurried at the thought of my brother. "Yes, hopefully soon. I'm waiting on a Faerie to alert us of when we need to collect them at the border of the Hinterdunes."

"Them?" Dhiren's eyes flashed.

"If the Faerie I sent delivers the message and he agrees, Don'Li Calbaeric will guide Felix to the border."

Dhirdre's eyebrows shot up and Dhiren slowly nodded as he looked at Rannoch. Rannoch waved a hand to dismiss anything Dhiren might say about Don'Li, apparently Don'Li truly was notorious.

I decided against keeping quiet. "He helped me cross the

Praegra Forest, I asked him to help Felix as well. Do you both remember Silvanis, from the battle in the mountain?"

"No, who is that?" Dhiren asked.

Kerenza breezed into the dining hall, spotted us, then headed straight over. She settled next to Rannoch and snatched a pastry from his plate. "Bonum mane! What are we talking about?"

"I was just about to tell them about Silvanis, who was apparently Opius's henchman. He may be positioning himself to take over as Generalis. I don't know if you all heard, but Dashelle was not killed that day, at the end of the battle. She tricked us and escaped. I believe he may be trying to complete the deal with her that Opius had started. If he manages, he will have Dashelle's support in taking over the Umorfae. Which also means he's trying to capture me, and Felix. He nearly did when I first got back, then again near the border of the Hinterdunes."

She chewed, then swallowed before answering. "This is not good news. Hopefully the fact that as he is an Umorfae means you will be safe, since he cannot cross the dunes. I would not mention this information to our faeder—yet. Oh, by the way, the Magna Culus King Ashwan has demanded your presence, Rannoch and Lily." She mocked an official gesture, twirling her hand in the air like she was delivering a proclamation.

I gulped as my mouth went dry.

"You should not say that so loud, Kerenza," Rannoch said sternly, stifling a laugh.

"I'm almost afraid to ask, what is a culus?" I asked.

"If he does one more faexhead thing, it is what will become part of his official title." Kerenza laughed. "It is, ahhh, an unseemly name for what we excrete solids from."

"Gross, Kerenza!" I wiped tears from my eyes as everyone nervously laughed. In truth, I was thankful Kerenza would make jokes. Finding out I had to finally go meet their faeder filled me with apprehension. Laughing eased it, at least a little. "Well, I guess we should go?" I asked Rannoch.

"Not before bacon!" Kerenza exclaimed as she took a piece from our plate. She crunched a bite. "What? Fresh bacon should always come first." She feigned innocence as Rannoch deadpanned at her.

He shrugged and nodded at last. "Not before bacon."

CHAPTER 27

My stomach dropped as we approached a set of gilded double doors at the end of an expansive hall lined with detailed mosaic pillars. The fine blue-and-cream tile patterns reflected the soft, flickering light of flames, which bloomed from the hammered gold sconces lining each side.

"Rannoch, should I have changed? I suddenly feel under-dressed."

"Not at all, I wouldn't change a thing." He squeezed my hand as we reached the entrance.

He went to push it open, when an Ignisfae shorter than I stepped out of an alcove.

"Prince Rannoch," he sneered, "I was told you were to request entrance, rather than just barging in like you normally do."

"Really, Eiulans, he demands our presence and then shuts the doors so I have to ask to come in?" *Sniveling bastard.*

I pursed my lips, holding back the nervous laughter at hearing Rannoch's interior thought.

"That is correct, Your Highness." Eiulans motioned to a handle embedded in the door. Rannoch sighed and stepped over to it. He pulled it out, revealing a honed blade which glinted like fire at the tip. I caught my breath as he motioned with it, the edge of it nearly grazing Eiulans's cheek in the process. Eiulans slowly closed his eyes once, entirely disinterested in Rannoch's maneuver. Rannoch angled it toward the door, then thrust it into a gap I hadn't noticed before. It clicked into place and caused a round panel to slide open, revealing interconnected metallic fittings. He rearranged the sliding pieces, when they fit together properly a button the width of a palm rose from the center of the door.

Rannoch rolled his eyes at me as he pressed it. We stood, and waited. And waited.

"He is in there, Eiulans?"

"Oh yes."

At last an unseen bar in the center of the door slid slowly over to unlatch it. Painfully slow. The sound of metal scraping against metal reverberated in my ears and sent an uncomfortable tingle down my spine.

The doors swung open at last, revealing a barren cathedral with a single form at the far end. He sat rigid, with his hands resting on each carved arm of his red stone throne. Rannoch held my hand tight as we walked towards the unflinching figure. He could have been Rannoch's brother, though dressed in ornate heavy robes, the face below his substantial crown nearly matched my mate's. His sinister underlying expression marred the beautiful exterior and offset him from his son.

I made a conscious effort to keep my breathing even, chin raised and shoulders squared. I remembered the first time I had approached a dais like this one, with a figure not nearly as imposing. Empress Celestine didn't have half the intimidating presence that King Ashwan had, but I refused to let the fear I had felt at her meeting overtake me. *I am worthy of your son, dammit.*

King Ashwan spoke at last, "So, finally mated are you? I began to think it would never happen. Of course you had to select one who was not an Ignisfae, was that one last shot at insubordination?"

My skin prickled and my nostrils flared, only one sentence in and I was already losing my grip on staying cool.

"Faeder-"

"Title!" the king bellowed.

Rannoch barely faltered before he restarted. "Your Highness King Ashwan, I present to you my mate, Her Highness Lily Brennanfalk."

He stared at Rannoch for what felt like an eternity, before finally shifting his eyes to me. Just as quickly he looked back at his son.

"I like her gold hair at least, it reminds me of wealth."

I lost my hold on my temper.

Fire erupted from my hands and flashed from my eyes. I stared him down, hard. I was half-tempted to stalk him all the way to his raised platform and force him to give me more than a passing glance. I'd show him that his little display of trying to tower over us didn't work.

Rannoch made no effort to quell the flames, though he spoke to me through our link. *He's doing this on purpose.*

"And a Fire Bringer? Perhaps she has more value than I first thought." King Ashwan rubbed his chin with his thumb and forefinger.

I pinched my lips together, I wanted to shout at him for his dismissive manner of me, for valuing me based on my ability and my blonde hair. I smirked at Rannoch at last, *Magna Culus is right.* Rannoch rolled his lips, trying to keep a laugh from escaping.

I let the flames die down as I turned my gaze slowly back to the king. He was watching me as I did, and I looked at him, unblinking. I could see him wordlessly measuring me, so I stood stock-still. I was not afraid, and was resolute in my newfound belief in myself. I had already served the Ignisfae people with a great deed. His own granddaughter was returned to them, in part because of my actions. And now, I was Rannoch's mate. I had earned the right to stand before him, and be recognized. I may be different, I may not know all their ways. But I was worthy. I wasn't about to let his treatment toward me diminish what I had done in any way.

His face was like stone as he looked at me, disinterested. At last, one corner of his mouth quirked up. I felt a twinge of relief from Rannoch. His faeder had relented, if ever so slightly. Yet still, why should I have to work so hard for his acceptance? Had I not garnered it, at least in some measure, before walking through those doors?

"You are both dismissed." King Ashwan waved his hand in the air.

I made an effort to not visibly roll my eyes at him, as Rannoch and I turned to leave. As we exited the golden doors, they clanged shut behind us. Eiulans gave us a withering look as he secured the thick slabs.

"That went well!" Rannoch said with an uncharacteristic grin, once we were a fair distance away.

"Was that a joke, Rannoch? Wow, your first joke! We should celebrate," I said as I practically stomped down the hall with him.

"I thought you might like it if I tried to make you laugh. I'm sorry about my faeder. I knew what he would be like going in there, so I'm not surprised in any way. Plus, it's his way of lashing back at me, because I never accepted any of the females he tried to persuade me to select. This was not about you, rather about he and I."

"I get that, but it doesn't change how it made me feel."

"Well, if this is the worst of our problems, we'll be just fine. Like I said, he cannot break a mating link, and my loyalty is to you now, in all things. You are what matters to me."

I smiled at last. His dad was an absolute prick. But Rannoch was wonderful, he was everything good in this world. I squeezed his hand and sighed. "We've barely arrived here in TerraIgni and I already feel like I need a break." I looked through an arched window out to the darkening sky. "Nightfall again." I let go of his hand and walked to the opening, then looked up at the misty, starless sky. "Why aren't there stars here? Why is it always mist? Will I never see the moon again?"

He settled to a stop next to me. "Do you regret your choice now?" His eyes dimmed and his ears tilted down.

"No, of course not, Rannoch. It's just, well that didn't go as I would have hoped—him making me feel so … unwanted really. And then when I saw the sky, I just got sad. The night sky was a big part of my human existence. I spent so many nights on the ranch stargazing, imagining what was out there. Everything is so different. But it's all worth it."

"Come, I have a surprise for you."

I lit up as he wrapped an arm around me. "Surprise?"

He beamed and nodded. "A really good one I think."

CHAPTER 28

He tugged my hand through the palace, then through a series of torch-lined rough tunnels. The roof of the passage intermittently opened up to the darkening sky above. I tried to ignore the fact that no twinkling stars shimmered through, just the endless gradation of dark purple and mist. At last an expansive area opened up, and my gaze fell on clusters of equus roaming a canyon.

Steren spotted him and trotted up. His massive hooves sent tremors through the ground as he stamped around happily. I backed up and smiled as I watched their reunion. I could have easily been sad for myself, my own bond with Apollo was yet another loss of staying in Alternis. But I knew all too well the joy of being so close to an equine that you could feel each other, trust each other implicitly. Rannoch positively beamed as he greeted him, and I realized that it had been some time since they had been together because of his trek through the Hinterdunes to find me.

After a few minutes of nuzzles from Steren and neck rubs from Rannoch, he walked over to me with Steren close behind.

"You must have missed him since coming to find me." I looked at his mount with longing as I thought of Apollo. I gulped and stifled a tear as a memory of him following me popped in my mind, my beautiful horse that I might see again—maybe—but would never ride again.

"I did. Though it's been longer than that. The equus are taken a different route, through the skies over the southernmost border of the Hinterdunes, through the mist. The clan splits, some go through the dunes hauling supplies, and some ride the equus. Those that are weakest or young return that way. I guided the warriors through the dunes, so I haven't seen him since we disassembled our camp."

"Well now aren't you the big burly Ignisfae, guiding all the warriors through the dunes."

He shot me a sideways glance, then laughed.

"Wow, Rannoch, I think you're actually learning about humor! This has been a big rotation for progress, at least in that department. You sure you don't need a nap or something?"

"I think you might be making fun of me."

I pursed my lips, then answered with a sigh, "I'm sorry. I miss Apollo. I was being snarky I guess. Sometimes I'm sarcastic to avoid feelings. It's an old habit. I'll … work on it."

He rubbed my arm. "I know a lot has changed for you. I imagine it's not easy, especially with what just happened with my faeder. Which is why I'm really looking forward to this surprise."

I perked up again. "I almost forgot!"

He grinned. "I have a feeling about something, come."

We walked hand in hand, with Steren trailing, over to a group of wandering equus. Zephyrine trotted over to Steren. After greeting him, she upturned her lip at me and sniffed. I laughed, equus apparently flipped their upper lip and inhaled just like horses—to suck in a scent from a person or another horse. I held my hand out, smiling as she wriggled her muzzle in my palm. She lifted her head, which swung high over me. I stood motionless, trying to figure out what she was doing. I knew from working with horses, maintaining composure around large herd animals was critical. Horses could sense doubt, they knew when a person wasn't sure about a situation. I had to assume the same could be true for equus. I didn't want to startle her with momentary worry, but I couldn't help my apprehension. Her towering size left me dwarfed below her chin. She could easily crack my skull if she quickly dropped her head on me. However, my concern washed away as she stepped back, then lowered. One leg extended toward me, she dipped her head and bowed, bending the other front leg.

I glanced at Rannoch. He beamed at me as she waited. "She remembers what you did for Steren when he was ill," he said as his eyes danced.

"So she's thanking me?"

"No, Lily. She's accepting you. She has never granted a rider. You are her first. She has picked you … to be her bonded rider."

"What?!" My mind reeled as guilt surged. Guilt because of the excitement and glee it immediately fostered. Moments before I had been missing Apollo, saddened by the thought that he was now on his way to Ithaca, perhaps to do no more than graze in a pasture. But, if I could step back from my emotions and look at it logically, I could rationalize the fact that—no matter what—I was not his rider anymore. Ill-fitting and abnormally large, my size would be a detriment to his frame. Circumstance had changed our rider-horse bond. I knew that when I had gone back to Black Oak and didn't shift back. It was one of the prevailing thoughts that had settled in my mind. The life that I knew was gone. And this, this was a gift.

"I thought she might," Rannoch said, "because of what you had done for Steren. I hoped she would, I should say. What better equus for my mate than the mate of my own mount?"

My eyes welled as I looked at him, then back to Zephyrine, still with her head lowered and waiting for something. "What do I do?" I whispered. I could feel I was supposed to confirm it somehow, and I wanted it so badly. Perhaps I was horrible for being ready to let go of one branch to take hold of another as I swung my rider spirit from one mount to another. But the need, the ever-present need for me to bond to a creature persisted. I'd always had that thread as a part of who I was at my core. Changing to a Fae hybrid hadn't erased that. Truth be told, it was not the first time I had done it. The reasons before were because of the horse I rode, either aged out of their prime or they no longer could compete at the level I had risen to. This was a wholly new twist, new territory I had galloped into when I charged into the Vale that very first time it changed me.

"Place your hand on her head for a moment, just below the forelock, then get on her back. That is all. Grip her mane and be ready. She will take her first flight as soon as your fingers grasp her hair."

I did just as instructed, my whole body shuddered as I touched her, the fine hairs of her head sending thousands of signals through my hand, the pinwheel that they radiated out from on the star pattern there sent a shockwave through me. I closed my eyes, then released my hand and walked around to her left side. I dropped my eyelids for one beat, *up into the mist we go.*

I swung my right leg up over her spine, then settled myself in the center as I wrapped my legs around her and tightened them around her girth. I wound my fingers through her flowing mane as she rose. I felt her haunches contract, before she sprang from the ground and into the air.

CHAPTER 29

The world rushed down away from us as her mighty wings flapped, propelling us into the sky. My stomach dropped as she banked, sending us in a different direction as she kicked her legs to twist her body and tossed her head into the turn and caused her flowing black mane to whipp the other direction over her dapple gray neck. I hazarded a glance over my shoulder as we righted, Rannoch flew close behind astride Steren. He released a howl after we locked eyes for a moment. I laughed and returned the call, as we flew through the vapor. We soared out of the canyon, into mist above the dunes beyond the city.

Rannoch and Steren pulled ahead, guiding us through the atmosphere. My blood rushed as we continued through the blocked sky. It dawned on me, I was not afraid, not one bit. Only my grip on her mane kept me secured, and who knew how high in the sky we flew? And yet, I felt totally safe—albeit exhilarated. I had no fear of falling off and tumbling down through the formless expanse, even the thought should have sent me into a panic attack.

Yet the fear and expected anxiety were not present. Only joy, freedom, and pure happiness were there. I smiled and rubbed her neck, I admired her powerful form as we sailed through the swirling mist. I felt a flicker through my mind from Zephyrine. A response to my touch and thought of her, a return feeling of gratitude and friendship. To bond so quickly to her almost felt like a cheat, or a shortcut. It took years to develop a bond like that with Apollo. Still, I relished it, clung to it and was grateful for the immediate closeness I felt with her.

We flew for hours, I was left to my wandering thoughts as wind whipped past my ears. We dropped below the mist at last and sailed down, onto a broad plateau surrounded by narrow rock spires that reached high into the air. The rich bronze-and-rust layered stone was a stark contrast to the grayish blue misty sky. Rannoch jumped off Steren's back, then rushed to me with a grin that split his face. I dismounted with a hop off of Zephyrine, he caught me before I landed and twirled me in the air, hugging me as we spun.

"Thank you for my surprise, Rannoch! I can't believe it, I'm so excited I want to scream!"

He pulled back to look at me. "That wasn't your surprise. I couldn't make her pick you. I certainly hoped she would, and thought you deserving of it. But I had no control over it. It had to be her choice."

I squinted an eye. "But then what-"

He lifted a finger to my lips. "It's better if I show you." He picked up my hand, then led me over to the tallest spire. Steren and Zephyrine followed, but were too busy nosing each other to walk quickly behind. As we approached, I saw a narrow platform jutting out from the side, which rose in a spiral up the entire rock formation.

The excitement simmered under my skin as we ascended. I had to guide myself with a hand on the warm stone interior wall as we climbed the steep stairs. Though the wall looked rough, it felt smooth as my fingers dragged along the inner spindle that the steps sprouted from. We had gone seven spirals up when I looked down over the open right side to see Steren and Zephyrine, nuzzled in each other's manes far below. The excitement switched to concern as I realized how high we were, and how much higher we had to go.

"Don't worry, it's just a little further," Rannoch said after seeing my face.

"I don't think I'll ever get used to you talking like me, using contractions and stuff, though I do really enjoy it," I joked, trying to shift the focus from my nerves. It was funny that I was fine riding Zephyrine in flight, but up on the spindle I felt unease. It may have been that there was little to grip to, and the stairs on the right side were completely open with a sheer drop, not to mention that they also sagged with age like drooping leaves off of a great stalk.

"I figured it might make you feel more at home, having me speak more like you. Plus, I've found I like it. It's a little more relaxed way of speaking, I guess."

I stared at him and nearly let go of the inner support. "That is … that is so romantic, Rannoch." I smiled to myself as we continued up the impossibly high rock formation.

At last we made it to the top. I wanted to crawl across the flat platform as we crested the last step, when my eyes fell on a telescope the size of an equus. I forgot my fear instantly and went straight to it, running my hands over the segmented metal body.

The lens was at least two feet wide, the fittings narrowed and widened intermittently. The whole apparatus was rooted into a large disc with a pedestal to sit on.

"Welcome to Starcrest." Rannoch beamed. "Try it out."

I lit up as I smiled at him. Stars. I would be able to look at the stars here. I sat down and peered through the eyepiece, but the usual adjustments I would expect from a manmade telescope were not there. This was Fae-made. There were handles and levers on either side.

"Maybe you could show me," I said as I tried turning knobs to no avail.

He chuckled, my ears twinging in glee as he sidled behind me. I sat up so that he could sit on the pedestal with me on his lap.

"Here, like this," he spoke softly, his lips against my ear. His breath against my skin sent a delighted shiver down my spine. I was tempted to turn around and kiss him, but the eyepiece flickered in response to his motions and my focus immediately returned to looking through the glass. The view at first was hazy, but gradually the scope pierced through the film of the Vale, to the galaxy beyond. I caught my breath as stars flecked into view, like thousands of glittering jewels in the velvety black space. On the eastern side of the sky, I caught a bright glow that blotted out the stars in the surrounding area. I waited with my breath held as it crept into view.

The Moon.

Tears welled at my waterline. I blinked them away so that I could see it clearly. I gulped as the tears brimmed up again, the fact that I still had some connection to the night sky, the one that I spent countless nights staring up at with Maris, or Josie, or Felix for that matter. It was one thing we all loved, and spent so many of our nights in our quiet town gazing at. I stared up at the night sky displayed with a kind of brilliance I had never seen. I may have watched the stars for nearly an hour before Rannoch finally broke the silence.

"This is the only place in Alternis where we can see through to the heavens." Rannoch's deep voice grazed my neck. "I have spent much time up here, anytime I needed peace or solace."

"How does it get through the mist? How can it even *do* that? "

I could hear his smile as he answered, "A remarkable Ignisfae you should meet had the idea for it, Yantzen J'Dun. He spent at least five cycles just drawing the plans. He and I made it together."

"You *made* this?!"

"Well, I forged the pieces as he instructed. Yantz is the one that figured it out. He is beyond brilliant. I'm just the one that swung the hammer."

"Does he still design stuff like this?"

"No, now he is a thread painter, an artist. He changes what he does. But whatever focus he chooses to have, it is always with the highest level of skill."

"I would love to meet him … and to see what thread painting is. I've never heard of it."

"I'll take you to meet him, and see the bazaar when we go back to TerraIgni. I can't wait to share everything our city has to offer you."

Our city. I melted.

I quirked the side of my mouth up as I turned to him. I twisted around to straddle him, my legs astride his so that I could gaze directly into his remarkable cognac eyes.

"You have ignited my heart, Lily. Our phrase, burn brightly, we say it as a reminder to live our lives to the fullest, to be the best we can be. I don't need the affirmation as I used to. Being with you, I simply *do* burn brightly."

His statement took my breath away. Tears stung my eyes as I raised my hand to his cheek. I leaned forward and caught his lips with my own. I yearned to be as close to him as possible, for our flesh to meld as one. At first the kiss was gentle, a slow caress of lips and tongue. It gradually increased, the heat from our skin rising with the escalating fervor.

I tapered it back again, wanting to savor it—savor him. I moved on top of him more completely, and wrapped my arms around his neck. He pulled me by the hips into himself, pressing his hardness up against me.

I groaned as he pushed my hips in a slow rhythm, and kissed my neck. He dragged his lips lower, along my collar bone, pausing on my now-healed bite marks. Then lower still. I lifted my arms and untied the dress from my neck, and allowed the top to flutter down to my exposed waist. He caught the tip of each breast with his lips, and flicked his tongue over the end. The sensation nearly sent me over the edge as I arched my back. I bent down and kissed him again, my attempt to reign in our heat had loosened as the ache between my legs grew more insistent.

He pulled the bottom of my skirt up, and yanked the band of his pants down. He thrust himself into me without waiting. It was beyond obvious what I wanted. His impressive length was sheathed completely in me in an instant. My release threatened to unfurl as he cupped my breast. I moved in a slow rhythm on top of him, there were few options for positions way up on this spire, sitting astride him with his arm hooked around my lower back seemed to be the only way. My toes barely touched the disc as I rode him, leaning forward to get a better angle. I bit his ear, which made him clench his fist into my side.

The misty sky rotated above us and everything flipped. He splayed me against the body of the telescope, the smooth metal warm against my skin. Rannoch pounded me against the very metal he had so painstakingly forged. I was wrong, there were definitely more positions to explore up here. He was relentless, the bite to his ear had untethered him. I was nothing short of liquid fire as he unleashed himself on me, in me. Rannoch was everything I wanted, everything I needed. Primal urges fought their way out as I wanted to bite and claw at him. I nearly punctured his shoulders with my nails as he threw his head back, his body going taut. His final plunge unchained me, as I shattered in waves.

He dropped on top of me, heaving as we caught our breath. I closed my eyes as I cradled his head.

I love you, Rannoch.

He shuddered at my thought. A tear slipped out and ran along my temple, making the smallest splash sound as it landed on the scope. Lucky. We were so damn lucky to have each other. When we were together, all the problems disappeared. I forgot about them, at least for a little bit. There was so much that needed to be fixed in this world, threats that needed to be removed, so many things that I myself needed to help right. I could rattle off a list that would ratchet up my anxiety, but for the moment, we could enjoy each other's companionship, love—*and holy fucking shit, great sex.*

He blurted a laugh.

"Are you listening to me think?!"

He lifted his head to look at me. "I couldn't help it. I just get small portions of what you're thinking sometimes, but you kind of projected that last part."

I closed my eyes and grinned. "It's true anyway. You might as well know how much you're rocking my world."

He chuckled as he drew lazy circles on my skin with his fingertip. "I don't think I'll ever tire of the funny expressions you say. How does one even rock a world?"

"Well, you manage it every time," I muttered as I started to fall asleep.

I woke up as a sudden chill crept over me, then blinked my eyes open to see Rannoch finish adjusting his pants. I stretched my arms, surprised that I had actually taken a nice nap on a giant telescope, with no kinks or sore spots which I would have expected.

"I think we should head down to check on the equus. We've been up here for quite awhile."

I tied my dress as I asked, "Why don't they just fly up here? Do we have to take the stairs down?"

"Unfortunately, yes. They don't like the spires, strange as it may seem. They are uncomfortable on narrow ledges. They need a bit more space to land and take off."

I groaned. "Well, fuck. Okay, let's head down."

My legs were shaky as we made the careful descent, both from nerves and from the expulsion of energy on the telescope. I smiled to myself as we crept down. At least thinking back on that eased the tension of the unnerving open stairway.

We reached the bottom at last, Steren and Zephyrine greeted us, both lowered so that we could mount up easily.

"Time to head home?" Rannoch asked.

"Yes." I smiled as I worked my fingers into her mane. "Home."

151

CHAPTER 30

It was a long flight back, but I welcomed the cooling mist on my skin. We arrived back in the equus canyon, then dismounted and gathered feed nets for them. I was glad to see that Rovan and the Ignisfae that tended the equus had stuck with my suggestion to feed them with the hay gathered off the ground. After giving Zephyrine some attention, I peeled myself away from her, then started the walk back to the city with Rannoch.

"Strange how fast I attached to her," I commented. "I'm having a hard time separating."

"That is normal, the bond is a close one. When it happens, a thread of their spirit imprints on you, and one from you imprints on them. Intertwined."

I nodded as I walked with him, then looked over my shoulder at her one last time before entering the tunnel pathway. She looked right back at me, her amber eyes connected with mine even from a distance. My chest expanded as I flooded with emotion, and longing to run back to her.

Rannoch stopped. "Do you want to stay longer with her? I understand, if so."

"Actually, I'm pretty hungry. I do want to stay, but let's go eat. I'd say we worked up quite an appetite."

He chuckled. "No argument there."

The busy dining hall filled with smells of warm cooked food welcomed me. My stomach rumbled as we approached the buffet. A variety of hot tortams were laid out, along with decanters of wine, and baskets of what looked to be some sort of steamed tuber vegetable. We loaded a tray, I made sure to grab an extra glass of vinirubrum for good measure.

"Good choice, always take one more," a female voice said from too-close behind me.

I nearly dropped my glass as I spun. "Kerenza!" I laughed. "I nearly threw my vinirubrum on you."

She giggled. "As long as some makes it in my mouth, I would be okay with that."

"You weirdo." I gave her a hug at last. "Come join us! I have news!"

She waggled her eyebrows, which I rolled my eyes and shook my head at. Rannoch carried our food over to an open table, then swung his leg over the seat back before sitting down in one motion.

"Such a boss, you don't even bother to pull out the chair," I snickered as I moved my chair to sit across from him.

"Never do. Takes too much time." He grinned from under an arched brow as he set the tray down.

Goddamn he's hot.

His ears twitched and the corner of his mouth tipped up.

"Sheesh, I can't get away with anything," I muttered as I raised my glass to my lips.

Kerenza's sideways smirk widened as she took a sip of wine. I stuffed a tortam in my mouth, as Dhiren and Dhirdre appeared at the buffet and started loading a tray. *Oh thank God.* Hopefully their arrival was enough distraction to sidestep my current discomfort. As much as I loved Kerenza, having the whole display play out before her was not something I was comfortable with. They walked over to our table a moment later.

"May we join?" Dhirdre asked.

"Always!" Kerenza answered as my mouth was still full. "Lily has news, and I cannot wait to hear what it might be." She swigged from her glass again as they sat down.

I swallowed my bite, then mimicked Kerenza and took a sip before answering. "Well"-I smiled and set my glass down-"Rannoch took me to visit the equus, and Zephyrine bonded with me. I took my first flight as her rider."

Kerenza coughed, and Dhirdre dropped her jaw.

I realized with dread that maybe that news wouldn't be so welcome to them, all those cycles and Zephyrine had never accepted an Ignisfae, but she accepted me. Worry crept in, that maybe they would think me unworthy. Afterall, how long had they cared for her? And here I come, then just swoop in and snatch that bond. This was perhaps exciting news for me, not them.

"Magna news, Lily!" Dhiren exclaimed. "We are all bonded riders. I, for one, would be honored to ride alongside you."

I released a heavy breath and flashed him an appreciative look. "Thank you, Dhiren. I worried that maybe this wouldn't be good news to you all."

He smiled and nodded, lifting his glass in a quick salute.

Kerenza spoke up, "It is a surprise, I suppose. I think we all just figured she never would select a rider. It *is* magna to hear, and I think I can speak for all of us when I say that we are happy to have you join us in the skies."

"You guys are the best, seriously. I suddenly felt like such an idiot," I said. Kerenza twisted her features, and I realized she didn't know that word. "Stultus, I guess," I added.

They all laughed, which sent a shockwave of relief through me as I laughed as well. I finished eating my tortam and potatoes, then drank the last of my wine.

Kerenza cleared her throat. "I have news as well, which I am willing to bet Rannoch forgot to tell you about. Remember the holiday I told you about when we first met?"

"Oh yea! The one where everyone weaves, dances, and drinks?"

She bobbed her head and beamed. "Yes! Praetexia. It is in nine rotations! We will begin preparations on the next rotation, then the fun begins!"

I opened my mouth to speak, when a familiar blue light shot into the dining hall, then encircled me. I laughed at the greeting, but then realized it was not the Faerie I knew, it was Don'Li's. Their tinkling sounds drifted into my ear, as understanding came through in short bursts. *Don'Li. Felix. Hinterdunes border.* Just as quickly, the Faerie darted away.

I dropped my jaw as I shot a glance at Rannoch.

He stood before I even said anything. "Let's go," he commanded.

I was already moving.

"What? Where are you going?" Kerenza asked.

"To the border of the Hinterdunes, to collect Felix," Rannoch answered. "He has arrived at last."

Dhiren stood so fast he bumped the table. "We should join you," he blurted, motioning between Dhirdre and himself.

Rannoch appraised him for a moment. "Agreed. We will all take our equus along the mist border, then cut north to the Hinterdunes juncture."

"I do not want to slow down your departure," Kerenza announced. "I need to take care of Emblyn, she has been … difficult lately. I will see you when you all return. Burn brightly, I look forward to welcoming Felix here."

"You and me both," I said as I hugged her goodbye.

Dhirdre and Dhiren split off from us as we headed to collect our things. We made quick work of grabbing weapons and packing supplies. Before long, we all met back up at the equus filled canyon. I walked with Rannoch over to Steren and Zephyrine, done with their hay and resting after our first adventure. Rannoch had no lead line, or any sort of tack to toss onto Steren for the long trip.

"Do you ever use saddles or something, for longer rides?"

"Saddles? What are they?"

"Oh … leather fittings, to make the seat more comfortable."

"No, never. We always ride in direct contact. We want it to be comfortable for the equus."

I thought for a second. "I see. Well, with horses, the saddle does actually make it easier for them over long rides."

Dhiren was already astride his mount and walked him over.

"We should set off, yes?" His forehead wrinkled with concern.

"Yes, definitely," I responded. "I don't want Felix waiting there. There could be more than one danger lurking. Dashelle, Silvanis, I would not want him facing either one alone."

Dhiren didn't wait, he kicked his equus's sides and took to the skies. Dhirdre, Rannoch, and myself launched a moment after. Rannoch pulled ahead, leading us all high toward the formless expanse. After a steep incline, we entered the mist and leveled out. The mighty black equus wings pumped the haze into swirls as we flew.

Time stretched as I tried to adjust my seat, I'd lost track of how many attempts I'd made to shift off of my pressure points throughout the lengthy ride. *Now I really wish I had a saddle.*

I glanced over my shoulder, then did a double take. Dhirdre was napping on her equus, her cheek resting on its withers and arms wrapped around its neck, with her legs trailing behind over the rump. Just as I frowned and thought I'd like to do that, a thought pinged in my head, one that wasn't my own. I realized it was Zephyrine, encouraging me to copy Dhirdre. I fought it for a moment, but it came again, and through it the sense that it would alleviate discomfort for her as well. *I guess it's not just my ass that's aching from this long ride.* I sensed from her that she was becoming tender as well. I reminded myself that this was new for her, she may become sore more easily from carrying me.

I leaned forward and allowed my legs to slip back, then carefully unthreaded my fingers from her mane so I could hug her neck. I closed my eyes as the sound of rushing wind mixed with the beat of the equus's wings, the pattern alternating between a rhythmic flap to near-silent gliding soar. The rocking movement, and caress of air lulled me to sleep.

A nudge to my thoughts roused me, I realized it was Zephyrine waking me as I blinked my eyes open. I gasped as I sat up and grabbed for her mane, having completely forgotten I was sleeping on a giant flying horse. Moments later we started to descend, the mist cleared and an expanse of land opened up below us. My stomach dropped when I saw the considerable height we were at as the equus started to spiral down. The land terminated along the southern side, a craggy cliff that disappeared into nothing. We sailed down, each equus taking a few strides to slow down as we landed just to the side of the drop off.

I was the last to dismount, my knees nearly buckled as I dropped. Rannoch was there in an instant, scooping his arm around me to steady my balance.

"Sorry, I'm fine. I just need to stretch. How long did we fly for?"

"Two rotations," he said as he brushed hair from my cheek with his thumb. "It was too long to go without touching you."

"Creep."

"What?!"

I laughed. "Just kidding. I'm just surprised how long it's been. How long until we reach Felix?"

"We need to let the equus rest, after we leave again, it will be another two rotations. They are *much* faster than we would be on land. But it still takes time, and they are tired."

"Of course," I responded quickly. Steren and Zephyrine must have been exhausted, to be asked to fly for so long soon after we had taken our selfish trip to Starcrest.

"No, don't think that, Lily. That was your first ride with her. And we visited somewhere very special. There is no reason to have any guilt for taking a slice of time for yourself for an escape."

I let go of a breath. "You're right." I smiled, in spite of the fact that it should have made me uneasy how he could hear my thoughts sometimes. The mental connection made me feel that much closer. I grabbed his hand as we walked over to Dhirdre and Dhiren, who were busy unrolling a thin blanket for us all to sit on.

I settled down cross-legged and looked around, it didn't appear that we had somewhere to sleep. Rannoch rummaged through a bag and pulled out some food, as Dhirdre procured a familiar looking leather pouch.

"What do you say to a game of ludens palas?" she asked with a huge grin.

"Oh fuck yea!" I exclaimed.

Rannoch chuckled. "We'll see about that beginner's luck this time. Though I certainly wouldn't mind if you won again."

I blushed, remembering my "winnings" from the first time I played. That would definitely *not* be the case here.

The game lasted what may have been hours, or half a rotation. By the end, we were all howling with laughter, and a little drunk, as Dhirdre took the win. She had startled Dhiren so badly when she screeched "Ludens!" he had fumbled his card and knocked the whole thing over. She cackled as Dhiren rolled his eyes.

"Magna, who knows how she will make me pay for this," Dhiren groaned as he stretched his legs. "Rannoch, do you think we should leave soon? I would bet the equus have rested enough."

Rannoch appraised him for a moment with the corner of his lip tipped up. "Yes, I think you are right, that should be enough rest. We will take turns sleeping once in the sky, two of us need to be awake at all times."

"I'll take first watch, I took a long rest before," I said. Though the vinirubrum was definitely taking effect, I was suddenly anxious about reaching Felix. It had already been several rotations since they reached the border, having to just sit and wait there increased the chances that Silvanis could find him. I didn't know if the wound Silvanis received from the Elvish blade had actually taken him out. I had to assume it didn't.

"I will as well," Dhiren announced, distracting me from my downward spiral.

"No, Dhiren," Dhirdre cut in, "you have not rested yet. Both Lily and I already did, I will take watch with her. Besides, I am hanging onto that ludens favor until I really need it!"

He rolled his eyes for the twenty-third time. "Magna."

We packed our supplies and were airborne within a few minutes.

CHAPTER 31

I was increasingly drowsy as we sailed through the mist. Rannoch and Dhiren had slept for who knew how long, all I had heard in that time was the flap of wings and rush of air.

"So, how does it feel to be our princess so suddenly?"

I snapped my gaze to Dhirdre, her eyes sparkled after asking the question.

I started to speak twice before answering, "The thought is overwhelming sometimes, to be honest. I just want to do right by the … responsibility. I never expected something like this. But I will always do my best." I cringed at my words, maybe I was supposed to feign confidence, no matter what.

She smiled. "I warned Rannoch this may be a lot for you. For anyone, really. I think it is one reason he waited so long to tell you. He did not want to scare you away. Also, the ability to pretend, just for a little bit, that so much did not rest on his shoulders … Well, I imagine that was quite an attractive idea for him. He has never taken to claiming his status."

"You seem close, you must have known him a long time."

"Yes, very long. Dhiren and I were born before him, but close enough that we were raised together in a sense. I consider him a brother, though I serve him. As twins are so rare, once we were born we were immediately promised to serve, and I gladly do it. Rannoch and Kerenza never made us feel less than they were."

"I didn't realize you and Dhiren were actually twins!"

"Oh! Yes, twins are quite an advantage in battle or other dealings. We can communicate silently. There are many situations where that can be beneficial."

"I can imagine," I said. "And that doesn't surprise me, that Rannoch and Kerenza made you feel equal. They are the most warm-hearted and kind individuals I've ever met. It's interesting, they are such powerful and formidable warriors. It's like an extreme contrast I would have never expected."

She nodded, then asked, "How did it go with King Ashwan?"

My face fell as I gulped. "Not good, he barely looked at me and definitely did not seem pleased. It was really disappointing. Actually, it made me pretty mad. He referred to the fact that I can Fire Bring like I was an asset. A thing, rather than a person."

She looked thoughtful for a moment. "Rannoch and his faeder have a complicated relationship. I think King Ashwan is bitter, he did not mate for love, and it did not end well. I imagine the reality that Rannoch chose a different path makes his faeder feel even less in control."

"Yes, Rannoch told me what happened to his maeder. It's horrible to think about, what the Umorfae did is unforgivable. My heart hurts for Rannoch and Kerenza."

Dhirdre's gaze sharpened. "That was the result of what had transpired before she even left TerraIgni to approach the Umorfae with an offer. Queen Deniza was trying to make up for a transgression. But, I suppose that is very old history at this point. Still, I think King Ashwan carries it with him. However, it is not my place to speculate, I merely serve them. I say, just give King Ashwan time."

I thought back to Rannoch's stories of the females that tried to corner him into marriage, how the king had facilitated the situation. Encouraged it. Anger boiled to the surface, why did I even want someone like that to accept me? Fuck that guy, he had put his own son on the auctioning block for someone to try and snag. He didn't want someone to love his son. Was it spite? Jealousy? He didn't have someone who loved him so Rannoch shouldn't either?

Zephyrine's withers scrunched as she tossed her head. "Oh! Sorry girl!" I yanked my hands away, I had nearly burned her when I lost control over my emotions. It was like a stab to the heart as I saw what my reaction had done to her. I could feel her wince at her smarting skin.

Three, two, one, you are calm. The fire quieted and I unthreaded a healing filament, casting it over the surface to soothe her. The glow faded from my hands as I sensed her ease, the momentary hurt vanished.

"I do not know if I will ever get used to seeing that," Dhirdre commented.

"I hope I learn to control Fire Bringing better. I get mad, and it comes out. I'm not sure how Fire Bringers learn to manage it. Do you know any, Dhirdre? Maybe someone can teach me."

"There are not many, it is a rare gift. I know of no others living. But, I will do my best to find one."

I slumped. Alone, I was alone with this *gift.* In TerraIgni, there was always fire nearby, it wasn't needed. And when had it truly benefited me? Perhaps in the battle with Opius, and Dashelle. Certainly it was what had first allowed me to escape the bindings that held me, when they had captured Rannoch and I.

My stomach clenched at the memory, the near-scrape we'd had when we hung over the pit that Naiya had been tossed into. It had been too close, and so many had lost their lives during that battle.

I changed the subject instead. "What do you like to do with your time, Dhirdre?"

She glanced at me, and flashed a coy smirk. "Dhiren hates it, but I am a dancer."

"Why would he hate that? Dancing is a beautiful art form."

"Oh, because I am usually unclothed and many times take someone home with me afterward."

I grinned as my cheeks reddened. "I can see why your brother wouldn't like that. I know mine would flip out." Speaking of Felix sparked a memory, we would be picking him up soon, and bringing him to TerraIgni.

"Dhirdre, I just remembered something, Don'Li said that the border of the Hinterdunes senses if you have fire ability. Felix doesn't, will he be safe to come with us?"

"He will. We will be crossing through the mist, on equus. Any Fae can be ferried that way. If he were on foot, yes, he could not cross the Hinterdunes into TerraIgni."

I blew out a relieved breath. At least he would be safe once we could head back, assuming he hadn't been tracked down by Silvanis, or Dashelle for that matter. I hardened my resolve as we flew. Thinking about the what-ifs would do no good. All I could do was get to them as soon as possible. And fortunately, with Don'Li with him, he would be better protected—and informed.

I focused on the steady beat of Zephyrine's wings, the swish of mist as we sailed, and the half-comfort that we would reach Felix soon.

CHAPTER 32

We began our descent in a single line formation, the spiral down funneled the mist in a corkscrew behind us, as land came into view. The dreaded lake with the rocky prison in the center popped up on the horizon. I honed my gaze straight down instead, ignoring the multicolored ore lump and azure water where so many had died during the battle alongside the Arbor Elves, against the Umorfae. So much loss to retrieve the children stolen by the Umorfae, taken at Dashelle's command.

We had prevailed, they were safe. *We* were safe. I could take heart in that. But the loss of Arbor Elves … Aolis. Watching Aolis die while I could do nothing, watching his *sacrifice,* giving his last moments to the fight. Guilt washed over me as I thought about his heroic end. Because what he had done *was* heroic. About to die, and with one useless arm that would prevent him from ever opening a fenestram again, he had taken down the archer that was picking them off one by one.

And the others. Some faces I couldn't even remember. But I remembered their names. Fenlaen, Auroris, and Aurelian's persistent injury. They had all made the difference in that battle, the one that returned Emblyn and the other young ones to the Ignisfae. We had succeeded, at a cost.

I shook the memory from my head as we cycled down to the ground. I stifled an exalted holler as two figures emerged, healthy, and unharmed.

I leapt off Zephyrine just as her hooves touched ground, then threw my arms around Felix. My brother. My heart burst with relief, I could have cried now that I knew he was safe. He laughed and returned the hug.

"We should go quickly, Lily." Felix said as he pulled away. "We fought Silvanis once already. He's one pissed-off dude. Don'Li was the reason we were able to get away from him. But I would bet he's not far off. Let's talk later, we should go."

Don'Li nodded his agreement. "He gave me a parting gift before we escaped," he said as he pulled down his collar, showing a deep knife wound to his lower neck. Though closed, the injury clearly still needed tending. "With the Elvish blade we struck him with, no less."

I cringed. Not unharmed after all. "Can I heal you first? That looks like it needs attention."

He waved me off. "Later, I am okay for now. That bastard is cunning and sneaky, I do not feel we have the time. Even with having the numbers in our favor now, I would not take the risk for it."

I wanted to express all my thanks to Don'Li, for all he had done, for myself and for Felix. But they were right, we needed to turn back to TerraIgni.

Dhiren was already dismounted and guided Felix to jump on his equus's back, he hopped up after after and settled himself with

Felix in front. Dhirdre did the same for Don'Li, though he sat astride behind her. I smiled at Rannoch, tempted to kiss him for all he had done to get to my brother in time. But we needed to leave. I twitched a smile at Rannoch, with the glimmer of promise in my eyes. Later for sure, I would make that gratefulness known. Perhaps with my lips around his fullness, perhaps on top of him—or both. He would know how much his effort meant to me. Not that it was my only means of showing my gratitude. But it certainly drove my desire for him. Through the roof and beyond.

We were all airborne in moments, as Rannoch led us away from the border, back to TerraIgni where we could have a proper reunion.

We stopped at the same rest point on the return trip. The equus were quick to huddle together for their half-rotation nap, as we met up after dismounting on the narrow strip of craggy land.

Felix spoke first. "Don'Li here deserves a medal or something. He found me almost right away when I climbed down the wall at the Tear. Told me everything. Not long after that Silvanis nearly caught us. After we got away, Don'Li taught me how to use my powers better. I didn't know we could create a current to run faster. If it weren't for that, well that dick Silvanis would for sure have caught me."

"I don't know how to thank you, Don'Li," I said. "There aren't adequate words."

Dhiren nodded and bowed to him, with a fist to his heart.

Rannoch cleared his throat. "I also owe you thanks. Lily told me what you did for her. I am in your debt." I could feel an ounce of regret and pain in his words, and I knew exactly why: the distrust that had crept in when I told him who had helped me. He flashed his glance to me, his eyes softening as I heard him speak silently to me. *You are right. I owe him my genuine appreciation.*

Don'Li smiled. "I was glad for the opportunity to lend help. Should the need arise, I would gladly do it again."

"I can show my thanks a bit," I said as I walked over to Don'Li, then motioned for him to pull his shirt open, exposing the injury. I raised my hand, letting the white light uncoil from deep inside me as my vision tunneled down into the brutal cut. Jagged pieces lined each side, like Silvanis had not just stabbed, but sawed at it. I felt his lingering malice as I soothed it, stitching it together as best I could. Unfortunately, since it had started healing on its own, the scar would definitely remain. As I finished up, I let the thread snap back inside, and my vision returned to normal. He rubbed at it, then gave me an appreciative nod.

"I'm going to have to take that knife back from that asshole at some point, no more stabbing my friends with a blade gifted to me by the Arbor Elves."

"Yea, sounds like a smart plan, Lily," Felix retorted.

I opened my mouth to respond, when Dhirdre spoke up, "How about we all have some fun?"

"Oh no," Dhiren groaned as he rolled his head skyward.

"So dramatic, Dhiren," Dhirdre laughed. I looked between the two of them, trying to figure out what she was suggesting. She bobbed her head with a smirk. "Two words. Ludens. Palas."

"Oh yea, doing it!" I agreed.

"What's that?" Felix asked.

"Only the best fuckin' game in this world," I responded.

Dhirdre was already unrolling her ludens set she brought, motioning for us to take a seat.

The rotations back were a blur of soaring, rambling thoughts, and the strange comfort of sleeping midair on a massive flying horse—spliced with the short respite at the halfway point. After the game of vinirubrum-filled ludens palas—in which Felix had secured a win against Dhiren—we were on our way. I laughed as I thought back on how Dhiren had grumbled at losing two matches in a row, and owing two ludens favors. Behind that eye-rolling exterior, I could feel Dhiren's smile below the surface. Somehow, with all the trauma and efforts we had all gone through together, we had become a group of friends.

It happened so subtly, so naturally. I had kept myself away from others for so long, I hadn't seen it developing until it was already in place. Had I realized, I probably would have resisted, hid myself, protected myself. With caring for someone comes the possibility of them being taken away. Another wound to add to the list of emotional scars. But scars are a funny thing. They're proof of a life lived, there is no way to live and not collect them, in one way or another. Scars are evidence that we can heal. They do not remain as some open, festering wound. They close up, but never go away. Forever branded from that life event, whether emotional or physical. That scar holds a memory.

I fingered the healed gash on my thigh, the one that hadn't disappeared from the battle with Dashelle. I had closed it too haphazardly, too quickly. I didn't have time to give it the attention it required in order to fade. Rannoch had needed me, he was too badly injured, so I had reserved my strength to save him. Spending time to heal my cut could have meant I wouldn't have enough for him. I proudly bore my old wound, I would wear it forever, as a reminder that I would always do what was necessary to protect those I love. It was a mark of honor. I had fought, and did not back down. It was my badge I would never try to erase. He had told me he would fight endlessly for me, but the reverse was also true. I would fight endlessly for him, for all of them. As long as there was fight left in me, I would use it to protect them all.

CHAPTER 33

TerraIgni came into view far below as we descended through the mist. Additional banners adorned the exterior of the fortress walls, bright gold sashes whipped as we sailed down. The celebration for Praetexia must have begun. Light was just beginning to brighten from the early morning rotation as we made our approach into the equus valley enclosure. I hoped we were in time to participate in the weaving, before the party started. I knew how much this event meant to Kerenza, and wanted to spend time with her, learning their ways and contributing to their extraordinary fabric making process.

Zephyrine landed on graceful hooves, then came to a stop. She had flown so long, and never once pinned her ears back in complaint. I rubbed her neck and sent a silent thank you to her, grateful for the passage, and the trust she had given me. I dismounted, then headed over to where everyone had congregated near the rocky tunnel exit.

"The Praetexia celebration is already underway," Rannoch said. "Dhiren, Dhirdre, will you go find Kerenza and see what she might need help with? Lily and I will take Felix to his quarters and get him settled."

They each flashed Felix a smile. "I am looking forward to welcoming you properly to TerraIgni at the party," Dhiren said.

Felix beamed. He was positively beautiful in the warm, early daylight. Relief washed over me yet again, he was *here*. We had picked him up without a hitch. With the way things usually went, I had expected something to go wrong. Granted they had battled Silvanis, but the fact that he wasn't directly on their tail at the moment we retrieved them felt like a true blessing.

"We have quarters for you as well, Don'Li," Rannoch said, as we made our way down the narrow, torch-lined path.

"Magna," Don'Li breathed a sigh, "I admit I am tired."

I slipped back, and whispered to Don'Li, "Do you need any extra … help? With your knees or back."

He patted my hand. "No, just some rest, and I will be fine."

We dropped Don'Li off first, he waved us away as he closed the heavy curtain doorway to the guest room.

When we arrived at the entrance to where Felix would apparently now live, he turned to Rannoch. "I need to speak to Lily alone for a bit. Can she come meet you afterward?"

Rannoch's eyes darted between the two of us. "Yes, of course. I will meet you in our room, Lily. Felix, I will have clothing sent here for you."

I nodded and kissed Rannoch's cheek, before he turned to walk away. I pushed past the draped partition, and held it open for Felix to follow. I glanced around the palatial room: a large bed with a plush woven cover took up nearly half the space, and two archways on the far walls opened up to other spaces. One was a breakfast nook which also took advantage of the canyon view, the other a bathing chamber. Gilded, unlit torches framed a balcony on the far side. A wide, overstuffed chair perfect for reading or enjoying the view off the balcony sat nearby.

"I'm legit jealous of that chair! I hope my room has one," I said as I ran my hand over the velour-like covering.

Felix scrunched his forehead. "Wouldn't you know already? I thought Rannoch said he'd meet you there. That would tell me you've already been there before. Also surprising that you apparently already share a room?"

I dropped my jaw. "Oh." I fumbled with my linteum. "Right, so I have really big news which I just realized I conveniently forgot to tell you. Rannoch and I are ... we're staying in this special room for the time being, which is meant for ... how do I say this ... newly-mated couples. Rannoch asked me to be his mate, and I said yes. They don't call it husbands and wives here."

"Holy shit what?! You're ... you're married?"

"Well, not really. There's no wedding ceremony that I know of, we promised each other to always be together and a bond formed. A link. An actual link that I can sense."

"What's involved with this promise?"

I cringed. *No way am I telling him all of that! Any of that.* "The only thing I'll say is there's a bite involved. I bit him and he bit me, and that mark is like ... a brand I guess?"

"He ... bit you. Do you know how weird that sounds?"

"It felt totally natural at the time, it was exactly what I wanted to do, was to bite him and be bitten. I know it sounds weird. But it didn't *feel* weird. Look, if you could just get over this whole bite thing before you see him again so it's not awkward, that would be great."

"Lily, you just dumped bomb-drop information on me. You have to let me process this. I just didn't expect it. But also," he crossed over to me and wrapped me in a huge hug, "congratulations. I am happy for you. Though, it is pretty fast. It seems impulsive, even for you."

I pulled away to look at him. "It honestly didn't feel impulsive to me. It felt like, for once, I actually knew what I wanted. I didn't feel lost, or unsure of what my decision should be. I *knew*, and I would say yes again. There is a lot for me to learn, about my role here in TerraIgni, about the Ignisfae and their customs—and don't even get me started about his dad. But even though there might be difficulties, I would still choose this."

He nodded, resigned. "Not to change the subject, but there is something I need to tell you. I had to leave Black Oak quickly, we were wrong to trust Barb Phillips. I heard her on the phone. She must not have realized how good my hearing is now. I don't know who she told, but someone—an authority of some kind—outside of Black Oak knows about us. I don't think we can safely go back."

I bobbed my head slowly, utterly disappointed by our lifelong neighbor. "Well, at least she helped Mom before screwing us over. I'm so glad you're here, and someone else is glad too, I bet."

His ears perked up and his face brightened. "Oh?"

I giggled. "Yea, Dhirdre was asking about you. I think she's into you."

His face dimmed. "Oh. I had hoped … well that's what I needed to talk to you about … before you came back to the Vale. It's not Dhirdre I wanted to come back to Alternis for." He paused, and pressed his lips into a thin line. Sucking in a breath, he leveled his gaze at me. "It's … Dhiren, her brother. He and I, well, we didn't even get to talk about it much, but there was something there. And I just never found that back home. Lil, I'm gay. I've known for a long time, but I hadn't found the right way to tell you."

My mouth dropped as I searched his face. I was such a jerk, how could I not know? How did I not see my own brother until now? "I'm so sorry, Felix!"

"You're ... sorry I'm gay?"

"No! That came out wrong, I mean I'm sorry I didn't ever realize. This is such a huge thing, and I feel like somehow I should have already known this about you. Thank you, for trusting me enough to tell me." I rushed forward and wrapped my arms around him before he had a chance to hug me back.

"Lily, you're crushing me!" he gasped. His skin trembled as I held him.

I released him as I thought back on the shared meals with Dhiren and Dhirdre. How he had jumped to his feet, the concern on his face and his insistence that they join. "Wow, I feel like an idiot. Dhiren was there when we found out you were at the border, he made sure he came with us. Now that I'm thinking about it, he almost overstepped with Rannoch."

Felix's face lit up. "Really?" he asked, blushing a bit.

"Well yes, he was pretty forceful about it. It seemed like he wasn't going to take no for an answer. And when we left TerraIgni, he was the first one in the air." The more I thought about it, the more I just wanted to facepalm myself as the realization set in that Dhirdre asked questions and made comments because of her brother's feelings, not hers. "I shouldn't say more, it's not my place. But, let's get you ready. It's almost time for the party to start. Kerenza has been talking about this ever since I first met her. Maybe this will be a good chance for you and Dhiren to spend some time together."

Rannoch's voice called out from behind the doorway. "I have clothes for Felix. May I come in?"

My eyes went round as I cringed at Felix, silently pleading for him to be cool. He waved a hand at me. "Come on in, *brother*."

The way he said "brother" made my stomach drop. I held my breath as Rannoch made his way in, bearing piles of folded clothing. He set it all down on the arm of the chair. *Is everything all right?* he silently asked me, no doubt noting the tension in the room.

I nodded as he turned to Felix and I.

"I want to understand why you bit my sister."

Great. "Felix! Come on!"

Felix flashed his glance at me. "I'm your brother and I want to know what's up with this. I think it's totally fair to ask why he's biting you. We weren't raised here, and we don't bite our partners."

"Bit. Once," I cut in. "And apparently, we do. Because I was *driven* to bite him, and for him to bite me. It was instinct, I felt it."

Rannoch spoke up, "If I can explain, what Lily says is true. It is instinct. Some ancient primal urge to bite when we select a mate. We have evolved, but that thread has never gone away. It's a mark that shows the choice we've made, and the link finishes forming because of it. I understand you may have concerns, but the bite is not to harm her. Yes it must heal after, but beyond that, it is finished. It's not something we continually do."

"You never know, Felix. Maybe you'll eventually feel that drive, too," I added. "We may have grown up as humans, but it's upbringing only."

His face reddened. "Well, I think I understand a little more now—maybe. I'd like to get ready now, so-" he motioned to the door.

"Of course," I answered. His lack of actual acceptance hung in the air. It was clear to me, even though he had said congratulations, he was not ready to accept Rannoch and I. He had spent years as my protector in the absence of our dad, I supposed it was natural. Still, I didn't expect it to hurt so bad. I hadn't even thought about it until I realized I hadn't told him, but once I did, it dawned on me why I had conveniently forgotten: my fear of his reaction. I made my way out of his room without another word, as Rannoch followed me.

We walked in silence until we reached our temporary room.

"I'm not sure I understand what happened," Rannoch said at last, once we were settled inside.

I sat on the bed and buried my face in my hands. "I guess he was caught off guard," I said, as I slid my fingers down my cheeks. "God, that was awkward. I get that it's surprising for him, to hear that we're not just together, but bound to each other. He was in the human world for like a day while I came back, and then we were still separated for ... who knows how many rotations. Plus all the time I spent with you before he even came here and met you. For him, it must seem like a lot less time has passed than it has for me. It all feels fast to him. I mean, it *is* fast, but it's also my life and my choice."

"Just give him time. It will be okay," Rannoch said as he rubbed my back.

"You're awfully chill about all this."

He smiled. "I suppose that means "all right". And yes, I am. You know how much has changed for you. Just as much has changed for Felix. He's being asked to adjust to this and let go of everything you both knew."

I shuttered my eyes. My mom. My aunt. They were all that was really left for me there, but how would I retain a connection to them? That was the only loss I couldn't bear, and *had* to find a fix for.

Rannoch held out his hand to me. "Come on, let's get ready. Praetexia awaits! Plus, I want to introduce you to the master himself."

CHAPTER 34

Dressed in the finest silk I had ever seen, we made our way out of the fortress and into the city commons. I adjusted the shimmering gold fabric wrapped over one shoulder in a wide swath, cinched at the waist with a heavily jeweled metal belt. The loose panels at the front and back flowed around my legs as we walked hand in hand, letting the under wrapping of soft white gauze peek through. Ignisfae dipped their heads in acknowledgement as we passed.

I resisted touching my hair—to be sure it was still in place—with each person that looked me over. Though there was no doubt, it was cleanly swept up into a twisted circlet, which transitioned to a double braid that draped over my bare left shoulder, the other shoulder covered by fabric. A new royal attendant had been assigned to me to help with my appearance or with daily duties. Warm, cheerful, and bright, Tanzara felt like an instant friend. And I made sure, well paid. Though completely opposite in every respect from Naiya, I couldn't help but think of her, and her subjugated people. I gulped at the memory, and at the fact that the Syrenni still endured dominion by the Umorfae. Every time she crossed my mind, I knew I needed to help somehow. I couldn't abide living in royal riches while an entire race of people withered under the crush of Umorfae taloned feet.

We approached a series of stalls, sheltered by the drape of extensive woven coverings. Rannoch walked us to one near the center, laden with large landscape paintings. Only the paint was not paint, rather it was thread. Tied, knotted, and looped to form the various features of the different depictions. One in particular caught my eye: a fluffy, wool-like substance was used for the mist layer which billowed on the upper portion in soft puffs, and fine brilliant threads speckled the lower half to represent some kind of magical flower field. Some of the fine petals seemed to glow against the warm red earth background, indicated by silky strands cast in horizontal lines.

My attention was fixated on the expertly crafted scene, when a rich-toned voice spoke up, "Rannoch, my filio! It is so magna to see you." I glanced up to see a stout Ignisfae, with a weathered face. His eyes creased as he grinned at Rannoch, though his face was wrinkled, his brilliant amber eyes sparkled with youth and life. He came forward, then crushed Rannoch in a tight embrace, before backing up to cross a fist to his chest with a bow. "I was wondering when I would hear from you, about your recent adventures, and of course the news that all have been talking about. I am so proud of you, for what you did to retrieve the children."

"It has been too long, Yantz. And yes, I have been up to a lot!" Rannoch said. His smile warmed my heart. Rannoch clasped the elder Ignisfae's shoulder. "I want to introduce you to my mate, Lily Brennanfalk. It's because of Lily that we were able to reach the children. Lily, this is Yantzen D'Jun."

I curved my lips at the simplicity of my name, as Yantz bowed again. No title, no precursor name denoting status. With Yantz I could just be Lily. "I've heard a lot about you Yantzen, I'm glad to meet you. Your paintings are beautiful! I've never seen anything like them. I wish I knew how to paint, I haven't heard of painting with thread before."

His eyes twinkled. "I can teach you, and please, call me Yantz. I am honored to meet you, Lily. And grateful for what you have done for us all." The way he motioned when he said "us all" made my chest swell, he had motioned at me as well, including me. "We could start small, here," he continued, "I even have a workstation you could use." Yantz pointed to a hammock-like seat, hung from the frame under the draped covering. A table directly in front had a swing arm attached to it, with what looked like an embroidery hoop on the end.

Rannoch cleared his throat. "I need to check on preparations for Praetexia, why don't you stay with Yantz and learn."

"Are you sure I shouldn't help you with that?" I asked.

He held up his hand. "Really, this stage is not critical, and I think you would enjoy this much more. Weaving has not started yet, and there are no expectations on you to make an appearance. If it were me, I would not pass up the chance to thread paint with Yantz! Though I'm terrible at it, as I'm sure he'll tell you once I'm out of earshot."

I let out a small laugh. "Okay, as long as there's no issue."

"I will be back soon, my love. Enjoy your time with Yantz." He bent down and lifted my chin with his hand, then kissed me. Everything disappeared. The thread painting stall, the bazaar, the whole world.

"My love," I muttered against his lips, forgetting where I was.

His eyes lit up as I looked at him. His gaze danced around my face, taking in every detail, before he let go, then left.

I turned around to find Yantz setting supplies on the table for me, conveniently not looking in my direction where Rannoch and I had been exchanging sweet murmurs. "I'm excited to learn, though I hope I can do it justice," I said as I walked over to him.

He pivoted to me, his eyes brilliant as he looked at me. Something about his gaze seemed to pierce right through me, into my soul. "It is not about doing it well, it is about releasing yourself to the thread's guidance. Let it flow through you. If you can paint, then you must. It is a light in this world, one we desperately need. We need the light to combat the darkness."

I gulped and clenched my fists as I thought once again about the darkness I had already experienced, the darkness that still needed to be vanquished. He opened his arm, directing me to the seat, effectively turning me away from the spiral I was about to mentally slide into. I blew out a breath as I sat, then wriggled into the plush cushion of the comfortable upright hammock. He slid his hanging seat over from the opposite side, the ropes looped over the support pole through a unique pulley system.

"That is so cool!" I exclaimed as I looked at the whole contraption.

He grinned. "Oh, just something I thought up, need is the maeder of creation. If I want to keep thread painting, I need it to be comfortable!"

I stopped adjusting in my seat as I looked at him. His comment reminded me of my dad, and the sayings he seemed to always have filed away for immediate use whenever they applied. *Necessity is the mother of invention,* he had said that to me when I had been particularly proud of myself for inventing a simple pull cart for the ranch.

Yantz laid a series of bundled strings out, then handed me a needle. "You must feel the thread first—without touching, cast your hand over it, and see which one pulls you. Closing your eyes can help, thread painting is about feel, try to sense the one that is meant to start the painting."

I nodded, then shifted my shoulders to settle in. As I passed my left hand over the thread, one tugged at me. I stopped, then opened my eyes to see a gray puffy floss waiting.

"Interesting," he murmured. "Why do you think it is this one?"

I looked at the thread for a moment. "I guess because I recently flew through the mist, and I am curious about it. Why does it cover this world? Why does it block our view of the stars? It's both oppressive and comforting, oxymorons that make no sense to me. How can it be comforting, when it's shielding something I love?"

He flashed his glance to me, eyes honing in sharp. "You can pierce it, I figured out how. You can see through it if you wish."

My cheeks flushed. "Yes, Rannoch took me to Starcrest. The experience was ... " what could I say that wouldn't give away what we had ended up doing at Starcrest. Yet, the ability to actually look through the film, to break through and see space beyond. I had been re-grounded because of it. "It was a gift I shall forever be thankful for. Your invention gave me peace and connection to my former life, which I will never stop appreciating."

He shifted his glance away from me. "I knew there was something out there. I do not understand why Vitus chose to cloud us with mist, but I am glad to be able to break through, in my small way."

"Vitus Augustus is responsible for the mist? He died long ago, can no one clear it now?"

"The mist is a mystery, it was created by an individual, so it should be able to be cleared by one as well. Yet it persists. Perhaps eventually there will be one who can do it. I may be considered the most innovative Ignisfae, but the mist is one thing I cannot banish. It covers the sky, and extends along all sides, encasing us in a massive dome. Let us begin. Pick up your chosen thread, as you slip it into the eye of the needle, set your mind to relinquish control to the direction of the needle and thread."

I nodded and poked the end of the thread through the eye. I started to knot the other end, as I had seen my grandmother do when she would embroider.

"Leave the end as it is," Yantz instructed as he watched, "the thread must remain unbound, there will be tails hanging from the back, but that is okay. Place your hand behind the canvas, release a breath, then plunge the needle. Pull it through so that the tail is long enough to not slip out, about four dekkates in length."

"How long is a dekkate?"

He held his fingers about an inch apart.

"Cool beans," I said.

He grinned. "I like how you speak. It is ... unique."

"Yea, Rannoch likes it, too. I think it amuses him. He says he finds it endearing." I settled my shoulders, then lifted my hand to start. Closing my eyes, I released a breath as Yantz had said, then started. I pulled the thread until the tail was the right length.

"Now, this part is where it can vary. I can show you what I might do for mist clouds. But you may find a different way. Be open to what feels right. Wind the thread around the needle many times, then push it back through about a half-dekkate away from the entry point."

I did as he said, but when I drew the needle through and tried to tighten it, it flopped in a pathetic wobbly line across the canvas. "Well that sucked."

He laughed. "It is okay! That was your first one. Hold the length of thread taut from behind until you have a few in place. Here, allow me to demonstrate." He sat down at his seat, then pulled over the canvas he had in progress on his swing arm. After pulling through a thread, he wound the string in a tight coil the whole length of the needle, then reinserted it back into the canvas, creating a texturally pleasing, corded line. He whipped out several more in quick succession, staggering their placement so that they started to form volumes to represent clouds. The thick and thin nature of the yarn-like cord added to the billowing look. His hands moved with a fluid speed, like a composer directing a symphony. Yantz laid out more layers, moving up each time so the upper ones overlapped just slightly. "For the sky, start at the horizon, then work up, allowing the forms to become larger as they reach the top. For the landscape, do the opposite. Start at the horizon again, then work down. Things toward the bottom represent that which is closest to the viewer, and therefore larger."

"Always?"

One corner of his mouth turned up. "No. But for this lesson, we will say yes. Just to keep it simpler."

I started again, but instead of winding the needle countless times like Yantz, I only did a few loops, then ran it back through the canvas near where I had inserted the needle. I liked the look of his clouds, but they felt like what you would see from the ground, looking across the land. I wanted to feel like I was in it, the mist curling from the beat of equus wings. I punched through more and more, adding swirls in a radiating pattern until my gray thread ran out, then I cast my hand to feel for my next choice. I opened my eyes when I felt it, a tremor in my pointer finger which called it down, like witching for water. A deep, rich blue rested under my fingertip, so dark it was almost black and seemed to swallow light. I pulled it up, threaded the needle, and was back to work. I stitched in a star pattern from a central point above the mist, varying the length as I worked outward to fill in all the blank space with the night sky. Lastly, a brilliant fine silver filament called to me. I added delicate stars dotted around in varying intensity and size. They sparkled and glowed against the lightless field.

I leaned back to look at my work. Though the whole piece was no bigger than the palm of my hand, I had managed to create something. It wasn't perfect, there were some minute gaps in the night sky, and some of the mist clouds could have been better shaped. Yet overall, I liked it. More than that, I got a feeling when I looked at it. Freedom, hope—for the future, and the past. The feeling of riding on Zephyrine through the mist, the hope I felt at seeing the stars while visiting Starcrest. Hope for the future, that maybe someday the mist could be cleared, that we could see the stars more easily. And longing for the past, spending time with Maris and Josie as we stargazed. It wasn't the best thread painting, but the *feeling* it gave me meant everything.

"I would say you have learned quickly! And learned to immediately break my lesson plan as well. No landscape, no horizon."

My stomach tightened. "Oh, wow I didn't even think ... I just sensed something and went with it. I'm sorry, Yantz."

He chuckled. "Listening to the thread is the first rule. I like that you have your own mind."

I saw Rannoch weaving through the crowd toward us. My heart leapt at the sight of him. Our eyes connected, I beamed as he approached. "I think Rannoch is here to collect me," I said to Yantz, finally tearing my eyes from Rannoch to look at him. "Thank you for teaching me, I hope I can come back, and maybe listen better next time. No promises though," I added with a big grin.

"I will be here whenever you want to learn more, from me or just by experimentation." Rannoch walked up just as Yantz finished his sentence. "Lily has done well! She did magna work, with none of what I suggested." His eyes twinkled at me with the inside joke.

"Sounds about right," Rannoch said as I coughed a laugh. "We will see you at Weaving, I trust? I set up your usual spot."

"Of course, my filio. I will see you there! Lily, I will frame your work for you."

Rannoch nodded to him, before turning to me. "Kerenza is excited to weave with you, but I have somewhere to take you first, and to tell you something."

CHAPTER 35

"I imagine you're hungry," he said as he leaned over to brush a kiss to my cheek.

"Starved," I said as I felt my stomach rumble.

"So dramatic," he murmured with his lips curved. I walked with him through the busy bazaar, stalls with various wares or food offerings bordered each side. We ate sticks speared with caramelized meat, wrapped miniature tortams filled with either puréed purple potato or stiff, rich cheese. We stopped at nearly every stall, greeting the attendants and trying their offerings of food, drink, or perusing the items on display. By the time we reached the end, I was stuffed, and Rannoch was laden with bags of gifts, mostly items to decorate our new home. Rannoch had told me as we walked that we were to move into it, right after Praetexia, along with another bit of information I was still pestering him about.

"So this ... parade, everyone walks behind us and chants, as we dance towards where we'll live?" I asked, as I finished a cold drink seasoned with spicy ground red pepper and squeezed citrus.

"Yes, it's tradition. The pompa is meant to guide us with their blessing, to show they are behind us in support of a fruitful life. It's exciting for anyone not usually meant to enter the inner keep. All Ignisfae are allowed to freely come for the pompa, as well as for the following three rotations, to place gifts at our doorstep.

My mouth dropped as I looked at him. Felix was right, I essentially was married. Or this was somehow a wedding event. I adjusted the gold panel that crossed my chest, and the jeweled belt that secured it in place to accommodate my over-full stomach. "Well," I said, using my clothing as a means to busy myself, "I didn't quite expect a ceremony for us, I thought this was about weaving."

"It usually is, but in this case the events coincide, since we were recently mated," he said in a soft tone. I looked at him carefully, noting the worry in his eyes at my hesitation. *I will do whatever you want, if you want no pompa, I will make it known.*

I inhaled a long, slow breath. "I don't want to cancel it. I just needed a moment to process the idea. Plus, with all these things for me to learn, each event is a chance for me to do right by your people, or for me to fuck up royally in front of all of them."

"Our people," he corrected. "Your skin may not match theirs, your hair may be different. But you belong here, you are welcomed and embraced. I know you feel pressure from this, but please know they look at you with kind eyes, and do not judge harshly for one wrong dance step, one missed gesture."

"That's not true for one in particular," I commented.

Rannoch sighed. "My faeder has earned my sister's name for him, he is close to no one. No friends, no one who actually loves him. Even Eiulans doesn't really seem to enjoy his company. My faeder pushes all away to keep himself separate by being a constant culus. So it is not you, it's him."

"My dad is gone, and your's hates me. I hope you can see how that would be hard for me. Here's a chance for me to have a father ... faeder figure. But no, he's too much of a dick for that."

"My faeder figure is Yantz, has been for a hundred and fifty cycles. And he accepts you, has already started teaching you."

My breath caught, as I thought back on his face, and his visible age. I remembered what Don'Li had told me about aging. *Visible aging only happens right before we Fade.*

Rannoch spoke up, "Yantz is somehow different there, with Fading. I sense your concern. But don't worry. He's looked old for ... I can't even remember now. At least a hundred cycles. He says as long as there's work for him to do, he will not Fade. He's the oldest known living Fae, and seems to have no intention of disappearing anytime soon. I think as long as life interests him and excites him, he will stay."

I released a relieved breath, then halted. "But what does the Fading really mean? Like, you actually just disappear?"

"Yes, exactly."

"What about Fae that are killed in battle? I never saw any of them disappear."

"That is different ... maybe. We don't really know. We believe when Fading happens, you go to the Ether, and exist without a form. But death in battle, it is not known. Maybe it's just blackness, or you cease to exist."

I stared at him, remembering when he had said he'd fight Opius to the death for me. Would accept that risk. He would have risked ceasing to exist completely for me. For our love.

"This is all very serious conversation, when we should be getting ready to celebrate," I said. "Let's get this party started. We should probably find Kerenza, right?"

"Yes, but first," Rannoch slipped his arm around my low back, drawing me in close, then pulled me even further from the eyes of the bazaar. We slid into a wide nook in the stone wall, away from the din of working Ignisfae. He caught my lips with his, then moved along my jaw, down my neck. His mouth roved over my exposed bite mark, now healed, the slight scar displayed like a trophy. He kissed it gently, reverently, before moving back up to my lips. When I opened my mouth to him and swept my tongue against his, I felt Rannoch's whole body ratchet up in fervor. The kiss—and my skin—heated. He gripped me tighter, his other hand now cupping my breast. He pulled away to look me in the eyes, then smiled and dropped his questionably placed hand, given that we were still technically in public—albeit hidden.

"I wanted you alone, if only for a moment," he said, then kissed my cheek. Come on, Kerenza has a surprise for you."

"Seriously, I don't need any more surprises."

"I think you'll like this one."

CHAPTER 36

He guided me away from the bazaar in the outermost ring of the city, to a wide, cobblestone square much closer to the inner keep. With festivities just beginning, this section seemed to be the main gathering spot for events in TerraIgni. Glinting swaths of fabric draped over the entire area, reflecting the light of torches far below. Strung gold beads that hung in vertically shined throughout, but what truly stopped me in my tracks was the looms.

Rows of them towered in lines, with ropes thread through the levers, each one connected to the last, with all ropes ending at a stage, bundled and held in place by giant bronze hooks. Mounds of brilliant thread sat next to each loom. Ignisfae rushed around, setting the last of the materials in place.

Kerenza spotted me as we walked through the center, then came forward with Emblyn to greet us. "It is almost time! We have our looms set up at the center front, soon the contest will begin!"

"Contest? This is the first I've heard about that."

She grinned. "First the males are up on stage, they all pull the ropes to flip the levers. Females do two hundred passes with the shuttle, while males pull the switch after each pass, then we alternate. Males come down to the looms and do their two hundred shuttle passes, while the females pull the ropes to flip the looms. By the end we have ten thousand rows complete, then they are judged. Really, it is not about who wins," she said as she smirked, then leaned closer to me and whispered, "though the females always have the better weaving!"

Rannoch belted out a laugh. "Oh sure! It's not because the males flip the levers well or anything. However Kerenza is right about *one* thing," he said as she narrowed her eyes at him, "it's not about who wins. It's really to share the work so that we can all get the weaving done, then celebrate!"

Kerenza nodded. "Yes, celebrate! I am so excited to dance with you, Lily! Now come, be my partner. We are supposed to work in pairs, I would be honored to weave with you." She looped her arm through mine, tugging me toward the event.

"One day I will be enough cycles old to run the shuttle, but my maeder says it is not time yet," Emblyn said, her voice slightly clipped with sadness. "But can I help at least?"

"Oh I will definitely need your help, Emblyn," I said. "I don't really know what I'm doing, so I'll need you to keep an eye on me and tell me if I'm about to make a mistake."

"Emblyn is a magna thread assistant," Kerenza added, "it is almost unfair we have her help." She leaned over and whispered to her daughter, "Help your Avuncul Rannoch, too. He will definitely need it."

"Kerenza!" Rannoch bellowed a laugh, then scooped Emblyn up and settled her on his shoulders. "She's right though, I will need it," he said quietly to Emblyn. Emblyn stifled a giggle with her hand, as we all set off toward the stage.

Rannoch deposited Emblyn next to the loom closest to the front, then headed up to the stage where others had already started gathering. Kerenza motioned for me to take the right side of the weaving apparatus, which was over twice my height. I looked back at Rannoch, who was starting to untie the ropes from the hooks. Felix and Dhiren climbed the stairs to the stage, Dhiren motioned around the square, apparently explaining how the weaving would work as they approached Rannoch. Felix beamed at Dhiren, his smile was so big his eyes crinkled.

Everyone settled in their place, but one was noticeably absent. King Ashwan was nowhere to be seen. I looked all around, then saw Don'Li toward the end of the square. I grinned and waved at him, he smiled back but stayed tucked far at the rear to observe. A struck gong took my attention back to the stage, where the king now stood. His presence swallowed the energy, everyone quieted as he waited, stock-still.

"Every cycle, we weave together as we weave our lives, the fabric binds us as Ignisfae," his voice boomed across the square, the acoustics amplifying it as it scattered over the cobblestone ground. He raised his hand, then called a wide plume of flame from one of the torches that marked the corners of the stage. He held the fire aloft with his outstretched palm, maintaining the flare in a steady stream that tapered off well above his head. "Let Praetexia commence, that we may burn brightly for yet another cycle!" He charged the flame in a mighty blast, sending it high into the air. The heat from it radiated out, kissing my cheeks in a flash before it dissipated into the sky. The crowded square erupted in a cheer, shouts of "burn brightly" were returned by all in attendance. I turned to find Kerenza holding the shuttle up, tied with the first thread already.

"Shall we?" she asked. I looked around, realizing that Ignisfae were watching, apparently for us to make the first pass. I gulped. *Great. Now it'll be painfully obvious I don't know what I'm doing.* "Do not worry," she murmured while smiling, keeping her voice low and face pleasant so no one caught on, "it is not hard, we just pass the shuttle back and forth, adding on a new thread when it becomes too short. Lift your arm to tell Rannoch when he can flip the mechanism, it will tighten the weave down. Once we do a pass everyone else will start."

I stood on the end of the loom closest to Rannoch, Kerenza made a show of readying the first run of the shuttle. She wound up, then threw it through the crossed vertical threads to me. I caught it, then raised my hand. Rannoch yanked the pulley, which switched the frame position, tamping down the thread. I tossed it back through to Kerenza, as the clack of the other looms clattered to life.

It became a dance in a way, throwing the weighty disk back and forth, synchronizing with Rannoch to continually add layers. Emblyn kept track as we worked, every twenty rows handing Kerenza a long stick to push the threads down from the top, aligning them before moving on to the next set. Before I knew it, we had completed our two hundred passes. Kerenza and I headed up to the stage, then switched with Rannoch. Dhiren had paired up with Felix to weave, so instead another familiar face partnered with Rannoch, Rovan settled himself on the far side of the loom. Once again we found our pace, switching the levers in a rhythmic cadence.

Sweat beaded on my brow as we completed our last set. One by one, all looms ceased movement. Once they stopped, I realized how noisy they had been, their constant racket now an obvious absence in the broad space. No more shifting parts to echo off the building walls that bordered the area.

Again appearing out of nowhere, the king—who hadn't deigned to actually participate—appeared on the stage. I wiped my forehead as I glanced at Kerenza, who looked equally annoyed by him.

"Congratulations all to a successful Praetexia! With the weaving complete, I announce the start of the feast!"

Ignisfae that hemmed the edge of the square rushed forward, then began dragging the looms out of the way, while tables were brought in. Trays of food and large decanters of wine were delivered within moments, as music started from somewhere unseen. The drum beat thudded with an infectious rhythm, the party started nearly the instant the king had declared it. A muscled arm swept around my side, spinning me in a circle before I had time to face my partner. But I already knew it was him, aside from the fact no one would dare dance with their prince's mate without consent, I sensed Rannoch's proximity before he was within three paces of me. My heart twanged at his closeness as we swung to the beat.

My earlier worries about making a mistake disappeared, everyone had launched into motion and cast aside inhibitions, moving with free-form ease.

The party went on for hours, round after round of dancing,

pausing to sip, to smoke, to eat. We danced in pairs, we danced in groups. By the time we were ready to stumble back to our room my body glistened with sweat. We struck out together, Don'Li laughing as Kerenza joked with him, Dhiren propping up both Felix and Dhirdre, though he also struggled to walk straight.

Ignisfae collected behind us, a wide stream of a cheering crowd. I had almost forgotten about the procession, and suddenly wished I wasn't swaying to keep myself steady. *Oh fuck, I'm pretty drunk!*

Rannoch's voice swept through my mind, laughing with each echoed word. *Me, too. Just keep walking.*

We pranced and staggered down the path, when I tripped on a cobblestone ledge that caught my toe. I laughed, collected myself, then proceeded forward, hoping all the Ignisfae didn't think I was ungraceful. After five paces, I did it again. I felt Rannoch's hand close around my arm to catch me, at the same time another caught me from the other side. They pulled me up before I fell flat on my face, as my eyes settled on who stood directly in my path.

King Ashwan's hardened gaze only further deepened, as he stared at me, then shifted his cold glare over my shoulder. "Who brought *him* here? He should have never set foot on TerraIgni soil!"

I looked behind me, to find Don'Li still holding my left arm, who didn't so much as blink as he stared back at the king. "I wished to come here, to show my desire to right the wrongs of the past. My actions have caused you and the Ignisfae pain, I wanted to make up for prior transgressions."

That last word struck a chord in my memory, though I couldn't place why I had heard it, or what it might have to do with TerraIgni. I held my breath as the two Fae continued their unblinking connection. My body tightened as I sensed King Ashwan's rage, his *hatred.* All of his anger, boiling to the surface, and directed at Don'Li.

In an instant, the king lunged forward, his rock-hard fist cracked Don'Li in the jaw so forcefully I swear I felt it through his hand, still gripping my arm. Don'Li's palm opened, releasing me as he staggered backward. King Ashwan threw another punch, which sailed wide, then struck through at a puff of mist where Don'Li had been a moment before.

"You only get one, King Ashwan. The first I gave you, you—and I—deserved it, but the second I will not abide," Don'Li said from a few feet away.

"I will have your blood before the end!" King Ashwan bellowed. "It is because of *you* that my queen is dead!"

The crowd gasped, and I dropped my jaw, swiveling my head to Rannoch. He looked equally stunned, and confused. "The Umorfae killed her, how is it his fault?" Rannoch asked. "He is Caelifae, they are our allies. Did she not go willingly to attempt trade with the Umorfae?"

Dread crept in, like a schadenfreude that delighted in saying, *I told you so.* One that nodded and pursed her lips, *this is why he helped you.* The inner voice that was sometimes harsh, brutal, and pretended to be your friend. The one that comforted, while at the same time scolding. I shook my head, realizing it was *me* that had facilitated him coming to TerraIgni. Somehow, he was connected to my mate's maeder's death, and I had invited him in.

Silence settled, no one spoke as the king heaved, his fists balled at his sides and ready to take another swing at any moment.

Don'Li opened his mouth, but didn't speak for some time. Finally he said, "I met her on an earlier trade expedition before the ill-fated one with the Umorfae, and she had my heart, immediately. I was so taken by her, yet her sadness I could not stand. She had no love, no care given to her from her mate. She was an object, a possession. A thing to be owned rather than a Fae to be loved. I gave her that love. But she was still tied to *him*. And she loved you both so much," he said, motioning to Kerenza and Rannoch. "Queen Deniza felt so much guilt over what had transpired, she attempted to make up for her-"

"Mistake," the king cut in with a dark undertone.

"The mistake was *yours*," Don'Li retorted. "You were mated to the most beautiful, wonderful Fae I have ever met, yet how did you treat her? Like you treat all others, I would bet."

"How dare you even suggest I did not love her! Of course I loved her!" the king exploded.

Don'Li lifted his chin, shaking his wispy white hair off his shoulder with a flick. "And yet, you accepted her preposterous idea to approach the Umorfae, because of your greed. She wanted to make up for her infidelity, and it got her killed. I have done wrong, but so have *you*. You starved her for love, and she found it elsewhere. Then you punished her for it."

The king shook with fury, then his glance shifted to the throng of Ignisfae watching. Watching, and hearing. Listening to the whole messy, personal history being laid out between the two of them. King Ashwan looked at Rannoch. "I came to your pompa to offer my gift, Prince Rannoch, but I must excuse myself. Dhiren, Dhirdre, escort this unwelcome guest away at your earliest convenience.``

He swept away without another word. My heart sank at what had just transpired. The knowledge that I had unknowingly been aided by someone who was inherently tied to what had happened to Rannoch's mother. I had opened this door. I needed Don'Li's help, he was critical in my survival, yet I now saw it came with a cost. A cost not agreed upon, one that Don'Li had slipped in without my knowing. He wanted to help me, so that he could feel better about what happened before. It all made sense now. I turned to look at Don'Li. Was he my friend? I had thought he was. Had he given something, to get something? He had been careful with his words so that I did not actually know the truth of his past. No, *he was* my friend, I was sure of it. I opened my mouth to say something, but he was gone already. I hadn't even felt the rush of wind as he had disappeared.

"Come, let's go to our new home," Rannoch said, trying to smile. But the weight was tangible, palpable. An old wound brought to the forefront on a momentous day. I imagined everything he thought he knew about his mother's loss was now in question.

We continued the parade to our doorstep, the crowd quieted as we arrived. He propped open the heavy fabric door, laden with beads as he swept me up into his arms, then crossed the threshold into our home.

CHAPTER 37

He fucked me with fury, he made love to me with care. Rannoch was relentless with his attention, as we experimented on every surface of the space we would now call home together. Every joining was an obvious attempt, he needed to prove he was not his father; he would show love, he would show consideration. I made good on the promise I had thought to myself earlier, to show my gratitude for all he had done, and this time, he let me go longer—much longer. With his fingers grasping my hair he had unleashed, shoving himself into my mouth. My jaw started to ache from his sheer size. But I didn't let up until he found his completion.

We finally collapsed in a heap in our ample, plush bed, the exquisite sheets woven with the thinnest, softest thread caressed my bare skin. I nodded off with my cheek resting on his broad chest, his arm wrapped around me, as if I couldn't get close enough for him.

But it was not peaceful sleep.

Images rolled through my dreams. What I pictured Rannoch's mother might have looked like, bowing at the feet of the Umorfae empress, before losing her life to their cruelty. Syrenni, so many

Syrenni, toiling under the Umorfae iron grip. A dominion gilded in a polished exterior. Beautiful faces, masking true demons beneath. "Water for life, water for life," their chant droned in my head.

It was their greatest lie.

It was their greatest threat.

They did not tout life, their affirmation was just like their masks, lovely words hiding the promise of subjugation and torture. Another endless march of Syrenni filled my mind, once depleted of usefulness to their masters, they trudged over a dark cliff. Death, death, death. That's all the Umorfae gave. No one had challenged them. They took the Petrafae castle, stole a birthright from them and squatted their pretty little Umorfae asses in it, assuming control of what wasn't theirs. None of it was theirs. The Syrenni weren't theirs.

I woke up, sweaty and panting, with tears rolling down my cheeks.

"My love, are you okay?" Rannoch placed his warm palm along my jaw, turning my face to look at him.

"No, I'm not. I can't be okay with everything that has happened. Part of me wants to hide in here with you. Pretend everything is all right and make love until the end of time. But I can't. I won't. I need to do something. I've made mistakes, they're haunting me. And there are people suffering."

He shuttered his eyes for a moment, and I sensed it. The fear. The dread. The knowing that I *had* to go, to act. The knowing of the inherent risk. The fear of loss.

I ran my hand along his check, cupping it and encouraged him to look at me. "I understand your fear. I'm not going to say I'm not scared. I am. But think of this. Naiya lost her life trying to save her people, and she now has a child growing up under the nose of the Umorfae. Her child will endure what she did, perhaps worse, because Neila said she is different. If Naiya had not been brave enough to do what she did, we would not be here. *I* would not be here. Emblyn and the other children would not be here. We both owe it to her." He gulped, then nodded. "They have much to pay for, my love, Don'Li reminded me of that," I said, my voice shaking. "He may have done wrong in some ways, but we can do right. We can make change."

"What do you intend to do?"

"To go to Lacausia Palace, and force their hand."

His eyes widened. "How?"

"With as many Petrafae as we can convince to come with us."

CHAPTER 38

We stood in a circle around a large round table, the thick wood top covered with a detailed map of the whole world of Alternis carefully wood-burned into its surface. Mountainous regions were shaded with fine, slanting lines, the expanse of the Praegra Forest indicated with large masses of voluminous shapes. I spread my fingertips over the work, the surface smoothed by a generous layer of resin to seal it in and polish it. I had never seen a map of this world, never had a bird's eye view of how it actually laid out. My eyes traveled to the west, to the Southwest Tear, where I had come through and started this whole crazy journey. The point where my life had been completely upended, then righted as I found out who—and what—I was.

Dhiren, Felix, and Dhirdre murmured to each other, while I stood staring at the map. Kerenza stood by my side, her arm linked with mine. Rannoch spoke first. "We have determined to make a bold move, one that would do two things: free the Syrenni, and unseat the Umorfae. This is Lily's idea, and I fully support it. We need to go over a plan of action."

"How many Ignisfae should we bring?" Dhiren asked.

"None," I answered. "None beyond those in this room. This plan won't be about Ignisfae numbers, it will be about Petrafae. I don't want a battle, I want a coup. The goal here is to get the Syrenni out. A large battle will equal a lot of casualties, on both sides. Plus to bring an army of Ignisfae, we'd have to involve King Ashwan, right? He'd have to sign off on the idea of an army marching to Lacausia Palace, wouldn't he?"

"Definitely," Rannoch answered.

"Then I say we treat this like you treated the endeavor with Naiya. Ask for forgiveness rather than ask for permission," I said.

"Lily, this sounds risky," Felix cut in. "Not only would this be dangerous, couldn't this be bad for your new ... status here? And with the king?"

"Yes, you're right, Felix. It is risky. But you weren't a part of a lot of what happened here, you haven't seen all of what I've seen. I *believe* we can make a difference for a whole race of people. I think we can do it. Yes, King Ashwan already doesn't like me, and this may mean real consequences for me here in TerraIgni. But I'll take the punishment, if I can help the Syrenni. I owe them that much." He stared at me for some time, his gold hazel eyes locked to mine. "You can stay here, you know. That would be totally fine."

"And let my sister go out there without me to protect her? And Dhiren? No, I don't think so," he shot back. Dhiren rubbed Felix's tense shoulder, then he leaned into Dhiren for comfort.

"I know I'm asking a lot," I added, "and this is more of an invitation to come, Rannoch and I are going, you can choose to come or not."

"Obviously I am coming," Kerenza chimed in. "Who else is better qualified to kick those culus Umorfae in their stupid faces?"

"My thoughts exactly," I said with a grin. "Dhirdre, Dhiren, did you already take Don'Li away?"

"No," Dhirdre said, inspecting her fingernails. "It was not convenient yet."

I scrunched my face at her. "Convenient?"

"Did you not hear the king's orders? He said "at your earliest convenience," I take his orders seriously. And literally," Dhirdre said, as she brushed her silken hair from her shoulder with an exaggerated swish. I almost busted out laughing, and would have, if the situation were not so serious. "Rannoch, I thought you might want to speak with him, I did not want to take away your chance to find out more, if you wanted."

He nodded. "Thank you, Dhirdre, and good thinking. I'd say he owes yet another favor, after lying by omission to Lily. And maybe he can give me more insight into my maeder."

"I agree," I said, "and he might be willing to help because of that. Especially considering this involves the Umorfae."

"Lily," Rannoch said, "you need to know that even though you intend this to be a coup, and not a war, casualties are still highly probable."

I gulped and blinked back tears. I knew that I couldn't promise success or safety. But I also couldn't be okay with doing nothing. "I understand." There had to be a way I could minimize losses on our side. I couldn't bear to lose any one of them.

Rannoch moved shiny black figurines of equus onto an arid region of the map. "We should fly straight to the Ignisfae settlement, we left a full cache when we were there last. We shouldn't have to bring anything with us beyond the food we would need for the flight there." He moved a set of carved red stone soldiers down from the northeast. "We already asked the Petrafae to meet us at camp. From there, we'll all march southwest to Lacausia Palace."

I looked out the window, the light barely beginning to wane. "How long will it take us to reach the camp?"

"Twelve rotations at least." Rannoch answered. "Hopefully the Petrafae have already left, so that they can plan to meet us there as soon as possible. It was good your Faerie friend came so quickly and agreed to take the message."

"You already called the Faerie, Lily?" Kerenza rubbed her chin with her fingers. "Twelve rotations will mean we will arrive there in the dead of night. That is good at least for stealth. We will be less likely to be seen."

"We should return to our quarters, take a rest, then gather what we'll need. Let's plan to meet at the armory in one-eighth rotation," Rannoch commanded.

Everyone nodded in agreement, except Felix. "Wait," he said, staring at the map, "I don't understand, why is it about the Petrafae? What's their part supposed to be if this is not a battle?"

I turned to face him. "We need their earth ability. We're going to ask them to surround the castle, and tear it down if the Umorfae don't give us what we want. Piece by piece until they relent."

CHAPTER 39

Back in our room I stripped down, about to slip into nightclothes to take a nap. Rannoch caught my hand as I reached for the folded set. I stopped, staring at him for a long moment. He searched my face, then lifted my chin with his hand.

"You are so brave, so selfless. I'm terrified to lose you, Lily. But I know you need to do this. And I'm proud of you for it."

"I think I would hate myself if I didn't." I had to admit there was a lot that could go wrong. We didn't even talk about the fact that Dashelle was still out there. What if she somehow popped into the picture? That was a factor we didn't need. But I reigned that thought in, tamped it down so that Rannoch wouldn't catch on. I didn't want him to have more to worry about. "I've learned a lot from you, Rannoch, and my brother, how to defend myself, how to fight. And the Vale gave me these gifts, why have them if I don't use them to do good? Otherwise ..." I trailed off, thinking about Dashelle. *Otherwise I'm no better than her.*

The feeling of absolute power I had felt when I came back through the Vale haunted me. I had a moment of realization of how much simmered below my skin, how much I could truly do.

For only that fleeting moment, I was drunk with it. And I could almost relate to Dashelle. That had scared me, how could I relate to a scheming murderer? I *had* to do good, to push off the potential desire to do the exact opposite.

He circled his arm behind my bare back, his pupils ignited as he looked at me. I felt my eyes heat in return, the sensation traveled down my body in a flushed wave. I opened my mouth to his, and kissed him. My response to him was immediate, the moment I tasted him, I needed him. On the verge of our mission—sacrifice perhaps—I needed him to imprint himself on me. How many more chances would I get? I hooked one leg around him as he gripped me tighter.

The movement untethered him. He wrapped his hand around my knee that I had lifted to his side, and dropped us to the bed. He was inside me in an instant, every decadent inch. I arched my back as he drove into me. My warrior.

As he moved in an ardent rhythm I realized, I would be the warrior. I would fight for those I loved. I would not let those I cared so much for sacrifice themselves for this cause. They could help me, but I would protect them.

Rannoch's shoulders tightened as his speed increased. My precipice loomed, like a thinly veiled promise of cascade, just barely on the edge of release.

It unfurled before I knew it was happening, a force I had lost control over. I was about to tell Rannoch to wait, to slow him, that I might keep him here with me longer. The sooner it was over, the sooner we would leave to peril. But my body had no care for that, it unleashed in a tide of pleasure. He found his release moments later, as I clutched him, encouraging it. I held him as he shuddered, and

I knew. There was no way I could let him risk his life in the attempt to save the Syrenni. There had to be a way to keep him safe.

I awoke to a rasping sound that shuffled under the bed. Rannoch was just beginning to wake as I leaned far over to see what had caused the sound. A lump under the bed near Rannoch's side was hidden in shadow, but then jumped and turned to me in an odd, sudden movement. I shrieked and sat up in bed, pulling the covers around me.

"What? What is it?" Rannoch asked, now fully alert.

"There's something under the bed! I heard it moving around before it went under there!"

"Oh, maybe that's just Octobo. I'll check." He swung his head over to look under. "There you are little filio! I was wondering when I'd see you."

A moment later, he came out and scuttled around the floor.

"What the fuck, Rannoch! I thought you told me there were no giant spiders here!" I clutched the sheets tighter around me.

He blinked, looking back and forth between the arachnid and me. "Oh ... *that's* a spider? Here he's called an aranea.

"No, that's one hundred percent a giant fucking spider. Why am I not surprised? And not only that, he's your pet?" I buried my face in my palms. *Nooooo.* I sighed and dropped my hands, realizing my mistake. I had said "insect" when I had asked him in the Hinterdunes, not arachnid. "Do they get any bigger? Like, is this the biggest they get in this realm? I want to be very clear. I asked about giant spiders before because in fiction books I've read it's always these disgustingly huge giant spiders, bigger than you." Octobo jumped around, his movements quirky and rapid. He was more of a jumping spider with a compact, crab-like body, rather than a creepy crawly spider with a large butt.

"This is pretty much it. He's about full grown. I don't think I've seen anything much bigger. Octobo is very loyal, and if you give him a chance, he will probably come to be your friend."

I snorted a laugh. "Friends with a spider? You clearly have a lot more to learn about me."

Octobo shifted again, his compound eyes seemed to take on more of a gleam as he faced me, widening like a cat begging for food or attention. My breath caught as I realized it reminded me of the arthropods from the ill-fated lake mountain. They looked like nightmares, but once I broke through, I saw their beauty. Octobo stamped his fuzzy paws, then pointed to his head with one leg.

"What's he doing?" I asked.

"He wants water. He likes to wear a large drop on his head and take some from it when he needs to." Rannoch reached over to a glass by the bedside, then carefully poured a small amount onto Octobo's head. Octobo pranced around with the bubble, displaying the sphere like it was a fancy hat.

"Oh my God, I think I've seen everything now." Octobo stopped, turned to me and stuck one of his paws in the drop, then put his foot in his mouth, drinking the small amount siphoned off. "Okay, he is pretty cute. Wait, where does he sleep? Am I going to walk into his web or something?" I shuddered, remembering when I wandered right through a massive spider web as a kid, the overgrown orb weaver spider ended up on my face. I had thrashed around like a maniac trying to get the nasty thing off.

"Web? No, he has a little hole with a trap door."

"Not sure that sounds any better. Blanket statement: no scaring me with his trap door, and he never gets in the bed, ever." I shook my head. *Pet spider. Of course.* "Maybe we should get ready to leave, it's probably time to meet up with the others. Octobo can stay ... here," I said with resignation.

Octobo stamped his front two feet in protest.

My jaw dropped. "Does he understand me?"

"Yes, he does. I'm not sure if he understands words, but he understands thoughts."

I cringed. *So all those negative thoughts I just had about spiders ... Great. Not only do I have to be nice, I have to think nice as well.* I looked at Octobo and sighed. *I will try, Rannoch loves you, I'll try for him.*

Octobo scampered away with his water drop balanced on his head, out to the balcony that offered a wide view of the canyon walls. A light click sound followed.

"His hole is outside?"

"Yes, he's very respectful, I promise."

I laughed. "A respectful spider ... er, aranea. Who would have ever thought." I turned to the large cabinet that took up one wall, then started going through it to find what clothes were there. I found a whole stack of fresh linteums in a variety of colors, as well as numerous beautiful dresses with sash tops. "Were these just brought in for me?"

Rannoch nodded. "I asked Tanzara to make sure you had everything you needed here. Clothing, bathing items, whatever females need."

I pursed my lips and stifled a laugh at the way he said the

last part with the slightest discomfort. I tossed a linteum over my shoulder as I walked to the bathroom. "Very thoughtful of you."

I stared at the carefully designed bathing chamber, the same brick red rock the fortress had been carved into was integrated in the bathroom as well, smooth-polished and pristine. Veins of sparkling cream ore laced the tub. Sheer drapes of the palest gray-blue hung from the ceiling. I glanced at myself in the mirror, hair a mess from sleeping and makeup under my eyes. I held off the interior voice that was about to say this might be the first and last time I see this beautiful bathroom.

CHAPTER 40

We met at the armory, Kerenza already laden with her usual selections: sais, a spear, and a short sword. Dhiren—armed with a sword, a bow, and a quiver of arrows—was helping Felix pick out a weapon while Dhirdre was adjusting the straps of a double baldric for two gleaming swords. Rannoch handed me my selwaer, he had kept it safe for me while I had returned to Black Oak Grove. The metal resonated against my skin as soon as I wrapped my hand around the hilt. A chord struck, like the twang of a harmonic tuning fork as the sound traveled through me, reconnecting me to the well-crafted blade. I smiled at the sensation, greeting the selwaer like it was sentient. The precision details made by Rannoch himself glinted in the light as I turned it to catch the highlight.

I turned to find Felix testing out a weighted staff. Though it had no pointed blade for impaling, the heavy, studded ends looked lethal as he swung it around. He anchored it to the ground, then blasted air funnels to whip himself around faster. I flashed him a look that showed my approval as he finished the move. Dhiren beamed at him as he spun back into place in front of him.

Dhirdre cleared her throat. "Rannoch, I brought Don'Li, in

case you'd like to speak to him. He's two doors down, in the private room."

His face hardened. "I will speak to him alone." I bit my lip as I looked at Rannoch, the things Don'Li probably had to divulge would not be easy for my mate. Yet, it was a chance to hear at least more than he previously knew. I nodded at him as he shifted his glance to me, before he turned to head out.

I found the baldric that fitted my blade while I waited, then tossed it over my head and tightened it down, spending more time than necessary to adjust the straps. Fidgeting with them helped stave off the worry about what Rannoch might be feeling, or the conflict the two of them might be having. I had to admit, even though I was a little mad at Don'Li, I cared for him. Cared what happened to him. And also hoped he would be willing to help us to right the wrong, as much as he could. Ultimately he was a central reason behind what had happened to Queen Deniza, which resulted in Rannoch losing his mother, though it wasn't Don'Li's fault. Not by any stretch. It was King Ashwan's. I tried to shake off the thought of her horrible demise as Kerenza approached.

She must have read the discomfort on my face as she spoke, "You should not feel guilt, you did not know. *We* did not know. We only knew Don'Li was a notorious lothario. And we knew that our maeder was attempting to make up for a misstep when she suggested the trade agreement with the Umorfae. We were never told what that misstep was. It was "private and not our concern" our faeder had said. I understand why now. Though he only pushed us further away, as he has always done. But, now I see, I think he was trying to retain his dignity by keeping it a secret. Then he slandered Don'Li so that even if all Fae knew of his tendency to convince females to his bed, they did not know the true reason behind it. Our faeder can be … calculating in that way."

"How do you know he slandered him?"

"I spoke to Don'Li first, I had my own questions. He told me my faeder had even sent Eiulans to the Caelifae and Petrafae. Being the Ignisfae king's highest ranking emissary, he had the ear of many amongst the Fae. He spread rumors about Don'Li, some based on truth, but others outright lies to discredit him."

"Eiulans … I knew I didn't like that prick. He was an ass when Rannoch and I were summoned to see King Ashwan."

Kerenza crossed her arms and nodded with the corner of her lip twitched up. "Magna Culus and his right hand, Lesser Culus. Those two are perfectly matched for each other."

I huffed a laugh at last. "I will never be able to look at him again and not think of him as Lesser Culus."

The fabric doorway swished aside, then Rannoch marched in, followed by a dejected-looking Don'Li. Rannoch's eyes were sharp, hard as he passed his glance over all who surrounded the room. His icy exterior had returned, which I hadn't felt since … I couldn't even remember when. He felt distant as my eyes welled, he had closed himself off because of what happened with Don'Li. Whatever had been said between the two of them had hurt enough to make him shield himself once again. I reined in the tears on the verge of spilling, as much as it was my fault that Don'Li had been brought to TerraIgni, I couldn't make the situation worse by crying.

"We will prepare to leave now. Don'Li will join us on the quest," Rannoch ordered, his voice rough.

Don'Li stepped up and crossed a fist to his chest. "I will do whatever I can to make amends." He turned to me, then lowered to one knee and bowed his head. "I did not deserve your friendship, I was not honest with you and I am sorry. I know I have done wrong, my deepest apologies."

He looked up at me, searching my face for forgiveness, waiting for an answer. A single nod of my head was all I gave him—all I could give him. If I tried to speak, I feared it would come out too shaky, too emotional. But my face did soften at him. He still deserved my friendship.

"Select a weapon, Don'Li, then we are departing," Rannoch commanded. I turned to look at Rannoch, but he was already turning away. No words or thoughts came through our link, not the slightest tremor that there was even a connection there. The distance felt like the expanse of an ocean, beyond holding me away at an arm's length, this was a veritable world away. My heart ached at the lack of closeness which I had grown accustomed to. Dread crept in and settled like a weighted cloak. I wasn't the only one blaming me, my blood iced as I realized that Rannoch blamed me, too.

I knew at that moment, I had to make it right. I had to protect them all, and make up for my mistake.

CHAPTER 41

The rotations passed in mind-numbing monotony as we flew through the mist. After a short stop at the rest point, we were off again. The first leg of the journey seemed to be just what Rannoch needed. By the time we landed to allow the equus to sleep, he seemed to have shaken off the ill feelings from the conversation with Don'Li.

After twelve grueling rotations, we finally arrived at the Ignis-fae camp. I could feel Zephyrine's exhaustion, and my own as I stretched my aching ass after I dismounted. I channeled a healing thread into the base of each of her wings, where I sensed the majority of her soreness. She dropped her head in relief as I pulsed the pain away. I rubbed her neck after I released the tension on the magic. It snapped back up my arm, coiling all the way back into my body. It was a strange sensation when I let go of it, both when I unfurled it, then called it back. It was only then that I could feel it, once it had retreated, it went to sleep, hidden and dormant as

I returned to myself. I didn't quite leave my body as I healed, but awareness was blocked out. Sight changed, I could see inside of bodies, but nothing outside of them, nothing of the environment I was in, nothing of the people that surrounded me.

She shook her head, then trotted over to Steren. The equus all walked over to the area where the corral sat empty, then started settling in as I joined the others.

"Let's get tents set up," Rannoch announced. "We'll set a circle of four to start, then add more when the Petrafae are near. For now, we should focus on only what we need."

"We should work in two groups, to speed the set up," Kerenza suggested. Rannoch nodded his agreement as she slung her arm around my shoulders. "Come on, my filia, I am on your team for sure." I smiled at her, as we headed over to where the cache must have been. Don'Li hung back with Felix, Dhiren, and Dhirdre, giving Rannoch and Kerenza ample space and a clear, unspoken message: he would not approach them unless asked.

Rannoch and I crawled down into the now-open chamber buried in the sand. We unloaded the leather wrapped poles from the cache, passing them down the line to where Dhiren stacked them neatly. After we pulled four tents out, Rannoch hopped up, then reached down to help me up. His warm hand in mine, and his eyes intently looking at me set my heart on fire. It was the closest I had felt to him since before the armory confrontation.

My love. It was all I heard through the link, but it was enough. Enough to flood my whole being with relief. I blinked back tears, *my mate,* I returned. He nodded and smiled as he helped me out.

We made quick work of assembling the temporary housing. Kerenza and I worked in tandem to secure the covers, while Rannoch held the poles steady. After they were complete, we returned to the cache, collected food, water skins, and presumably wine skins as well, judging by Kerenza's glee as she lifted them.

After all shelters were outfitted with provisions and blankets, we gathered outside to the seating ring, which Kerenza had just finished assembling. I plopped down on one of the folding stools, and just about melted into it as the fire came to life in the pit. Kerenza lowered her hand from the Ignisphaera, I hadn't seen her twist open the glass bauble that held an ever-burning flame to light it. My eyes glazed over with exhaustion as my body warmed. Dried food was passed around, along with wine. But every time it came to me, I only took the smallest sip. Even though the Petrafae were not expected for at least two more rotations, I did not want to just fall asleep from vinirubrum. Everyone else, though, seemed to feel otherwise. Perhaps they thought it was their last chance to enjoy, before they needed to be mentally sharp, honed to match the blades they carried. It was the last respite, the last moment to be friends talking around a fire. Even Don'Li seemed to be accepted now, the hardness Rannoch had displayed toward him whisked away, the sense that we were all friends did seem to be silently agreed upon. I smiled slightly at them all, my friends, my family. The family that I would protect.

After everyone had their fill of food and drink, we split off to our respective tents. I nuzzled in close to Rannoch, listening to him breathe, watching his chest rise and fall as he stroked my arm. His hand fell away at last, and his breathing pattern lightened. I waited, holding onto the moment just a little longer. Staying close to his warmth so that I could soak it in. When I was sure he wouldn't wake, I slipped out of the bed.

I took one last look over at him, the faint candlelight rimming his features in soft orange. He was so beautiful as I gazed at him. Opening yourself to love means inviting vulnerability. I had finally been brave enough to allow it. But I couldn't lose another that I loved. I wasn't brave enough for that.

I tightened my fist as I gripped the tent flap, before I pushed it aside, and left.

CHAPTER 42

I marched straight to Zephryine, who stood napping with Steren. Before I woke her, I called my Faerie friend, Livi, who had told me their name the last time I called.

Livi zipped around me in an exuberant greeting, their feet trailing my cheeks as I laughed. But it was a halted laugh, there was much on my mind as I had asked them to come to me yet again.

"Hello my friend, thank you for coming. I was hoping you would take a message to the Petrafae. They should be nearing the point where they would have to change direction, to come here to the Ignisfae camp. Please tell them, do not come to camp, go directly to Lacausia Palace."

Livi cocked their head at me a moment, weighing my words. They nodded at last, then zipped away, leaving their sparkling trail of blue light in their wake. Asking the Petrafae to go straight to the palace would trim a full two rotations off of their trek. They would arrive much sooner without the deviation to camp.

I turned to Zephryine, still sleeping. I frowned at the fact that she still needed rest. I walked up, then placed my hand on her neck.

She awoke in an instant, then scanned the area in case there were threats. "It's okay, girl. I need your help. I know you are tired, but I hoped you would be able to do this. I need you to fly me somewhere."

The thought returned to me right away: agreement, confirmation from her. She would do whatever I asked.

I smiled at her as she bowed, lowering herself so that I could mount up easier. I swung my leg over her back, then gripped her mane. "Take me to the bridge of Lacausia Palace."

I hopped off of Zephyrine as we arrived at the eerily familiar path, which lead to the castle. "Go, now. Fly back and get into the mist as fast as you can." I smacked her rump, causing her to launch into the air faster. I didn't want any Umorfae archers taking her down if they caught sight of her. Zephyrine disappeared in a swirl of mist. I breathed a sigh as she was now out of sight, on her way back to camp with little chance something would happen to her. I gulped as I straightened my shoulders.

I hardened my gaze as I walked, approaching the sweeping stone bridge that marked the border of the castle proper. Just beyond it, guards would be waiting. It was then that I felt the tug, the insistent call through the link.

No! What are you doing? Why did you leave? We had a plan!

I halted, holding back tears as I felt his desperation. But I couldn't risk him, risk any of them. They had taken me as far as I wanted them to. *I told you, I am selfish. This is the only way I can keep you safe. I love you.*

I cut myself off from anything he might try to shout at me

through the link, any way he might try to dissuade me. This was my path. I would save the Syrenni, and keep my family safe. That was all that mattered.

I lifted my head higher, as I stepped onto the bridge.

CHAPTER 43

I had hoped that I could demand an audience outside the castle, that I could persuade Silvanis to come out, and keep myself from entering the confines of the palace walls.

I knew it was a fool's hope. Guards surrounded me in an instant.

I tilted my chin up. "Take me to Empress Celestine. I'm unarmed, and I want to talk."

I heard the pounding again through the link, and felt the raw fear that tore through Rannoch as I had deposited myself at the enemy's doorstep. I was about to send a thought back, when a glint of silver caught my eye.

A millisecond later, I was blinded by pain. Pain so white-hot, I couldn't think, couldn't even grasp what had happened. My sight came speckling back, as I looked down to my leg. The same leg that had been scarred during the battle with the Umorfae separatists and Dashelle. I shrieked when I saw a thick bolt punched through the meat of my thigh, right below the skirt of my linteum. Blood rushed down my bare skin, pooling around my foot, in between my toes.

I looked up, just as Silvanis slung his bow across his shoulder, marching toward me.

"Well, caught you at last." He smirked, tossing his opal white braid with a haughty flick of his chin.

I gritted my teeth through the pain, hunched over my wounded leg. I couldn't even stand to face the bastard fully. "I'd say that's a generous way to put it," I ground out as I gripped my leg, "considering you only caught me when I surrendered." I nearly passed out from the pain, and wanted to scream in agony. Somehow, I reined it in enough to deliver one last burn. "I wonder if the empress knows how incompetent you are. I'll have to tell her."

Another blinding flash filled my vision, all I saw were his feet as he struck me in the cheek. This was no open hand slap. It was a full-on brutal punch. My head whiplashed back, so forcefully that my chin hit my chest on the return.

I blinked as I fell to the knee of my uninjured leg, the world tipped as I lost my balance, toppling over sideways. My head lolled twice, before my eyes closed. Muffled sounds were all that filtered in, as everything slowly shut out.

On my knees with an arrow jutting out of my thigh, my head pounding from the punch—and woozy from blood loss—I seriously doubted my sanity as I stared up at Empress Celestine. She smirked from above, while Silvanis stood haughtily below the dais. I had come to only moments before, my blood smeared into the pristine marble floor around me as I had struggled to right myself. My wrists bound in chains made it even harder to move. *How the*

fuck did I think this was a good idea.

"So," she said at last, her face just as placid as the last time I had seen her, "the traitorous Lily has returned. Or is it murderous? Both, I declare. You have been found guilty, you impertinent, Elf-skinned harpie. You are to face prime punishment."

I cringed, the bolt in my thigh throbbed as blood seeped further. I sucked in a breath, trying to combat the nearly uncontrollable desire to collapse and cradle my wound. I balled my fists, and spoke from nothing short of rage in order to respond, "Seriously? Elf-skinned? Was that supposed to be an insult? Elves are beautiful. That was poorly worded, you preening egg guzzler."

I staggered to standing, staring her down the whole time as I worked to get my legs under me. Once I did, I looked at the arrow, and winced at what I had to do. I couldn't believe I'd been shot, that this was where I was. Impaled by an arrow and being tried for treason in a magical realm. But I needed to keep my focus, I couldn't give in and retreat into my mind in order to escape the present. *I sure hope I don't pass out from this, this is going to hurt like a bitch.*

I gripped the arrow with two fists in front of my leg, the hand closest to my skin to prevent wiggling, while I used the outer hand to snap the shaft. The chains shifted just enough to allow me to twist my hand sideways. I screamed as I broke it, the movement causing the wound further damage was altogether unavoidable. My chest heaved as I released the frayed fletching to the floor. My nostrils flared as I gripped the arrow from the back of my leg, then slid out the length until it was clear of my torn flesh. I nearly lost consciousness again, the pain was unlike anything I had ever felt. I held the arrow head tight, as I looked back up at Empress Celestine. I let her see my rage, my hate as I lifted the broken arrow up. I didn't tear my gaze away as I unwound a healing thread to my leg. It was a risk, they would know that I had this ability if I used it in front of them. They might realize how it could be utilized to their benefit. But it was also highly probable they already knew. Silvanis had seen it himself when I had used it on him. As my sight tunneled into my skin, I didn't look away from her. I could feel my eyes glow as I did it, and hoped that pretending to hold her line of sight was enough. Enough that they didn't know I couldn't actually see them.

I released the filament as soon as I could, only to find Silvanis mid-swing, about to strike me as my vision returned. I dodged and staggered out of the way. I hadn't recovered, not by a long shot, hopefully I could evade him long enough that I could regenerate to the point where I could actually defend myself.

I shuffled away from him, my leg ached from the wound which had now mostly closed. He lunged repeatedly, each time I managed to skirt his attacks. I readjusted the arrow in my hand, trying to wriggle my wrists into a more comfortable position.

Silvanis backed up, taking me in with a long look as I gulped air. "No ropes for you this time," he taunted. "Solid metal which you have no chance of burning. I learned from Opius's mistake." He launched at me once again, but this time, I was ready. I deflected his strike, pushing his arm up with both hands, exposing his ribs. I shoved the arrowhead into his side, driving it deep. He flailed an arm, which knocked me in the head and sent me careening off-balance. He fell to the ground, then crawled away.

I finally noticed the crowd of Umorfae lining the pews of the west tower, probably the same ones which had sneered at me the first time I entered this chamber, that time long ago when I didn't understand what I was, or what the Umorfae were truly capable of. The crowd's angered and aghast faces fueled my strength, as they watched me best their new Generalis.

I stalked up to the dais, Celestine's face finally showing some semblance of emotion. "I am not here for a trial. I came for the Syrenni. I came to make you an offer," I said as I settled to a stop in front of her. I rested my hand on my injury, letting a thread out for a moment to abate the last of the pain.

"An offer? There is no offer that I would accept from *you*," she seethed.

"My offer is that I will not tear down *this* castle, if you let the Syrenni go free, now. I say "this" because it is not yours. Say no, and it will be torn apart, piece by piece."

She laughed. "Foolish filia, how could you possibly accomplish such a feat? This castle has stood for eons."

"I wouldn't do it myself. It will be taken down the same way it was created, with the Petrafae that are surrounding it, right now."

She dropped her jaw, and I finally saw it: fear. Pure fear crossed her perfect features. *I really hope I'm not just bullshitting and the Petrafae are here!* I closed my eyes, then started the call, the one that emanated from deep within me, to ask Livi to come to me once again. They arrived in short order, with news.

Petrafae, here.

I let the smallest breath escape at my relief. *Tell them to tear off the west tower, if you don't hear otherwise from me very soon.* They zipped away, as I looked back to the false leader sitting on her throne.

The empress had composed herself, and sat straighter with a

satisfied smirk. "Bring her out," Celestine ordered a guard to her left. I tried to keep my face neutral, but I couldn't help letting my confusion show. Was she talking about me? It made no sense. The guard marched off, through a hallway to the rear of the expansive space.

We waited, and waited. I didn't tear my eyes from her once, not even when Silvanis had limped back to his previous spot. She motioned with two fingers, wordlessly telling him to take his post. I set my jaw as worry took over, trying not to let it show. What if they had Neila? They had to know she was Naiya's sister, had they interrogated her, or worse, harmed her or the baby? My fists tightened as my mind spun through all the what-ifs.

Footsteps sounded at last, ratcheting up my anxiety. I expected the slight build of Naiya's sister to appear through the hallway at any moment.

I dropped my jaw as the guard entered with someone entirely different, unknown, and yet all-too-familiar at the same time.

Empress Celestine clapped. "Ah, *Your Highness*, you have finally arrived."

CHAPTER 44

She shifted her blazing cognac eyes from the empress to me. My breath caught as I stared, feeling like I was looking at Kerenza. But it wasn't her, hair blunt cut below the shoulders, her features leaner, and a bit gaunt.

I stilled as I looked at Rannoch and Kerenza's mother, utterly beautiful, yet hardened with time. It had been so long ago she was thought killed. Had they truly kept her here all that time without the Ignisfae finding out? She eyed me for a moment, appraising me before turning back to Celestine.

"You really should join us more often, Deniza," Celestine drawled, as she trailed her fingers up the arm of her throne. "Why, it has been ages it seems! How many cycles has it been? I forget. I am sure you must be interested to meet this female, just as I am sure you know exactly who she has taken up with—based on her scent. I can barely tell the difference between her scent and your filio's. Shame, perhaps you may have seen him again, but alas, she intends to tear down our beautiful castle. With you in it."

My blood iced as I realized Celestine's angle. It wouldn't just be me going down with the castle, it would be her as well. I would be taking away Rannoch and Kerenza's chance at discovering their maeder was alive. Alive all this time, only to die in the rubble.

My plan weakened, the more I thought about it, the more it turned to dust in my mind. This was never a good plan. Somehow, I had actually believed that I wouldn't be sacrificing myself at all, that if I could just show the Umorfae they were going to lose the castle, then they would relent. And I would just walk away? I shook my head, how could I have thought that this would protect my friends, my *family*, my love. No, now I was trapped, without options, and either about to die, or be imprisoned. Just like they imprisoned her. To be used when it benefited the Umorfae the most. How had I underestimated their level of cunning deviousness? I was going to leave this strange world the same way I came into it, as a fool. A dumbly altruistic, overly-optimistic fool. One that had turned a blind eye from the countless warnings I should have caught onto with Opius. One that had given herself over to the enemy with the idea that she could leverage the Syrenni free.

My heart sank, sank until it shattered. I nearly collapsed to the ground with despair and self-loathing. I knew I had made a fatal error, and would pay the price for it. I opened my mouth to speak to the empress, but what could I even say? What would even work? She had called my bluff, then heightened the stakes.

She smirked at me with that insufferable simper as she knew she had cornered me. She raised a hand as she spoke, "The trial is complete, we have proven her threat to the Umorfae to be substantial, she shall endure-"

A crack echoed through the room, shuddering through the tiles of the floor. The sensation climbed my legs as I struggled to keep my balance. Everything shifted as the walls groaned.

Oh fuck! I forgot to tell Livi to halt the Petrafae! I had already de- cided against the idea to tear down the castle. I couldn't let Queen Deniza perish that way.

The west tower banked backward, half of the throng of Umor- fae screamed as the entire section they were seated in separated from the main chamber. The whole west piece hung for a moment, before it tore off and fell straight down. Terrified shrieks filled my ears as the area to my left opened up to the misty air. The ones that didn't perish in the destruction scrambled out of their seats, huddling in what remained on the side of the imposing tower.

The tension in the silence that followed after the crash was pal- pable. Celestine gripped her throne, heaving as she processed what had just happened. She spoke at last through gritted teeth, "You will submit. And take the well-deserved punishment. Or I will kill her"-she thrust her finger at Rannoch's maeder- "right now."

I glanced at Queen Deniza, who had barely flinched though the whole ordeal. She shook her head once to me, as our eyes locked. I knew, as much as I would have loved to speak with her, I could sense she did not want me to do as Celestine commanded. She wanted me to fight. With even the slimmest chance of seeing her children again, *we* should fight, even if we might die during the effort.

"I will do no such thing. You will release the Syrenni, and you will release us," I said with firm resolve.

Empress Celestine laughed again. A dry, sick laugh that sent chills up my back. She held out a hand, scrawling her fingers in crooked shapes, and pulled a rivulet of water from a raised basin, then formed a large globe. She paused a moment as she stared me down, holding the ball above her hand in midair, then shifted her steely gaze to Queen Deniza. "You may have noticed, not a single torch is lit. No fire for you to draw from, Deniza." A single twitch of the corner of Celestine's mouth was her only movement, before the sphere rushed to Deniza.

I screamed as the ball was about to envelop her head, it would only be a few moments before she drowned inside of it.

Flame erupted from Queen Deniza's hands, shooting upward just as the sphere was about to overtake her. The ball evaporated with a hiss, and the bonds that held her wrists withered.

Rope bonds.

My jaw hung open as I stared at the standoff between the two females. Celestine's knuckles whitened as she gripped her throne.

"All these cycles, and you never knew," Deniza said as she stalked toward the empress. "I am the master of my mind, and it gave me power, the power to shield the fact that I am a Fire Bringer." She snapped her hands apart, the disintegrated ropes fluttered to the ground in a pile of ash.

"Praetors!" Celestine cried. A wave of armed Umorfae lined up in front of the dais. Deniza never tore her eyes from Celestine as she drew closer, completely ignoring the raised spears now nearly at her throat. A torrent of water flew from the side, crashing into the queen and knocking her off balance. The water continued to pummel her. I looked over my shoulder to see Silvanis drawing the water from an unseen source in a continuous, brutal stream.

My anger boiled as I launched myself at him. The bastard that lied to the empress about me, hunted me across this world, hunted my brother, stabbed Don'Li, and finally, shot me after I had already surrendered; this son of a bitch was going down.

Flames burst from my palms as I reached him, I drove them

into his chest as he tried to eliminate Deniza. He shrieked and faltered, still bleeding from his side where I had stabbed him with the arrowhead.

It only took him a moment to recover. Silvanis snapped his sharp gaze to mine and circled me, wounded in more ways than one, he was still lethal as he prowled. He reached into a sheath at his side, then flashed a grin as he pulled a large, glinting knife out.

My knife, the one gifted to me from the Arbor Elves. He clutched the carefully carved hilt in his meaty hands. "Time for your retribution, cunne. I am going to make this hurt."

I retreated a step, then everything happened at once as he thrust forward to slice at me. Time slowed as Celestine screamed, I heard the telltale sound of fabric igniting, a loud crack echoed through the room as the floor split to my left. The southwest portion of the remaining tower detached as all the walls shuddered. Shards of crystals rained from above like shattered glass. I lifted my arms to cover my head, as Silvanis's arc downward faltered and went wide as he tried to catch his balance. The horrified shouts of the falling Umorfae courtiers sounded far off, as Silvanis's blow was about to land true.

I shoved my bound hands up into the area below his shoulder, blocking his strike, then crouched and spun low, sweeping his legs from underneath him. But he was too big, I hadn't managed to topple him. I scrambled backward away from him, as he quickly regained his footing, then stalked forward, gripping the knife tighter.

The open air from the exposed tower kissed my skin, as mist drifted in. I looked over my shoulder at Queen Deniza, backed all the way against the far wall. Spears from the guards angled back, about to strike as Celestine hollered, "Take her down!"

A gale force wind blew past, knocking Silvanis into the wall of the dais, his cheekbone cracked against the marble. His hand flew up, striking the corner of the raised surface. I followed the flash of metal as his hand opened, releasing the blade involuntarily. I traced the path it was headed before it even landed, tumbled toward it and snatched it out of the air. In a heartbeat I was in front of him, about to drive the blade in.

Another crack sounded. The tower was splitting in two. Silvanis tried to lunge at me. My head cleared as the subtle knowing of my next moves quelled any fear. In one motion I took one step to the side and crouched down low with one foot out for balance. I managed to curl my fingers to hold the knife and connect to the water suspended in him at the same time. I yanked his blood from within. He lost control over his forward motion, as the open wound on his side spurted from the pull. I thrust my hands toward his chest as he lurched.

Silvanis slumped on top of me as we dropped to the floor.

Voices streamed in, shouts echoed all around. I struggled under the weight of him, as the tiles shifted below me. Warm liquid oozed over me. I tried to wriggle free from his immobile body.

I realized with dread that we were going down with the section. This is what it had come to. I may have taken Silvanis down, but I was going down, too. Time practically halted as the whole floor kinked at an angle, and I started to slide with him.

A hand wrapped around my upper arm, another broader palm gripped the other. Both of my hands were still bound, stuck under my enemy.

The floor gave way at last, and fell away to the rocky cliff side far below. I watched as it crashed into the ground, watched Silvanis fall like a rag doll. I looked at the destruction, my feet dangling in the open air, my hands still gripping the blade, tainted with thick blue blood.

The hands hauled me up onto the remaining section of the tower. I collapsed onto my back and stared up, as Rannoch and Kerenza came into view.

Metal sang in the air, I angled my head back to see Felix, Dhiren, and Dhirdre finishing off the last of the Umorfae guards. Then another sight made my heart plummet.

Queen Deniza crouched on the ground, cradling Don'Li's head. An Umorfae spear rended clean through his chest. I struggled to get up, but Rannoch and Kerenza held me down while they worked off the chains.

"I can't believe you did this, Lily," Rannoch muttered as he got one hand free. "You could have *died.*"

"Maybe you can be mad at me later," I said as he pulled the chains off. I scrambled to get up, then rushed over to Don'Li.

Rannoch and Kerenza halted in their tracks, as they finally saw their maeder in the room. Queen Deniza locked eyes with her children, tears brimmed as she looked at them. The others gathered around Don'Li, wiping their blades clean. Dhirdre and Dhiren each dropped to a knee, bowing to their queen.

I looked over my shoulder at Celestine at last, then did a double-take. She stood shaking, as far back on the dais as she could get, with the lower part her face burned and the hair on the right side fried off. Her dress only partially covered her body, lace had been melted into her skin in intricate patterns at an angle up her legs and across one arm. Deniza had damaged her terribly when she spouted fire at her.

She was the only Umorfae left in the tower, so I turned back to Don'Li, who lay gasping on the floor.

"We can fix this," I breathed. "Please, help me, Rannoch. We can cut the spear off and-"

"No," Don'Li rasped. "No, I do not wish that. I was given the greatest gift, to discover Deniza still lived, to protect her from injury, and to be able to tell her how sorry I was." His words were choppy as he struggled to speak.

Queen Deniza wiped his forehead. "You do not owe an apology. And what you did, taking the spear meant for me, I wish you did not do it, but am forever grateful that it meant I get to see my children again." She looked up at them again and smiled as tears spilled at last. She looked back to Don'Li, and held his hand. His face aged in an instant. "Go easy, to the Fading. You are noble, and showed me true kindness. Live on in the Ether, that I may see you again."

He opened his mouth, but no words came. His eyes widened, before they turned a milky white. He looked like he could see something beyond, as he stared off into nothing. "It is ... beautiful," he whispered at last.

Then, I saw it start, the Fading. His skin turned transparent, before he diminished into nothingness. His body was *gone,* just ... vanished. But I felt him. I couldn't see anything of a spirit, but I knew he was there for a moment, pain free and light. His blend of warmth mixed with his wispy cool soul hung on a little longer, and I could sense his smile—even if I couldn't see it.

It took several moments after he disappeared for any of us to speak. Queen Deniza stood at last, then embraced her children. The children that she had not seen in nearly one hundred and fifty cycles. So much of their lives had passed, so much time lost. But at long last, they had her back. Now we just had to get the hell out of this castle.

I sucked in a breath, trying to calm the tears that wanted to flow at the loss of Don'Li, and the raging emotions of all that had transpired. I turned to Celestine, who still quavered on the dais.

"We are going, and we are taking the Syrenni with us. Release them *now*, or after we leave this castle the Petrafae will finish tearing this place apart."

She dropped her hands that had been covering her partially ruined face. "No!" She thrust her palm out, and called another sphere of water which she flung to me in the blink of an eye. It enveloped my head before I could react, distorting the room and all the faces that I could see shriek, but their sound was muffled. I saw Rannoch race to hoist himself onto the platform, presumably to fight her so that she would lose control over the globe that was already starting to strangle the life out of me.

I lifted my hands, and pushed the water up, freeing my face to the open air. Celestine's jaw dropped as I stood, the globe held aloft while I glared at her. I threw it aside with carelessness, as if she hadn't just tried to kill me with it. I didn't look away from her as the splash—and her heaving breath—was the only sound in the room.

I took a step toward her, she flinched as I raised my finger. "As I said before, we are leaving, and we are taking the Syrenni. If they do not immediately come streaming out of this castle, we're taking this place down."

I called Livi, then gave the message to tell the Petrafae we were on our way out, and to hold off any further destruction while we waited.

Celestine rushed to the edge of the platform as Livi disappeared, drawing another sphere of water from the basin. "I will not let you do this to me!"

I heard the unmistakable sound of a sword being drawn. From the corner of my eye I saw Queen Deniza pounce, with Dhirdre's blade in hand. She leapt onto the dais with ease, and angled the sharp tip at Empress Celestine's throat. "Perhaps I should do to you what you did to me. Drag you to TerraIgni and imprison you for an eon. Or perhaps I should end you right here. You certainly deserve it." Celestine opened her mouth to speak, then dropped to the floor and cowered. She was nothing more than a quivering lump hiding beyond her throne, a stone throne she was never meant to sit upon. "I will do neither, though. I will grant you what you took from me. I know you have young ones. You will live your remaining cycles with the memory of what you did to me burned into your skin. But you will be here for them. It is only for them that I do this. Release the Syrenni, and you—and your children—will live."

Deniza lowered Dhirdre's sword, then turned and jumped down. Leaving Celestine there to quake at nearly being killed for her atrocities.

Queen Deniza walked past me with her head held high. I turned and followed, giving Celestine my back, as we all walked out. Leaving the false empress there to realize the control she had lost.

CHAPTER 45

I nearly gasped when we got to the stairs, half of them were gone, having been sheared off when the Petrafae took down the tower. We crowded at the lip of the landing platform, peering over at the substantial drop. The staircase was intact halfway down, but we only had three ledges in between that we could jump to.

"Think we can make it?" I asked Rannoch.

"It's pretty far, and looks like we'd fall shy."

Naiya's lifeless body falling into the chasm flashed in my mind. My fists balled at the thought and my breath quickened. Rannoch gave me a sideways glance, his face softened as he must have caught a thread of what I was thinking.

"I have an idea," Felix spoke up. "We go one at a time, I'll give a boost each time to clear the next landing. Just like when I helped Rannoch when he was coming down from those restraints, remember? He wasn't going to land and I pushed him the extra distance."

"Good thinking," I said. "I'll go first."

"Wait," Felix said. "I'll go first. I'll need to be below, to send the boost up. I can't do it the other way around." He handed his staff to Dhiren. "I'll need both hands, can you take this?" Dhiren's eyes gleamed at him as he took it.

"I definitely accept," Dhiren answered. The corner of Felix's lips curved up as he leapt off the edge, blasting a current to sail down onto the first landing thirty feet below. He landed on light feet. I jumped off the platform next, the rush of falling made my stomach rise. Halfway down, the current of air surrounded me, pushed me a bit farther and slowed my descent. Felix caught me as I landed, sending us crashing into the wall behind him. His back smacked against it as he grunted. "Sorry, Felix. Thanks. Clearly I'm not as graceful as you."

He laughed. "Clearly."

One by one the rest followed. It was a far drop, but Felix managed to assist everyone down with ease. The next platform was on the opposite side of the tower, not as long of a drop as the first, but the distance between was greater.

He eyed the gap and said, "You'll need a running start, I think. This one may be a close call." He took three paces, then leapt off. Having a blast of air he could use the whole way made his arrival easier than ours would be. We'd be more than halfway across the open expanse before he'd be able to lend assistance.

I ran, then jumped next. As I fell in an arc, it didn't take long for my mind to calculate that I would definitely fall short. He shot a current at last, which lifted me higher—just not enough. My hands caught the edge of the lip just as I was about to fall past it. He clasped my wrists and hauled me up.

"That was too close," I panted, as I struggled to catch my breath. I peered over at the remaining drop, at least another hundred feet down. I gulped at how close I had come to falling the whole way. "We need to be ready to catch each person." Kerenza jumped next, easily hitting the landing after Felix gave her a funnel of upward air. I rolled my eyes, and smiled at the same time. "Of course you land perfectly."

She flicked an invisible speck of dust off her shoulder. "I do everything with style." I laughed at her stupid grin, the too-beautiful smile that said she was entirely too pleased with her jump and the line she delivered after. Queen Deniza came next, I had to keep my jaw from dropping at her fluid grace as she sailed down, barely needing any help from Felix. All this time in captivity, she must have spent most of it keeping herself chiseled. Dhiren and Dhirdre both fell just a little shy, Kerenza and I were ready to grab them to pull them safely onto the tile.

Rannoch took two huge strides before jumping, but I could tell right away, he did not make it far enough out. My heart thudded as I knew he'd be too far away to even grab. "Felix!" I yelled. Felix churned air as hard as he could, but there still was not enough lift. Rannoch's body size—combined with the weight of his weapons—had been too much for Felix to give proper aid this time.

"Hold her!" Deniza shouted. Before I knew what was happening, she scaled my shoulders, reaching out to extend the distance. Arms immediately wrapped around my legs, anchoring me to the platform. Rannoch grasped his maeder's hands as he came falling down, my breath flew out of me and my stomach dropped as his freefall made us all pivot downward. I clenched my eyes as I gripped Deniza's legs. We swung upside down for a moment before the others started pulling us slowly up.

"I have you, my filio," she said to him. It felt like it took way too long until we righted and pulled from the abyss. Once we were safe and settled, my heart raced as I tried to calm myself. I had nearly lost Rannoch when I hadn't expected it. I knew I had a close shave, but I figured he would land just as easily as Kerenza. I cried, then laughed, then cried again as I hugged both he and his mother. Saved by his maeder and his mate, because of her quick thinking.

"Okay, one more platform to go. Let's get out of here," I said between emotional fits.

"Thank God," Felix said. "I'm getting tired." He stood, then rocked his head side to side to unkink his neck. "Okay, one more round."

He jumped down, the next landing was at a much easier angle than the last, but still a fair drop. He sent two blasts of air to slow his descent and smooth his approach, but the air sputtered at the last moment. His knees buckled as he landed, his head dropped and he practically collapsed. I raised my hand to my mouth as I realized he had reached burnout. He had used too much from his well to help us, and was suddenly expiring. Footsteps sounded on the stairs to the landing he knelt on.

"No! Felix!" I screamed.

Praetors charged toward my brother, who struggled to rise. The twang of metal sounded as a blade arced down to his unprotected neck. I went to jump, when an arrow sailed past my face, then another sent with such lighting speed I didn't know how someone could string a bow so fast. Six arrows flew in rapid succession, each one finding their mark at the same moment that Dhiren dropped his bow and jumped the distance, blade out as he sailed into the fray. The guard that was about to take Felix down lay next to him, seeping bright cerulean blood as Dhiren landed. Dhiren's lip curled as he faced off with the remaining Praetors, blocking their access to Felix.

Dhiren moved faster than I had ever seen, I could barely track his sword as he spun through those who remained. I was about to join, to help, when Rannoch caught my arm. "Let Dhiren do this, they dared to try and take Felix from him, let him finish it." I opened my mouth to protest, that I was his sister, that I had just as much right. But something told me, this was their way. The sibling bond moved down a notch when the heart was involved. I nodded, then looked back to see Dhiren already finished killing them, and helping Felix up. "You see? He is more than capable."

Dhirdre jumped down, carrying Dhiren's discarded bow. She made the landing easily, though it was clear the impact was harder without Felix's assistance. She holstered Dhiren's sword as he checked over Felix, getting Felix's weight comfortably over his shoulder to help him down the stairs. One by one, the rest of us made the leap, across the great drop and onto the last platform.

There were no more guards that appeared, no footsteps of charging Praetors or even any Syrenni in sight. I led the way out, the way that I knew from that time long ago when I had visited this castle. We raced through the empty, brilliant structure. I shuddered at the time I had spent here, how I had actually enjoyed it, and been enthralled by it. Certainly it was beautiful, but it was not of their making. The Umorfae's whole existence was built on a sham. One lie after another. Taking the Petrafae castle as their own, enslaving a whole race to do their work so that they may lounge about, spending their time scheming and calculating their next move. Take, take, take. It was their way of life.

We reached the grand entryway, and the massive doors that were at least twenty feet tall. I turned to look at the expansive room, remembering how I had felt the first time I saw it. There to the right was the sweeping staircase that led to Opius's block of rooms. I cringed at the memory of how I felt during my first visit. Everything would be different if things had not happened as they did, I would not be with Rannoch, I may not even still be alive. Guilt surged at the thought that I couldn't completely regret things because of the outcome for me. It was the outcome for others that stabbed at my heart. Josie, and Naiya, and all others who had suffered because of Dashelle's, Opius's, and the Umorfae's greed. I had lost Josie because of my inaction. I hadn't followed her when I should have. I didn't do something soon enough. This time, for the Syrenni, I hadn't waited. I acted. Foolishly perhaps, but I had done something. I just hoped it was enough.

I passed my gaze over the pristine entryway again, remembering all I didn't know the first time I had seen it. The way I had marveled at the amount of methodically grown crystal, the perfect stair risers that grew out of sparkling calcite points. The flowing waterfalls alongside the gleaming white-and-lilac veined translucent platforms. I turned my back on those stairs, and left them where they belonged: in the past.

CHAPTER 46

We stopped just past the bridge, out of range of arrows in case the Umorfae decided to fire from the castle. I gave Rannoch and Kerenza space, as they reunited with their mother. I still couldn't believe it, after all this time and thought dead for so long, she had been rescued. In all honesty, she played a fair part in rescuing herself—and me. I smiled at how Celestine's idea to use her against me failed. *Talk about playing the long game.* What kind of person could do that to someone? Imprisoning an individual just so they could use them as a failsafe when it served their evil schemes. It was abhorrent, and turned my stomach. So much had been taken from Rannoch and his family. I couldn't believe Deniza had decided to let Celestine live, but then perhaps that showed how deep Queen Deniza's morals were. Yes, Deniza left her with scars for the rest of Celestine's wretched life, but Empress Celestine also would be there for her children. The very thing that had been specifically taken away from Queen Deniza. For as much as I hated killing, I would have ended her. Any Umorfae I knew had proven themselves to me to be undeserving of a second chance. What would Celestine do with this opportunity? Would she squander it, take vengeance, or rebuild and move forward? I could easily assume what her choice would be.

Queen Deniza turned to me as our eyes locked. I hadn't gotten a chance to say anything to her. Things had spun into chaos in the castle, and then we were racing through it to make our escape. She left her children then walked over to me. I held my breath as she stared at me for a long moment, her face unreadable. She took my hand and dropped to one knee, the same gesture Kerenza had done when we returned to TerraIgni from the Hinterdunes.

"I am honored to meet you, Lily, and proudly accept you as Rannoch's mate. It fills my heart with joy, knowing that he has found someone who loves him. You are brave, and deserving of your place in this familia."

The waterline of my eyes stung as I looked at her, then looked at Rannoch and Kerenza. They smiled and nodded. I may have had a steep climb to reach this resolution with their faeder, but with Deniza, she had freely accepted. A wave of emotion flooded as she stood.

Tears threatened to overflow as I wrapped my arms around her. I sucked in a breath at last, tamping down the emotions about to unfurl. God how I wanted to though, to just hold all of them and cry. I would, when I was alone with Rannoch and could let go, I definitely would. I hugged her instead. She faltered a moment, and I realized it may have not been tradition. She also had been imprisoned for so long, the touch of a person may have been for-eign to her at this point. After a long pause, she raised her arms and enveloped me.

I dropped my arms at last and gave her a respectful bow with my fist across my chest. "You fought bravely. I can see where your son—filio—gets it. And you are a Fire Bringer. I am as well. I was hoping … would you teach me? There is so much I don't know, and I lack the ability to control it sometimes. Will you be my guide?"

She blinked in surprise, before she responded, "I would be honored."

Gratefulness, respect, and perhaps excitement filled me as she spoke. At last, I would have a teacher for this gift, it had to be a gift, one that I could use when it mattered.

I looked over my shoulder, scanning the trees for the Petrafae. I picked out a flash of copper hair or tawny skin every so often, hidden in the trees in a wide circle surrounding their former home.

"Do you think Celestine might send the remaining Praetors out here?" I asked Rannoch. "We're pretty exposed."

"We'd have time to run, we can see the doors, and the Petrafae are ready, potentially they can pull down the portcullis, or the bridge, to prevent them from reaching us."

"Good point."

We waited for what felt like an eternity. There was no movement, not a single sign that Celestine would either cave to my demand, or retaliate. Perhaps she was calling my bluff again. Because if the Petrafae did finish the job of destroying the palace, the Syrenni would die, too. She had to know that. If my ultimate motivation was their safe release, why would I let them die that way?

"I remember Naiya telling me that they lived below the castle, and came up to work. Perhaps if we tell the Petrafae to only pull down the top portion the Syrenni could be rescued that way?"

"Any Syrenni in the upper portion of the castle would also be lost," Queen Deniza spoke. "And any held in their cells, which are at the top rear of the stronghold. The loss of life would be significant."

I winced and nodded. We couldn't do that. "Perhaps if we-"

A bell tolled; one single, long drone. It echoed throughout the remaining walls.

"What was that?" I asked as we all stared toward the now-silent castle.

"The summoning bell," Deniza answered. "It is used to call the Syrenni. I have never heard just one ring. I always heard either three or four."

"So … what does one bell mean?"

Deniza shook her head. "I do not know."

A moment passed, then through the doors we heard echoes of voices. I clutched Rannoch's arm as a single Syrenni came into view. Then another. Then many, many more. I scanned the approaching crowd for Neila, but so far I had only seen Syrenni I didn't recognize. My breath snagged, had something happened to her before I made my way here? There was certainly time for it, was I too late to save Naiya's sister? I couldn't lie to myself. I had wanted to help the Syrenni as a whole, but I was driven to help Neila, and Naiya's child.

Syrenni reached the bridge, huddled in a crowd as their clouded eyes darted between us on the opposite side. Rannoch nudged me with an arm, and I realized he was urging me to speak up. I hadn't thought about what to say, or that I would need to. It dawned on me I hadn't planned a single thing beyond trying to wrest them away from Umorfae control. Now that they were here, what would we do? My blood went cold as they all stared at us, fidgeting in the early morning air, the darkness of night finally starting to retreat.

I pored over each face that looked back at me, but none seemed recognizable. My heart dropped as I realized I didn't see Neila there. I looked again, there were at least two hundred Syrenni, maybe more. Perhaps I had skipped over her.

One last Syrenni appeared through the great doors, struggling with a baby on her hip. My hand flew to my mouth as I recognized her face, and the unmistakable opal glint of Umorfae hair on the child. She made her way through the crowd, all the way to the front.

Neila settled to a stop in front of me, her black eyes clear and sharp as she gave one nod of her head, and smiled. "Naiya would be thankful. My sisterhood is free. We have much to do to start a new life, and I do not know where we will go. But we will live. Naiya's child will live."

The baby turned her precious face to me as I held back tears. She was so clearly Naiya and Locrien's child. Naiya's eyes, Locrien's hair and mouth. There was no denying it.

"Her name is Sereia, named for our lost queen," Neila said as she gazed at the baby. "I was so fearful the Umorfae would find her. I could not have hidden her for much longer. You can see what she is, there is no doubt what the Umorfae would have done to her. I do not know what she will do with her life, but I do know, she will bring change for the Syrenni. She is strong, perhaps she will do more than that. Perhaps she will change all of Alternis."

"I will do all I can to help her, and help the Syrenni." I didn't even know what I was promising, I had to get them out of Lacausia first. I cleared my throat, my mind tumbling through the various reassurances I could try and offer, but what were we going to actually be able to do? We had freed them, but they needed a home; a place where they could build a new life. Clarity struck, and I knew exactly what we could offer them, and where we could take them. As long as the Petrafae agreed to help again. "Take your people to the river, meet us at the spot where you had found me ... back when you warned me about Silvanis. It will take us some time on foot, but we will be able to help guide you to a new home once we're there."

She nodded, then turned to guide her people down the rocky embankment, to the rushing current below the bridge. They leapt into the water, into their freedom, and disappeared. It only took seconds for the hundreds of Syrenni to slip below the depth. I watched for a moment, waiting to catch any sign of them. I smiled, they were *gone*. Released from their millennia-long servitude, they swam toward a new life. Perhaps there was still much uncertainty surrounding it, but at least it would not be lorded over by hateful Umorfae. They had lost their grip on the Syrenni, and I would make damn sure things would stay that way.

"What are we going to do now?" Felix asked, following my line of sight to the river beyond.

I interlaced my fingers. "We're going to ask the Petrafae for another favor."

CHAPTER 47

"Asmi, Hiret," Rannoch greeted his friends as the Petrafae gathered around us, "I am indebted to you once again."

"As am I," I spoke up, "I would have been screwed without your help." The corner of Rannoch's mouth tipped up, and I almost smacked his shoulder.

Asmi seemed to not even notice as he said, "I have to admit, it felt magna to unseat the Umorfae and damage the castle in a way they cannot repair. The Petrafae are not vengeful, and would have left the castle as it is—in spite of the Umorfae taking it for themselves. I see our ancestor's mistake now, they built it for beauty, not function. It was too easy for the Umorfae to invade and take over."

"I'm surprised you didn't want to take it back," I said, "kick them out and keep it for good."

Hiret shook his head. "Adrilan is our home now, and has been for hundreds of cycles. As Asmi mentioned, we built our new home so that only a Petrafae can reach it. The Umorfae can never do what they did to us again. We have enough satisfaction from that. They can have this relic." He tossed a hand at the structure, then turned his back on it. "I suppose our work here is done."

"Actually," I said, "I realized we—and the Syrenni—need your help, if you are willing to give it. They have left the area already, but the river will only take them so far. They will be too close to Lacausia if they linger there. They need a new home, a place where they can thrive and return to what they once were. But we don't have the resources to get them there ourselves. I was hoping you would help guide them with us."

"Where do you intend to take them?" Kerenza asked.

I arched an eyebrow. "I think you'll like this idea."

"Oh?" Her eyes glimmered.

I nodded. "To the lake surrounding that dreaded cave. I wanted to ask the Petrafae to transform it into a habitat for them. With the Syrenni patrolling the lake—once they are recovered and established—the Umorfae will never be able to use the cave for what they did before, when they took the children."

She twitched the corner of her lips. "Oh, yes, I like this plan."

Asmi spoke up, "But how can we help move the Syrenni there?"

"I'll tell you my idea as we walk to meet them." I lifted my open palm to the path ahead, so that we could leave the damaged castle behind us, and the remaining Umorfae who were no doubt steaming mad over their loss.

Rannoch held me back as the others marched ahead. I smiled as I watched Kerenza beam at her mother. It was still so unbelievable, we had gotten her back. I looked at Rannoch expecting to find a happy face. My stomach fell when I took in his set jaw, and his hardened glance.

I didn't say anything for a long moment. At last I said, "We should catch up to the others, we're still close to the castle."

"No, I want you to stay here and talk to me. I need to hear you promise me that you will *never* do something like that again. You nearly got yourself killed!" he said with a stern voice. I opened my mouth to protest, what I had done was foolish and didn't go as I thought it might. But we *were* victorious, in more ways than one. "No," he said, "I can hear your argument you're about to give me. You shut me out, and did this alone. And got shot in the process."

I winced at that. I had healed it mostly, but it was a major injury and was still readily visible, as was the dried blood caked on my leg. I dropped my head and turned from him. Tears welled as I remembered coming to on the floor below Empress Celestine, with my blood smeared around me, and the crushing realization at the mistake I had made. "I …" I gulped, there were no adequate words as self-loathing took over again.

"You what? Did the right thing? Weren't wrong? I could have protected you, and you just delivered yourself to their doorstep!"

I crossed my arms and spun toward him. "I can't stand myself!" I shouted. I blinked and backed up a step as my words settled over me, pooling like a dark, weighted—yet intangible—shroud. "I feel like a terrible person. I have so much guilt, in so many ways. I did practically nothing for Josie, and she's gone. Or did too little too late. I was totally unaware what was happening with the Syrenni, and I actually *enjoyed* my time here," I said as I threw my hand in the direction of the castle. "I like how I look now, yet when I was home I scared my mother, I could even smell her fear, my looks terrified her. My mother is alone, while I am here creating this new life with you. My home there is gone, and I now have TerraIgni, which I am a fucking *princess* of now. Apollo is no longer my horse, that bond is broken, but suddenly I have Zephyrine and it's so strong, that connection. Can you imagine how all of that would make me feel? My guilt is already more than I can bear. The thought of losing any one of you, I did it for *me*, because I selfishly did not want to lose another. And now Don'Li is gone. Yes, I admit, I didn't do the right thing. I had good intentions, but the road to hell is paved with good intentions." I scoffed at myself, at using another of my dad's phrases without thinking about it. He had always said that, anytime one of us messed up trying to do something that went awry for one reason or another.

I looked across the way to our group disappearing on the trail, where Felix lingered, not letting me out of his sight. I cried at last. "I am sorry, Rannoch. I just … *couldn't* lose you."

"And what about me? I *can't* lose you. Imagine how I felt when I woke up alone in our bed, and realized what you were doing, right when you were about to give yourself over to them. The helplessness that I felt. You were gone, and I couldn't protect you. Then I felt the arrow strike, and I dropped to the ground when it happened. I could barely speak, Kerenza had to drag me up to get even a word out of me. It was she who rallied everyone right away, I could not do it. She led us. I was always the one ready to take charge, and when you were in jeopardy, all I could think about was you. She took the lead, and because of her, we came to you."

"I messed up, again. I admit it. I hated myself when I realized what had happened, when I woke up after being shot. Even though we won in the end, I knew I went about it the wrong way. You always say things like "you're selfless" or "you always think about others" … I don't know if it's that you're overestimating me, or if you wish those traits on me—to see what you want to see. Because I wanted to save the Syrenni not just for them, but for me. To deal

with *my* guilt. I'm just not as good of a person as you think I am."
I sagged as tears slipped over my cheeks. I knew the deeper reason
I wanted to save them, even if I couldn't say it out loud.

He gave me a soft smile and took a step toward me, tucking
in a loose hair behind my ear. "Yes, you are, Lily. I am here to
remind you of that. I will always remind you. Yes, I was … I don't
even have a word to describe how I felt when I realized you left.
Terrified, angry—so angry, frustrated, helpless … a combination
of all those feelings. But the only thing that matters is, I love you.
I wonder, what tells you we're a match? Not just attraction, but
beyond that."

I searched his eyes, then turned away and folded my arms
across my chest. I knew why. But I was still too mad at myself.
"That we balance each other," I whispered. And it was true. He
could be so serious sometimes, and I brought humor, a way to
divert that hardened warrior facade he sometimes slipped into.
His wounds, his deep-cut unseen wounds to his heart; I could
touch them, mend them, when no one else could. But … I almost
couldn't face the part of me that he was there to lift up.

"I know, Lily. You are a healer, have had that as a part of who
you are probably since the beginning. To have these choices thrust
upon you, many of them not actual choices, but situations. Events
that there is no bargaining with, they happened, and you were unable to make any change. It is *because you care about others* that they
hold a grasp on you. If you were not good, not caring, not selfless,
they would not have such an effect on you. You are not responsible
for other's evil deeds. I do not overestimate you, I *see* you."

I cried out and threw my arms around him. He held me as I
sobbed. All the emotions of the events that had sprung from my

misguided decision flowed from me in a crashing wave. Turbulent and chaotic, both victorious and defeated. I looked up at him through tear-soaked lashes.

"Come, my love. Time to guide the Syrenni as you wanted, to their new home. What plan did you come up with for this?"

I sniffled, calming the last of my tears. "Oh, I wouldn't want to spoil the surprise just yet."

He chuckled and kissed my head, as we headed towards our waiting friends. "Now why does that not surprise me?"

CHAPTER 48

We walked down the trail to our group, who turned to us as we approached. Felix looked me over with a concerned glance, I merely nodded a wordless "I'm okay."

Asmi spoke up, "So, what is this idea you have, and how are we needed?" He motioned to the group of twenty-five Petrafae behind him.

"The river can take them only so far," I answered, "and there isn't a safe way to live so close to Umorfae territory. They need water to make the journey to the lake, I'm not even sure how long it would take us to get there. They would die on the way there. I thought—and maybe this is a crazy idea—that you all could make a slab of earth big enough for them to ride on, with depressions in it to hold water for them. I could funnel the water from the river into the pits. Then you all push it, or lift it? The whole way to the lake."

Kerenza burst out laughing. "How do you come up with these magna ideas, Lily? Platforms with little lakes. Fucking brilliant."

I dropped my jaw at her. "Kerenza! I have never once heard you swear like me."

She twitched a sideways smile. "It's not just Rannoch you have changed."

I shook my head and huffed a laugh. "And used a contraction no less. I'm up in here just wrecking your linguistics. All joking aside," I turned to Asmi and Hiret, "can it be done? Is that too ridiculous? I know it's a long way, and would take so much of your energy to sustain it for that long."

Hiret rubbed his thumb and forefinger along his jaw. "It is a good idea, but I think if we split it up it would be more manageable. Perhaps groups of four?" he asked Asmi.

"Yes, I think you are right. But I think five platforms, with the Syrenni split evenly between them. It will make navigating much easier than one large one. We will have to rotate rest breaks as well, so that none of us reach burnout," Asmi answered.

Burnout. I remembered Felix collapsing after he jumped, and how he still didn't know about what burnout was, or what it could mean. I needed to have that conversation with him as soon as possible.

"Yes, magna idea, Lily," Rannoch said and smiled at me. "We have one other issue: food and water for ourselves. We are not equipped, and also what of food for the Syrenni?"

I tapped my foot. That was a problem. In fact it was a pressing one I hadn't even thought about. We would need water soon after leaving the river. And food shortly after that. "How far away is Adrilan? If we asked for help, how long would it take them to reach us?"

"We can cross the land on a slab much faster than on foot, yet still it would take much too long," Hiret answered. "We only have enough provisions for ourselves. We could share, but it would run out well before any Petrafae could reach us if we did."

The other Petrafae murmured to each other, and dread crept in that the idea of helping with the risk of starvation may mean they'd ultimately decline. "Wait!" I exclaimed. "The Arbor Elves! Aurelian had told me if I ever needed anything, all I had to do was ask. They might be able to open a portal and meet us at the river!"

Dhirdre nodded her approval and grinned. "Oh yes, Rannoch, you have a smart mate indeed. Even managed to establish a relationship with the Arbor Elves." She tapped her temple then pointed at me.

I laughed, then exhaled a breath. Poor Livi, I had asked them to zip all over this world again and again. They were the real hero, without their assistance, virtually every piece of this unbelievable puzzle would have been lost. When it was over, I needed to find some way to show my gratitude. I focused in on the node in my throat, then started the call to ask Livi to come to me. It rolled out in melodic waves. I was surprised to feel the ping almost immediately. They had stayed close by. I smiled at that, as I sensed the reason.

They appeared in moments, circling me with glee. As they touched their nose to mine, I felt the confirmation. They were worried about me, and wanted to be sure I was safe. Their face shifted male, and kissed my cheek. *I hope this is my last request for awhile. Please, if you are willing, go to the Arbor Elves and ask for their assistance. A group of around thirty Fae are guiding over two hundred Syrenni to their new home, at the lake where we fought the Umorfae. We need food and water for all. Please meet us at the end of the Lacausia river.*

After flourishing a bow which made me grin, they departed in an instant. I turned to my companions, my close-knit group who had seen me through thick and thin. I looked over each of their faces, as my mistake truly settled. I had tried to protect myself by approaching the Umorfae alone. But really, I hadn't trusted my inner circle. They were all skilled. They were all adept. I had blocked not only Rannoch, but all of them as well. I may have taken the step forward in life to allow people in, but the moment they might have been in jeopardy, I had recoiled. Offered myself instead to the enemy, that I might spare myself the pain of losing one of them. Two steps forward, one step back.

Don'Li had been lost as a result of my actions. I knew I could have healed him if he let me, it would have taken all my strength to do it, but I could have. He had teetered near the Fading for so long, he was finally ready to let go. Yet still, his death marked me, it would forever be a reminder to trust my friends. Perhaps he would still be here if I hadn't taken the role of the sacrificial lamb. Or perhaps more of us would have been lost. There was no way to know, but one thing I was sure of: I would take this lesson, and not let it wreck me. It easily could, by allowing it to eat me alive from the inside out, let the self-loathing fester.

They all stared at me, waiting. I sensed they knew I was in a personal crisis, and paused for me, giving me time. I cleared my throat at last. "I owe you all an apology. I shouldn't have done what I did—given myself over to the Umorfae to bargain for the Syrenni. I thought I could prevent you all from being hurt or killed that way, and I didn't want anyone to suffer because I had this driving need to free them. I should have trusted you all, to do what you are so great at—to fight for the side of right and justice."

Dhirdre walked to me, and wrapped her arms around my

shoulders. Kerenza came next, and embraced both of us. One by one, each of my friends added themselves to the hug. My friends. My family. My *everything*. I closed my eyes as one tear slipped over my cheek. No one said anything for a long moment. I took it all in: the chance to center myself, to process what had transpired, and to focus myself to move us toward the next goal. Guiding the Syrenni would be a grueling, long journey. I hoped that the Arbor Elves would be willing and able to help with supplies, not having food would make the trek an impossibility.

We released the embrace. Felix cleared his throat. "Well, thanks for the apology. I mean, I did follow you here, then you went and tried to go die on me!?" My mouth dropped, when his grin spread and he laughed. "I am *always* here for you," he said in all seriousness.

Dhirdre said, "I forgive you, Lily. I understand your reasons. But know that I am willing and happy to fight by your side. I am here for you, always, too."

Dhiren echoed the sentiment. Kerenza slung her spear over her shoulder. "And I am *always* ready to kick some enemy culuses with you."

I snorted. Even Rannoch laughed at that. "We should go," he said as he took my hand, "time to help the Syrenni make a new life for themselves."

I smiled at him. We had done it. They were freed. Now came the monumental task of actually getting them to the lake.

CHAPTER 49

By the time we arrived at the termination of the river, the Syrenni had already been there for two rotations. I caught up with Neila who informed me of how her kind were faring, and some of what she told me was concerning to say the least. I told her of our plan, then marched over to Rannoch and Kerenza to discuss with them.

"The Syrenni are restless, Neila told me some are debating about going back to the castle. They've already eaten all the fish they could find here, and are saying that at least they were fed there. I think they spent so long serving that freedom is scary and uncomfortable. For as terrible as it was, it's all they've known. Neila told me that all living Syrenni at this point were born in the castle. We need to get them some food, or we might find they did not actually want to be saved."

Kerenza rubbed her forehead. "I did not consider that possibility. They cannot truly want to go back, can they?"

"We freed them in order to have their own will, I guess if they decide to go back, we wouldn't be much better than the Umorfae if we told them they couldn't," I said, though I couldn't deny my disappointment at that thought. It would all be such a waste.

"This can't all be for nothing," Rannoch said. "I'll speak to the Petrafae, to see if they'll split off some of their rations for them." He walked over to Asmi and Hiret, while I stayed with Kerenza.

"Well, this could be a real issue if we cannot get them food," she said as we watched Rannoch argue with Asmi.

I scratched my scalp hard with all of my fingers. "Yea, this is a fucking mess. We got them out and now they're so hungry they're actually considering going back to the Umorfae. How could we win just to fail? Goddammit my planning skills suck."

She rubbed my shoulder. "This is not all on you. Did you ever aid in the release of an entire race before? I doubt it. Don't be so hard on yourself."

"Okay, sort of fair point. However, we did all discuss breaking them out. I feel like I should have better thought out what happens after. If they decide to go back ..." My face fell as Rannoch gave up talking and dropped his hands. I could tell it wasn't going well. And honestly I wasn't surprised. Even if they gave a fair amount of their food, it wouldn't be much to assuage their hunger for long—if it was even enough for all of them for one meal. I looked behind me at all of the dull-eyed and downtrodden Syrenni. Only two hundred or so. *This* was their entire race. A few hundred scared creatures, diminished to the point of being ready to return to their former masters. Their numbers were so heartbreakingly low, essentially endangered. The nagging thought of whether or not they would be successful and thrive crept in. They had been kept in captivity so long, they had no skills to survive in the outside world.

The Syrenni stood partially submerged in the waning river. A little further and it dwindled to nothing. If they turned back, water was plentiful, they had shelter, food … but it also came at a high price. Though the issue of not having food was huge, the fact that the river all but dried up from here on out must be equally terrifying to them. I knew firsthand what happened to a Syrenni when they went without water for too long. They would have to trust in us that our platform plan would work.

Several turned back, heading into the river, toward Lacausia. Neila's voice rose from the center of the crowd. She shouted, "Have faith! We can overcome this! Think of Queen Sereia. What would she have done? She would have led us to freedom!" She lifted the babe high, the child's hair glinting in the light. "We have a new Sereia. Follow her! She represents a new way of life. Do not give up this chance."

"We are supposed to follow her? She is half Umorfae. And barely older than spawn. We might as well return," responded one of the Syrenni near her.

"At least we were not hungry in the castle!" shouted another.

More moved away as Neila continued to plead with them. My stomach clenched as I watched them retreat. All we had done, and lost, to have them decide to go back in the end.

I whipped my head at the sound of electric currents sparking behind me. The familiar bright white-and-rainbow crackling openings hung in midair, widening to reveal beautiful mottled bark faces on the other side.

Arbor Elves had come in droves. I spotted several familiar faces on the other side: Dendris, Kaerlan, Illaran, and many more that I didn't recognize. Dendris spun through, bearing a bulky sack on her back. As I looked them over, I realized all of them carried substantial supplies. The knot in my stomach loosened with relief.

"Stop!" I shouted to the retreating Syrenni. "There is food for you here! Do not return to the castle. We can help you. Please, let us try."

Several of the closer Syrenni halted, then turned slowly. But others moved further away, paying no heed to me.

"Listen!" Neila yelled, pointing at me. "She is the reason for your freedom!"

More stopped, then looked at me. I straightened my back. "*Many* worked hard to secure your release. We lost someone in the process. Please give us the chance to help you make a new life. You don't have to be held under the sway of the Umorfae any longer. We *will* help you."

Neila's sharp black eyes twinkled at me in appreciation. Murmurs rippled through the crowd, and they finally started moving closer. I ushered them over to the waiting Arbor Elves, who were busy opening bundles of food.

I walked over to Dendris, then wrapped her in a tight hug. She froze at the contact, then lifted her arms to encircle my back. I backed up to look at her as I clutched her hand. "I am *so* glad to see you again. I could cry that you came and brought all this food for everyone."

She smiled at me at last, her rigid nature finally giving way to my persistence. "Aurelian was happy to grant assistance, it took us some time to gather everything needed. We do not have fish to offer, but we foraged for as much of the bisporus as we could find, it is the closest we have to meat. Hopefully it will do." She had finished laying out a spread of an unusual-looking spongy plant, which was some sort of mushroom.

"Honestly that looks pretty good to me, I-"

Syrenni swarmed and devoured what was there.

I smiled at their now-satiated bellies after the Syrenni had consumed everything, one problem handled. But then another creeping realization set in. "How will we have enough to make the trek? They've already eaten everything you brought!"

"I bring not only food, but also an additional offer."

"Oh?"

She nodded slowly. "One I think you will all welcome."

CHAPTER 50

"There is no need to make the long trek," Dendris said. "We will guide you all to the lake by fenestram and help settle the Syrenni there. We brought not only food, but also seeds. We will teach them how to cultivate. While many of us gathered bisporus for the bulk of their food, Aurelian sent a small party to scout an area. We found a suitable location along the northwest bank, far from the cave entrance. The water of the lake may be shallow for them, but it is plentiful nonetheless."

I practically collapsed with relief as I threw my arms around her again. "That is amazing!" At the same time, I wanted to facepalm myself. My "brilliant" idea would have exhausted the Petrafae, and us, meanwhile the obvious was staring me in the face. The Arbor Elves were coming to us to bring food, and had been to the lake before. They knew the endpoint, thereby being able to open portals there. How had I not thought about asking them to take us there? I shook my head at myself.

I thanked Dendris, then excused myself to find Neila and catch her up on the development. Neila's membranes flashed over her eyes as I told her. "This may be startling for your people, it's a strange sensation to step through a fenestram. If you could prepare them for what the transition will be like, that would help. The best thing you could say is that the passage is immediate. They will walk through to their new home, and be spared the hardship of a long journey. You will all be far from the threat of Umorfae, and be able to live in peace."

She nodded, then walked over to the Syrenni who all lounged at the water's edge.

I headed over to where my group was gathered. Rannoch's gaze sharpened as I told them everything. Kerenza slapped the heel of her hand to her forehead. "I feel like such a stultus! Why didn't we think of that before?" she exclaimed.

"Seriously, I thought the same thing," I said as I laughed.

"We should ask them to bring us to our camp afterward," Rannoch announced. "Or as close to it as they can get, so that we can pick up the equus to make our trip back to TerraIgni, once we've settled the Syrenni." I nodded as I moved closer to him, to feel his solid presence. He wrapped an arm around my waist, pulling me closer as we searched each other's eyes. We were almost through the weeds we had thrown ourselves into. Soon, we would be able to go home—to my new home—and move forward. I took his hand and clasped it, we were so damn close to achieving what my heart had ached to do: to free the Syrenni, and give them a fresh start. It had taken all of us, effort from so many in order to make it a possibility.

I stepped away and glanced at Queen Deniza, we would be making quite the surprise return to TerraIgni with her. The corners of her lips turned up as she looked at me. "You have developed relations with the Arbor Elves. The Ignisfae never managed to do that. You are clearly a skilled diplomat, and obviously a caring mate for my filio. The Ignisfae are lucky you have joined us."

I swallowed as my mouth went dry. Acceptance from their faeder may be lacking, but their maeder offered it freely. I held back tears at the gratitude I felt for the gesture. "I am glad to call the Arbor Elves our friends, and I am honored to be Rannoch's mate."

Kerenza stepped up and slung an arm across my shoulders. "She has done *much* more than that, maeder. She worked with Rannoch and I to rescue Ignisfae children from a terrible threat. And one of them … was my own. My filia, Emblyn, will be so happy to meet you when we return."

Deniza covered her mouth with her hand as her eyes welled. "A filia? I have missed so much. There are too many things I was not there for. And you must have a mate, then! I cannot wait to meet him."

Kerenza's face fell. "Well, I did. But that story does not have a happy ending."

Deniza reached forward and cupped her daughter's face. "I am sorry I have not been here to help you through these times, but I am now." Kerenza hugged her and buried her face in her hair. Pangs of conflicting emotions washed over me: sadness and guilt for the fact that it had not been that long since she had lost Kenneder—not even a full cycle yet, and here she had to watch Rannoch and I and our unfolding love story. And I had to admit, I also felt a twinge of jealousy that she was reuniting with her mother. I still had no idea how I was going to be able to do that with my own mom. I had promised that I would find a way, but as to what that would even entail … I frowned at myself, I should only have happiness for Kerenza for this moment she had assumed would never happen. She had thought her maeder gone, her return was nothing short of a miracle. I shook my head, to try and empty it of the small bitterness.

It's okay to feel that way. To miss your own maeder.

I snapped my head to Rannoch, who's eyes softened at me as he reached for my hand. I sighed, then nodded. He was right. Emotions are complex, missing my mom didn't mean I wasn't happy for Kerenza to have this moment when she had lost so much. She deserved it. She deserved much more, too.

The crackle of fenestrams pulled my attention, and I smiled as I saw the first of the Syrenni stepping through; into the mysterious portals that would whisk them to their new home, far from the reaches of the Umorfae.

I looked around at everyone, all who had made the difference to make this moment a reality. Dhirdre smiled at me, crossed her fist to her heart, then nodded. I was speechless at everything they had all done to help us get to this point: the moment where the Syrenni could truly live without fear.

Rannoch offered his arm. "Well, my love? Shall we join them?"

"Abso-fucken-lutely," I said with a grin.

CHAPTER 51

I blinked as I looked across the lake, there stood the massive peacock ore mountain—the same one that had imprisoned the children and still housed the arthropods. I turned to look at the wide beach, and the crystal cove that the Syrenni could now call home. The only problem was the depth of the water. I remembered sloshing through it when we had battled the Umorfae separatists. The whole lake floor was no more than knee deep at best—unless there was another area like the abyss to the cave entrance. The Petrafae had been brought to the water's edge by the Elves. I walked over to Asmi, who stood appraising the area.

"Do you think you can transform it for them?" I asked. "Push the lake bed so that it is deeper."

He tapped his chin. "We can. It will inherently change the balance of water, though. Water will retreat from the edges of the rest of the lake. Hiret and I will scout the perimeter, if there is life that will be affected by this change, we should not do it."

I cringed and nodded. I hadn't thought about how it would change the ecosystem. I walked over to where Dendris stood talking with Neila. She motioned to the distant tree line as I approached.

"Ah, Lily, I was just explaining to Neila where we advise them to grow their food supply. We will stay with them as we teach them our ways. There are fish and shelled creatures in the lake, but it will not be enough to sustain them. Plus, they must not allow themselves to eat too many of those, they could easily deplete the population to nothing."

"Asmi and Hiret are checking the lake edge for signs of life, if it's clear, they will adjust the lake floor to give you all more room to swim. Dendris makes a good point, the addition of your people here will inherently affect the ecosystem. It will be important that you remain aware of other living things and how they are faring."

She looked down at Sereia, who sat patting mounds of sand with her chubby webbed fingers. "We have much to learn. Everything will be different now, for the better, I think. But it will not be easy."

"No, it certainly won't," I said. "But we will return every so often to check on you and aid you as we can."

"As will we," Dendris assured. I smiled at the beautiful Elf, their generosity was remarkable. So quickly they had launched into action, gathering food. I thought about how Aurelian even planned ahead as to where they could actually settle. That is what a great leader does. I had much to learn, and fortunately, I had solid guides that I could look to.

Asmi and Hiret returned with good news, the east bank was home to smaller amphibious creatures, which could easily shift their location when the water level changed. Other than that, there shouldn't be any noticeable impact. All Petrafae made quick work of reforming the lake bottom, pushing only the northwest portion down and creating recessed hollows along the newly created wall opposite the shore, enough for each Syrenni to have a nook to call their own.

We had done all we could for the moment, and were waiting to be escorted back to our camp. The Petrafae were being whisked back to Adrilan already. I stood alone on a small rise, watching the Syrenni play in the water and settle into their new home. I should have been smiling, been relieved. But I wasn't. I was tempted to call some water to myself, or to release a little flame that simmered under my skin. My well had built up from not using it for over two rotations. I bounced a knee as nervous energy spiked. Dashelle's crooked grin flashed in my mind. I was pretty damn sure she had been driven mad by the amount of power she held. It had turned her. Or was she already evil? One thing I knew: that potential to become like her scared me. Rannoch's constant praise of my character wasn't totally correct, I knew I was not infallible. It wasn't only my guilt that drove me to help the Syrenni. It was also to side-step the monster I could become. I looked far to the southeast, to the too-still water near the cave entrance, where dozens Umorfae bodies probably lay rotting. Some of whom I had killed myself. I grimaced, we had done what we had to do, and yet they represented steps down a path which I could not backtrack. "The means justify the end" sounded like a perfect way to accidentally become that monster. How many more times would I have to kill in order to protect those I loved? There were still threats out there. And at what point would I find it wasn't as hard to kill anymore, not as disturbing, not as vile? I shook my head as an image popped in my mind of a future me that sliced through an enemy with complete precision, without an ounce of regret. A power-hungry Lily who had lost her humanity. Her empathy. A splatter of blood slashed across her slanted eyebrows as she completed the quick kill.

I tightened my fists as Rannoch approached, he eyed me with each step he took. "The Arbor Elves are ready to take us to our camp. They have been only to the edge of the Praegra Forest nearest there, so we will have a trek to the equus," he said.

I nodded and unclenched my hands, then wiped an unseen tear. "I'm ready."

"Are you okay?"

"Yes," I lied. "Let's go home."

CHAPTER 52

We thanked the Arbor Elves after they deposited us at the farthest edge of the Praegra Forest, before they portaled back to the Arbor Boles. I eyed the prehensile vines swaying from the trees as we started our journey to camp—the same vines that had caught me after I became separated from Opius. I cringed at the thought of him, and realized that it was because of the vines that I had ventured out of the forest. I had ended up in that canyon, where Rannoch and Kerenza had found me.

My mind wandered as we raced through the woods, thinking over all that had transpired, how much I had changed since then. How much more I knew about this world, and about myself. Though fear still nipped at me with the possibility of finding myself walking down the path to darkness like Dashelle, I could recount the things that I had done—the good deeds, and see that my actions were not borne of evil.

The forest gave way at last to the rocky, dry landscape and arid canyons. Our group ran on tired feet, but we continued. At this pace, it would be perhaps another rotation to reach camp. I marveled at Queen Deniza, the way she charged ahead, trailing her children. She had not faltered once, and never questioned them. I knew Rannoch and Kerenza were far older than I, but it was heartening to see a parent as strong and experienced as her so respectfully hand over leadership. All I had known was the human handling of parenthood, and really, I was still so young. I had never been granted that kind of take-charge behavior. Perhaps though, with time, my own mother eventually would have treated me that way. I hoped that I would someday be blessed enough to find out.

Progress slowed as the sand became deeper, and hotter. We pulled into a nook of the canyon walls to take a drink and catch our breath.

"It has been so long since I traveled this path," Deniza said as she ran a hand along the crumbly rock wall. "It looks just as I remember it. I had started to think I would never see it again."

"We are all fortunate beyond measure that you do get to see it again," Rannoch said. "It will not be long before we reach camp, then we can rest before taking the final trip to our home. TerraIgni awaits you, maeder."

She nodded. "And … of your faeder? What …" she trailed off as she glanced between Kerenza and Rannoch. I could feel the question hanging in the air before she even asked it. "Has he taken a new queen? What am I to expect when we return?"

"No, he never did," Kerenza answered. "He is as disagreeable as ever, yet he did not choose another. He keeps us at an arm's distance, always. There is much we don't know about what he's thinking most of the time."

Deniza nodded. "So he has not changed. Well … I hope that I will get to remain near you both, that we may make up for lost time."

Rannoch frowned, as did I. I hadn't thought about anything other than the Ignisfae being delighted at her return. How King Ashwan might react … that was another story.

We started our run through the rough landscape again, with renewed vigor to our goal. Just a little while longer and we could be heading back to TerraIgni. Perhaps problems awaited us there, but at least once we were flying over the Hinterdunes, threats from those that could be anywhere in this realm all but vanished. For as dangerous as the dunes were, the buffer it provided was a safety net that I sorely missed.

We arrived at camp, the tents untouched and quiet just like I had last seen them. My legs ached and I desperately wanted to rest, but something nagged at me. I had the sense that we shouldn't stop for too long. Our camp may be remote, but it was not untouchable. We had no defense perimeter, and there were not many of us should Umorfae seek us out here. Or Dashelle. We could not become complacent to the fact that someone so powerful, so bent on revenge, also had me squarely at the top of her kill list. It put us all at risk.

"We should eat, sleep, then be off once we are up," Rannoch announced to all.

"No," I countered. "I don't think it's safe to sleep here. Eat, yes. We need food. Clean up. Change of clothing. But then we should go, and rest mid-air in shifts."

Dhirdre dropped her jaw at what may have been perceived as a challenge to his authority. I was not trying to subvert him, to make myself the one in charge, but I truly believed it wasn't safe to sleep here. We did all need rest, desperately. But we could sleep on the equus. It wouldn't be as restful as a bed, it also wouldn't run the risk of us being surrounded while we slept.

Rannoch tilted his head at me, then nodded. "Good thinking, I agree. It will not be easy to make the crossing, but it will be safer in the long run. Rest awaits us in TerraIgni. Let's gather supplies and something to eat. Felix, Dhiren, and Dhirdre, will you three manage a meal for us all? The rest of us will pack supplies for the return flight. After we've cleaned up, we will all break down the tents and stow them in the cache."

The corners of my mouth turned up as I looked at him. I had to admit, I was impressed with how smoothly he took my stepping in and giving a different suggestion. He had been their leader for who knew how long—well before I was even alive. And yet, he reinforced our equality by so easily accepting it. I reached out for his hand. Then he, his mother, sister, and I all made our way to the cache to collect what we would need. As a family. It wasn't my complete family, but a family nonetheless.

CHAPTER 53

The flight to TerraIgni was long, painful, and tiring. Every muscle in my body ached as we dropped out of the mist and banked toward the city hewn into the walls of the crescent moon canyon. Gone were the gold banners from Praetexia. Had they known who we were returning with, the glinting panels probably would have remained, to welcome their long lost queen home.

As we cycled in a corkscrew down, Ignisfae appeared on terraces and balconies, shouting and pointing toward us. A blast of flame charged sky high from the battlement, alerting our arrival to anyone who hadn't already noticed. On the widest palatial balcony, King Ashwan appeared. My stomach clenched the moment I saw him, as he scanned the faces of us all. He and Deniza locked eyes for a moment, and I swore I felt a twang in the air.

We flew over the city, with the cheers of Ignisfae trailing us the whole way. Rannoch led the pack, we swooped down into the valley where the equus lived. One by one each creature landed, taking several pounding strides to slow themselves. Each one sent a sharp pain up my backside. I cringed as Zephyrine settled to a stop at last. Rannoch dismounted, then was by my side in an instant to help me down. I slid off and into his waiting arms.

"Oh my God, my ass hurts so bad! I-"

I dropped my jaw as I saw over Rannoch's shoulder the unmistakable silhouette of King Ashwan, standing rigid. His towering presence filled the narrow passageway. Torchlight glimmered in his eyes as he stared at Queen Deniza.

I flicked my eyes to Deniza, she stopped walking and stared right back, her face hard as stone as she looked at him. I glanced back to him, but all I saw was a streak of color racing toward us.

He was on the ground at her feet at that same moment. Sobbing. "Deniza! I cannot believe it. I am so sorry, Deniza. I owe you a thousand apologies. More." He choked back tears as he kissed each foot, before lifting his eyes to her. "The mistake was mine, I see that now. I treated you terribly. I will spend the rest of my time before I Fade making it up to you."

Her face softened, she raised her hand to touch his cheek, but stopped shy of it. "Ashwan. We always had the mate connection. It is real, our link, and powerful. Yet you denied the true closeness of it. That broke my heart, that denial. If we are to heal, you cannot avoid what the bond means. Holding me—us" -she motioned to Rannoch, Kerenza … and me- "at a distance, it will not be possible to move forward."

He gripped her hand. "I promise, Deniza. The Gods have given me another chance. By some miracle, you are alive. I have been …" he glanced at Kerenza, then Rannoch, and finally to me. "I have made mistakes, and I will atone for them."

"It is not some miracle. The Umorfae held me for all these cycles. It is because of Lily, and your children, that I am free." She pulled her hand back as he looked at each of us again. "You had been granted what I was not, time with our children. How did you spend it?"

He blinked at her, speechless.

"I already know the answer. You squandered it. You had the chance to be a part of their lives, instead you did not invest yourself the way you should have. You made ruling paramount, and let them find their own way."

He opened his hands to her. "You are right. I squandered it. I cannot make it right with a few words now. But I *can* work to make amends." He stood, then lifted a hand near her face. "They cut your beautiful hair at some point, those culuses." He blanched, as realization must have set in. "That was how they tricked us into believing you were dead. They had left the bodies of the Ignisfae who accompanied you in a mangled heap, we could not tell them apart, but your hair was among them, with your crown."

"I figured as much, sadly. They tried to dishonor me by taking my hair, but it only strengthened my resolve to eventually break free." She pulled her head back a little as she refocused on him. "You have much to do, I think. How did you console Kerenza, when she lost her mate?"

He looked at her with nothing short of pure guilt. "I said nothing."

Kerenza held back tears as Deniza nodded, then added, "And Rannoch's mate. How did you welcome her?"

He grimaced at us both. "I suppose I did not welcome her. Though, I did attend their pompa."

I wanted to shout that it wasn't enough to make up for how he had treated me.

"You were disrespectful to my mate when you met her,"

Rannoch said, "I should have stood up for her then. That was my mistake. I should not have let you force me into accepting that was how you were going to address her. You *will not* do that again, ever." My lips circled up at the sides as I glanced at Rannoch. Perhaps he should have at the time, but, his faeder had not been in the mindset that he was now. King Ashwan probably wouldn't have listened anyway, and it would have only further angered him.

I had to admit, I was enjoying the dressing-down he was getting from Queen Deniza. Gone for so many cycles, she comes back and puts him in his place. Maybe that made me spiteful, and wretched. But at the moment I didn't care. He had been harsh and uncaring toward me, and referred to me as if I were a possession. He alienated Rannoch and Kerenza for all this time. He didn't deserve an easy reunion. And Queen Deniza wielded her position flawlessly.

Queen Deniza stood taller. "I will consider rejoining you, by your side, if you *do* make amends as you have said you would. Amends to *all*. And if I do, it will be with equal voice, ruling as equals. Though I am glad to see you are in good health, and TerraIgni has prospered under your rule. I am not, however, happy to hear of how you have spent your time."

His eyes darted around the equus canyon. Unlike our pompa, which had throngs of Ignisfae to watch the uncomfortable exchange between him and Don'Li, now there was only our small group. "I ... was afraid," King Ashwan admitted. "Afraid that showing how much I cared would be used against me, against my familia. I thought that by holding back, and shielding my feelings, they would not be known and wielded against me. I thought I was protecting you all by doing that."

"Protecting us?" Kerenza cut in. "How does that even make sense? You have been horrible to us. My mate *died* and you leave me, your filia, to suffer without so much as an arm around my shoulders, nothing. Our maeder"-she motioned to Rannoch-"gone, lost. You say *nothing* to console us." She folded her arms and turned from him. My lip wobbled for her. When I had endured loss, my mother, Felix and I comforted each other. My mom was there for me. Kerenza didn't have that. Instead she had a father that made her think she didn't have his love at all. It must have been like a living death of a family member. Forever there as a reminder of what she didn't have with him.

He crossed over to her, then placed his broad hand on her shoulder. "Kerenza, my filia. I owe you as many apologies as I owe your maeder. I will strive—I promise, I will—to be the faeder you have always deserved. I have been misguided."

She spun to him. "Misguided? Don't you dare try to say this was someone else, like this was Eiulans's fault or something. This was *you.*"

King Ashwan held up his hands. "No, no one else can take the blame. Misguided by my own fears. I take the responsibility for my … long running mistakes. I know this will take time for you to accept me. I have hardened my heart for so long that it may be awhile before you believe my authenticity. But I hope you will, eventually."

"I think you will be waiting longer than you expect," her voice icy as she narrowed her eyes at him. "If that will be all, *Your Highness,* I will excuse myself." She smirked and mocked an excessive curtsy, then turned without his permission.

He opened his mouth to say something, I had to stop myself

from covering my face at her brazenness. Right out of the gate, she was testing his limits, daring him to rain a verbal attack on her. I remembered how he had shouted at Rannoch for something as simple as not using his title. Now, Kerenza was clearly sassing him.

Kerenza made it three paces when she halted, then glanced back at him in confusion. I knew then that she had taunted him to demand her obedience and respect, and had expected him to take the bait.

King Ashwan clasped his hands behind his back. "My amends start immediately. I will earn your respect, eventually I hope, rather than demand it. I realize right now you are not ready to accept that, but I do hope you will join me in celebration. We need to welcome our queen—your maeder— home properly."

Kerenza tilted her head. "I will join," she said, then turned to leave.

"Get ready to spend half of your coffers to make it spectacular," Queen Deniza said as she watched Kerenza enter the tunnel, then disappear to the city beyond. She turned back to King Ashwan. "I will accept nothing less."

He grinned. "For you, my mate, anything."

He held out his hand, which she took, though it felt like an awkward exchange between them. It was clear that—though Deniza said she would consider trying to reconnect with him—it would not be easy for them. She stopped, and gasped a breath at their lightly clasped hands, then looked at King Ashwan. A slight smile tugged at her mouth.

Queen Deniza looked between all of us who were still in attendance. "Come, let us celebrate with the whole city. It has been too long since I have been amongst our kind. Time to light the torches and burn brightly."

CHAPTER 54

I twitched a tired smile at myself in the bathroom mirror. The same bathroom that I had thought I might never see again, with its beautiful veined smooth tub, still releasing steam into the air after taking a long soak. The realization finally settled: we were back, we had accomplished so much. I had made missteps, there were losses, there were difficult moments—too many. But we had prevailed. I nearly started crying again, as I had three times before finally going in to wash up. Rannoch had comforted me each time. Had been there to stroke my back and hold me. There was so much bottled up inside. It had finally uncorked, and once it did, it didn't stop. I closed my eyes and steadied myself, there were still major problems to deal with, but we were okay. We had survived. We would *live*.

I left the bathroom after brushing my hair, only to find Rannoch playing with Octobo. The large spider had climbed up onto Rannoch's shoulder and was nuzzling his face. I tried not to shudder at what it would feel like to have his fuzzy legs pawing on my arm, but at the same time smiled at how happy they both looked.

"Octobo was worried about you. He's very glad you're home," Rannoch said.

I gave him a skeptical look. "I think you mean he's glad *you're* home."

"I swear! I got a thought from him that was clearly about you."

Octobo scampered down Rannoch's arm, then came over to me. I looked down at him as his four eyes reflected my distorted image. "All right," I said with a sigh, "I'm glad to see you, too, Octobo." I bent over and lightly patted his head, which was surprisingly soft. He leaned into the touch, then wriggled with glee. I huffed a laugh as he scuttled outside to his hole in the wall.

Rannoch's arm circled my waist and pulled me close, I could feel his breath on my skin as I looked out the balcony door, to the craggy canyon view opposite the great citadel. I actually *felt* like I was home. For as foreign as it was, with its towering height and levels upon levels carved into the interior stone fortress, its rugged beauty calmed my nerves and lifted my spirits. I smiled at two large potted citrus trees flanking each side of the expansive balcony, the cream ceramic basins painted with detailed blue patterns.

"Are those trees new? They weren't here before," I commented.

His lips brushed my ear. "I asked Tanzara to arrange for them. I remembered you talking about the fruit trees that grew on your family land. I thought it would make you feel more at home."

I spun to him. "You are so thoughtful, I love them. I do feel at home. I feel … calmer, at peace. Not just because of them, but, let's get more plants, a lot more. I want to fill the balcony until they are spilling over."

He laughed. "Gladly." A knock sounded on the wall outside the draped door. I scrunched my eyebrows at Rannoch. "Tanzara, she's here to help you dress for the party."

"Oh, right." I motioned for him to let her in. Rannoch excused himself, then headed to the bathing chamber to get ready.

She breezed in laden with silken fabrics and glittering jewels. I smiled at the hearty, one-arm hug she gave me before busying herself with helping me get ready. "Everyone else is ready! The whole city is absolutely bursting to welcome their queen home."

"I can only imagine," I said through a smile.

"They are all saying how much you have done. Because of you, we have her back."

I opened my mouth, unsure what to even say to that. "Queen Deniza did a lot to rescue herself. I may have opened the door, but *she* did a lot to turn things to our favor. And the efforts of everyone else involved, I don't want the misconception that it was all me."

She squeezed me again with both arms this time. "We know, believe me that we all know there are many to thank. But you also must see that these events also coincide with you becoming one of us."

I grinned at her, so quickly Tanzara had warmed to me and gotten to know me. She finished tying an exquisite, asymmetrical dress of brilliant gold. Looking at it before she had put it on me, I would have thought the fabric would irritate my skin, yet it was as soft as finely woven sheets. After painting my lips a saturated red and coating my lashes black, she braided my hair to one side.

I stood and looked at myself in the hall mirror, my reflection nearly took my breath away. I looked positively … regal. Rannoch came out of the bathroom wearing a draped suit made of the same fabric, with a matching sash that wrapped around his waist, then gathered at one shoulder over a white shirt. I gasped as my gaze landed on the crown on his head, polished gold reflected the torchlight of the room, and a single, large ruby placed at the pointed center blazed with its own fire.

Tanzara bowed before leaving, which I saw out of the corner of my eye. Rannoch and I didn't look away from each other as she left.

His eyes softened as he looked at me, the fire in his pupils smoldered as he took in every detail of my body, my face. "I know this might be a little … unexpected for you. I want you to know that you are loved and welcomed by the Ignisfae. My faeder made his mistakes with his approach, but he is making efforts to attone."

"How?"

Rannoch smiled and offered his arm. "With a gift, one that you very much deserve."

Rannoch and I left our room, only to find Kerenza, Felix, Dhiren and Dhirdre all waiting for us outside.

"Are we late?" I joked.

"Always," Felix said with a smirk.

"Never," Kerenza amended. She wore a diadem that nearly matched Rannoch's. "This is your time, when you are ready, we are ready."

I flashed her a confused glance, when Rannoch added, "It *is* your time, Lily. It's not just a party to welcome my maeder home. It is also to celebrate who you are to the Ignisfae." My stomach dropped and I swear I stopped breathing. I could feel my eyes were as round as saucers, as he took both of my hands. "You are to be crowned."

Okay, I was definitely not breathing.

"If you are willing, my faeder will crown you now," Rannoch said.

I gripped his hands as I looked at him. I loved him, I loved his people. Our people. I knew I would work hard for them. That was what really mattered for such a title, right?

A took a breath to collect myself. "I am ready." I slipped my hand into his bent arm he offered, as we proceeded towards the festivities. I *was* ready.

We walked down the wide hallway lined with massive pillars, dressed in matching gold finery, headed toward this monumental moment. Felix grinned at me as I shot him a glance over my shoulder. My gaze darted around all who walked with us, each step nearly slow motion for me as we proceeded, our tight-knit group marching toward my coronation.

Kerenza nodded to me, assuring me of her support, as we stepped onto the platform of the raised dais that King Ashwan and Queen Deniza stood upon. The same platform that had over-looked the weaving of Praetexia.

"We come together to not only welcome Queen Deniza home to TerraIgni, but also to welcome Her Highness Lily Brennanfalk!" King Ashwan announced to the thousands of gathered Ignisfae. I looked out to the crowd, and realized there were more than thousands, there were tens of thousands. My blood froze as he motioned me forward.

I walked toward him while Rannoch hung back. Tanzara was there, with a round box made from intricately detailed tooled leather. She lifted the lid off, then King Ashwan reached in to pull a plush pillow from it. A crown matching Rannoch's sat atop the velvet weave. He motioned for me to kneel after he lifted it out.

"For your undeniable service to the Ignisfae, for your commitment to my filio, Prince Rannoch, and for your unyielding tenacity to do right, it is my honor to crown you princess."

I lifted my eyes to his, which sparkled with warmth. My breath caught as I felt his welcome at last. I didn't care about the crown. It was beautiful, of course. The jewel at the peak of the gold which bloomed with unparalleled light demanded my attention, yet what truly caught my eye was how he looked at me. With pride. Tears brimmed my eyes as I looked up at him.

Queen Deniza stepped forward and placed her hand on the other side of the crown. "For your bravery, and your willingness to put other's safety ahead of your own, it is our honor to welcome you to our familia. Burn brightly, Princess Lily Brennanfalk."

I closed my eyes as they lowered the crown in place, and tears fell at last. The circlet settled with ease and was surprisingly light as I looked up to Rannoch's smiling parents. A cheer erupted from the crowd which rolled through with a droning thunder. Thousands of feet stomped the ground. The flaming basins of every carved Ignisfae statue, which bordered the gathering, churned high into the sky, illuminating the whole area in a brilliant flash.

Rannoch came forward and took my hand to help me rise. The air charged as I looked at him, his brilliant smile was absolutely electric as I settled to standing next to his side. He raised my hand high, just as he had done the first time we arrived at TerraIgni.

Rannoch's piercing gaze never left mine, as his people—

our people—exploded in cheers once again, and he mouthed the word to me, *home.*

Pronunciation Guide

Lily lil-EE

Felix FEE-licks

Rannoch ran-NUCK

Kerenza keh-ren-ZA

Deniza den-ih-ZA

Ashwan ash-WAHN

Eiulans EW-lens

Aurelian ar-RIL-ee-an

Tenaeran Ten-AIR-an

Don'Li Don-LEE

Yantzen Yant-ZEN

Tanzara Tan-ZAR-a

Umorfae -oo-MOR-fay

Ignisfae - Ig-NIS-fay

Petrafae - Pe-TRA-fay

Caelifae - kal-E-fay

Syrenni sir-REN-ee

Amabilis a-mah-BIL-is

Pythonissamul pie-THON-iss-ah-mool

Bad words!

Stultus - stuhl-TUS meaning: dumbass, idiot

Faex - Fay meaning: shit

Culus - KUL-us meaning: asshole

Cunne -QUE-nh -one syllable meaning: bitch, cunt

ACKNOWLEDGEMENTS

To my husband Kirt, I owe you so many thanks and acknowledgments. Thank you for all that you do, for supporting me and for being the incredible spouse and father that you are. I've learned what a great partner is by how you endeavor to support me every day. While I finished this book I fell in love with you all over again. Your dedication to me and our children is everything, and I'm so appreciative to have you in my life. You are so talented and I'm so proud to be married to you. Here we go, to the moon and beyond in our crystal castle!

Laura! I always have inexhaustible thanks to give you. To all our adventures in friendship and in writing, thank you for being my bestie through thick and thin.

To That Bitch Robyn, I'm so excited to actually use your stage name in print! You're captivating, you're wonderful, you're admirable. You give so much to those around you, and you are a beacon of how to live a life well balanced. I'm so grateful for our lifelong friendship and sisterhood. Now go twirl that pole girl (just kidding, I know you're not a pole dancer, yet!)

To my family and friends who have shown me their support. It means so much to me and I am grateful to have such wonderful humans in my life.

My endlessly talented editor, David Martin Lins, thank you for helping me craft a story I'm proud of. I'm so lucky to work with you and I have learned so much from you. You always help me see what I write in a different light, and I learn by your example how to make my stories more compelling and to retain the human experience.

To the best beta team ever! You are all so fantastic, and I appreciate all of your time and advice:

Chris Sanchez, I owe you so many thanks, and that's an understatement. I'll narrow it down to this book. I'm not going to lie, your rally of excitement helped me finish this book when I was doubting myself. Thank you for your insights and friendship.

Laura Quinn, my favorite Scottish Mummy's Vampire! Thank you for your careful editorial catches, for your thoughts, and most of all for your cheerleading spirit. Your enthusiasm is infectious, and your notes are spot on!

Sofia Vale Cruz, getting your messages after you read the first book meant everything to me! Thanks for your feedback and editorial notes, they are so helpful! Thank you from the bottom of my heart for your friendship and excitement for what I write. I love talking about books with you, I can't wait to read your book once it's ready and to be the fan girl that you have been for me!

Kelly Shannon, thank you for your thoughtful and meticulous feedback, your advice both on the small and large scales helped me hone this story. You're awesome!

Paige Ritchey, reading your play-by-play reactions in your feedback was so fun! Thank you for your suggestions for pacing and editorial notes. It was all so helpful and I'm very grateful.

Jessica, thank you for reading all of my books multiple times! I really appreciate your dedication and careful attention so that you gave succinct notes, it was all helpful and benefited the readers immensely. Your responses helped me refine the book to a better place!

Gina Melchiorri, thank you for your copy edit catches, and most of all thank you for your enthusiasm! Now I'm going to gush a little of my own enthusiasm and thank you for being the voice of Vale Born and the upcoming audiobooks. You are so talented and we (me, audiobook listeners, THE WORLD) are so lucky you will be breathing audible life into the characters of this series!

To my parents, Jay and Carla Zilka. Your support has been paramount to my success. You are both such incredible role models and inspiring guides for me to look to. I appreciate all you have done for me, and continue to do. Side note: I really hope you didn't just read all the smut I wrote! I'm cringing at the thought, but also appreciate that you both read everything I write.

And finally, I want to acknowledge you, the reader. It's because of your willingness to follow me on this journey that I'm able to keep bringing you stories. Keep coming back, because whoa baby, do we have an adventure on the horizon!

Thank you for reading! If you enjoyed this book, I'd be very grateful if you posted a short review. Your support really does make a difference, I read all reviews personally and use them to keep bringing you great stories. Thanks again for your support!

Get updates on release information, exclusive giveaways, and insider info by signing up for my newsletter at www.lorinpetrazilka.com

About the Author

Raised in a rural town called Elfin Forest, magic and inspiration surrounded Lorin throughout her childhood. Fantastical stories permeated her existence, and eventually she started writing her own. An award-winning fantasy and science fiction author, Lorin loves weaving epic tales that retain human-relatable experiences with a kernel of truth. She believes the vastness of the human spirit can be explored through fiction, and through character-driven fantasy we can discover more about ourselves. Lorin can always be found with a book nearby, absorbing stories or crafting words of her own. She lives in Southern California with her husband and three kids, loves the outdoors, and is always doing something creative.